MORE MYSTERIES FROM THE
BERKLEY PUBLISHING GROUP...

INSPECTOR KENWORTHY MYSTERIES: Scotland Yard's consummate master of investigation lets no one get away with murder. "In the best tradition of British detective fiction!" —*Boston Globe*

by John Buxton Hilton

HANGMAN'S TIDE	TWICE DEAD
FATAL CURTAIN	RANSOM GAME
PLAYGROUND OF DEATH	FOCUS ON CRIME
CRADLE OF CRIME	CORRIDORS OF GUILT
HOLIDAY FOR MURDER	DEAD MAN'S PATH
LESSON IN MURDER	DEATH IN MIDWINTER
TARGET OF SUSPICION	

DOG LOVERS' MYSTERIES STARRING JACKIE WALSH: She's starting a new life with her son and an ex–police dog named Jake ... teaching film classes and solving crimes!

by Melissa Cleary

A TAIL OF TWO MURDERS	HOUNDED TO DEATH
DOG COLLAR CRIME	

GARTH RYLAND MYSTERIES: Newsman Garth Ryland digs up the dirt in a serene small town—that isn't as peaceful as it looks ... "A writer with real imagination!" —*The New York Times*

by John R. Riggs

HUNTING GROUND	ONE MAN'S POISON
HAUNT OF THE NIGHTINGALE	THE LAST LAUGH
WOLF IN SHEEP'S CLOTHING	LET SLEEPING DOGS LIE
DEAD LETTER	A DRAGON LIVES FOREVER

PETER BRICHTER MYSTERIES: A midwestern police detective stars in "a highly unusual, exceptionally erudite mystery series!" —*Minneapolis Star Tribune*

by Mary Monica Pulver

KNIGHT FALL	ORIGINAL SIN
THE UNFORGIVING MINUTES	SHOW STOPPER
ASHES TO ASHES	

CALEY BURKE, P.I., MYSTERIES: This California private investigator has a brand-new license, a gun in her purse, and a knack for solving even the trickiest cases!

by Bridget McKenna

MURDER BEACH

JACK HAGEE, P.I., MYSTERIES: Classic detective fiction with "raw vitality ... Henderson is a born storyteller." —*Armchair Detective*

by C.J Henderson

NO FREE LUNCH	NOTHING LASTS FOREVER
SOMETHING FOR NOTHING	

FREDDIE O'NEAL, P.I., MYSTERIES: You can bet that this appealing Reno P.I will get her man ... "A winner." —*Linda Grant*

by Catherine Dain

LAY IT ON THE LINE	SING A SONG OF DEATH
WALK A CROOKED MILE	

SISTER FREVISSE MYSTERIES: Medieval mystery in the tradition of Ellis Peters ...

by Margaret Frazer

THE NOVICE'S TALE	THE SERVANT'S TALE

HEADHUNT

CAROL BRENNAN

BERKLEY PRIME CRIME, NEW YORK

This Berkley Prime Crime Book contains the complete text of the original hardcover edition. It has been completely reset in a typeface designed for easy reading, and was printed from new film.

HEADHUNT

A Berkley Prime Crime Book/published by arrangement with Carroll & Graf Publishers, Inc.

PRINTING HISTORY
Carroll & Graf edition published 1991
Berkley Prime Crime edition/May 1994

ISBN: 0-425-14125-X

Berkley Prime Crime Books are published
by The Berkley Publishing Group,
200 Madison Avenue, New York, NY 10016.
The name BERKLEY PRIME CRIME and
the BERKLEY PRIME CRIME design
are trademarks of Berkley Publishing Corporation.

PRINTED IN THE UNITED STATES OF AMERICA

10 9 8 7 6 5 4 3 2 1

For my father, Will Gertzman,
who'd have loved that I wrote a book,
and my mother, Irene,
who always says yes.

Acknowledgments

Margaret Norton, my editor, for her expert guidance, delivered with a gentle touch; Anita Diamant, agent *extraordinaire*; Richard Gallen, whose smarts and generosity made a big difference; Nancy Ringler Lucas, for being the best definition I've heard yet of the word *friend*; Joanna Maddock, without whose encouragement and bullying her mother would have never learned to use a word processor; and last but never least— Eamon Brennan, husband, colleague, friend—in the order that best suits the moment.

1

A SMALL UNFRIENDLY ANIMAL WAS TRYING HARD TO make its way out of my right temple. I woke, not knowing for the moment where I was. I opened my left eye and got that straight pretty fast. I was in Douglas's apartment—Douglas's bed, in fact. I worked my other eye open. The animal didn't like that. He liked it even less when I suddenly sat bolt upright. The stab of pain drew my protective hand to my forehead. No Douglas next to me. I could see from where I sat that the bathroom door was open, so he wasn't in there. Douglas never used bathrooms with open doors at any time for any reason.

I knew somehow that I had to get up and moving, no matter how I felt. Then I remembered the meeting. I was to meet Kingman Carter at seven-thirty. If the radio alarm on Douglas's side of the bed was to be trusted—and it always could be—I had an hour and seven minutes to make it. That was a relief.

Then I saw the bag. It was sitting at the foot of the bed on Douglas's side. I don't know how I'd missed seeing it first thing, probably the brandy. Only brandy gives me a hangover quite like that. It was a large Bloomingdale's bag with a self-congratulatory "Bloomie's" in huge letters running down one side. It was stapled shut, and the staple also held a white envelope bearing my name: "Liz."

As I reached for it and opened the unsealed flap, I knew what it would contain. In one extravagantly painful headthrob, last night came back to me.

CAROL BRENNAN

I'd arrived at Douglas's East 74th Street apartment an hour late and in a contentious mood. My Monday at the office had been more than usually frustrating. Some days are like that in public relations, which is the way I earn my keep and most of my two children's (their father's contributions had grown a bit sluggish of late). Anyway, three clients had had brush fires to be put out simultaneously; I'd been crashing on two new business proposals; Angela was off cosseting a *Vogue* editor with nectar and ambrosia at La Grenouille and Seth was at an extended session with his shrink, so no backup was in sight—at least not at the level I needed. The final straw was a last minute phone call from King Carter summoning me to this seven-thirty meeting with not a clue about the why or what of it.

If you're me you worry when a client, sounding ominous, calls a sudden unexplained meeting, because you *know* that the agency's going to be fired. After four and a half years, something's really ticked him off and good-bye account. In this case, for one Elizabeth Wareham, it would be an expensive good-bye. I had brought the Carter Consultants account into the agency and thus was paid an eight-percent commission on the annual fees it generated. At current billings that was better than twelve thousand dollars—a noticeable chunk of the Brown and Stanford tuitions I was responsible for.

I pulled the envelope free from the Bloomie's bag and opened it. The creamy, heavy notepaper, at first glance, looked like a genteel thank-you note for a lovely dinner or just the right kind of gift. It didn't sound all that different either. What Douglas's impeccable script said was:

Dear Liz,

This may seem harsh, but I think it better for both of us that we make a clean break right now. I simply can't take the casual disorder and emotional pyrotechnics on which you seem to thrive. This isn't meant to be critical, though you'll probably interpret it that way. Many thanks for the good times we've had. I wish you only the best.

It was signed Douglas. And it *was* Douglas: concise, reasonable, sane—which is, I guess, a helpful thing for a psychiatrist to be. Not meant to be critical, my ass. Inside the bag were a collection of Liz Wareham miscellanea that had found its way gradually into Douglas Friedlaender's sleek apartment over the course of two years. I dumped it out on the kingsize bed: a dark green wool bathrobe and a plaid cotton one, two toothbrushes, some makeup remover and moisturizer, deodorant, cosmetics, plus a couple of bras and spare pantyhose, as well as Ruth Rendell and Anita Brookner paperbacks, both of which I was in the middle of reading.

Shit! I took a deep breath and let it out slowly. The tears started in the back of my nose, where they burned. I'd gone too far. My mother always warned me that my big mouth would get me into trouble. And it always did. I climbed out of bed onto the deep white carpet. The creature inside my skull issued one more sharp complaint and then settled down to a monotonous rocking—uncomfortable but bearable.

A shower. I padded into the bathroom, clutching my shampoo and conditioner, retrieved from the pile on the bed. Douglas had one of the world's great showers in his round jacuzzi tub, and I turned it on gloriously hot and full blast, gulped down a glass of water and two Extra-Strength Excedrin, and climbed in. As the water sluiced over me, pieces of last night came back:

"Do you know what time it is, Liz? You might have called."

"Oh God. I meant to. The time just got away. It was a bitch of a day. I never even came up for air. Could I use a drink—and a kiss if you've got one."

"Is that all? You're over an hour late and you want a drink and a kiss. You're—"

"Douglas, I said I was sorry and—"

"No, you didn't."

"Okay, I'm sorry. But you weren't standing on a street corner. I mean you were in your very comfortable apartment. You could read a book or listen to a record or—"

"That's beside the point, Liz. You are inconsiderate—like

3

a child, and you've made me your fath—"

"Douglas, knock it off. You may be a shrink, but you're not *my* fucking shrink."

From that beginning, the evening didn't have too far down to go, but it managed. Many angry home truths beginning with "you always" or "you never" were exchanged. It wasn't the first time we'd had one of these sessions. During the last six months or so the times between the good evenings chewing over the film we'd just seen or trying new wines had grown longer. And the gap between bouts of good sex, even longer than that.

I squirted some shampoo into my hand and worked up a good lather. It felt wonderful. The Excedrin was starting to work. If I looked at it honestly, Douglas and I had clearly been on the way out. As he'd said in his note, better for both of us to make a clean break, right?

I stepped under the pneumatic spray and let it rinse my hair. The crying feeling stabbed at the back of my nose and my eyes filled up. Why did I feel so rotten, then? So rejected and alone . . . and scared?

I rubbed in a little hair conditioner, stepped out of the shower, and wrapped myself in an oversized towel. I'm not too good at fooling myself, and I realized as I rubbed my body dry that it wasn't Douglas I was crying about, it was me: the prospect of being alone—really alone—for the first time in my life.

I'd gone from living with my parents to living with my husband. After the divorce I'd lived with my children. A second husband joined us for four bumpily memorable years and then it had been the kids and me again. After Scott went off to Brown, it had been Sarah and me. I'd looked forward to my forthcoming freedom with a relish that had made me feel a bit guilty. But Sarah'd been gone a month now and I was surprised how much I missed her.

I defogged the mirror with a corner of the towel and fingered my mop of mahogany curls into more or less acceptable shape. My hair had been a bane of my existence from the onset of female vanity at ten or so until I'd liberated it at twenty-eight from a regimen of punishing chemical straighteners, painful plastic rollers, and searing dryers and just let it be its carefree self.

My face, unfortunately, was far from carefree this morning, I noted, as bloodshot green eyes looked back at me from the mirror. I fished some Visine out of the medicine cabinet, zapped each eye twice for good measure, and went back into the bedroom to dress. The odds and ends on the bed included a clean pair of run-free black pantyhose. Fortunately, I'd worn a knit dress—black turtleneck with long skinny sleeves—which looked okay for a second day's duty, despite its night on the floor. I noted as I pulled it over my head that I hadn't taken off the large silver peacock brooch first. God, I didn't even remember getting undressed. I stuffed everything back into the shopping bag except the two novels, which I added to the clutter in my oversized black leather bag-cum-briefcase.

My throat felt lumpy and I swallowed hard. Had Douglas gone off and slept at the Yale Club after I'd passed out? I checked his side of the bed. It had been slept in. He must have gotten up really early then and hightailed it to his office after packing the good-bye bag and writing his note. As I looked at Douglas's pillow with its faint impression of his head still visible, I could see him lying there turning slightly to the right, as he did. And then I remembered something else about last night—quite faintly, dreamlike. We'd made love. I'd been three-quarters asleep, but the instant memory felt so sweet. Goddamn you, Douglas. Why'd you have to do that?

My eyes started to tear again and threatened to undo the Visine benefits and I made myself turn it all off. I glanced at the clock and it was still only five to seven, so I was fine for time. King's townhouse, which we all called the Manse, was only a ten-block walk downtown from Douglas's.

As I was putting the finishing touches on my makeup, I realized I was ravenous and remembered that we'd never actually gotten around to dinner during last night's hostilities. My watch told me it was seven-ten, which left me no time to make breakfast. Besides, the idea of messing around Douglas's gleaming white kitchen preparing food seemed an unattractive prospect, all things considered. I settled for the lone banana resting in a large crystal bowl of oranges and ate it as I looked out the kitchen window at the slate sky and steady rain.

I hadn't come prepared, and neither had my new blue cashmere blazer. Yesterday's *Times* had proclaimed "sunny skies and seasonable temperatures" until Thursday. I grabbed an umbrella out of Douglas's front closet—a three-dollar streetcorner special, but in decent working order—and left. I stopped at the trash closet near the freight elevator and, after the briefest pause, put down the Bloomie's bag, closed the door, walked back around to the passenger elevator, and rang.

2

....

I BOUNCED DOWN THIRD AVENUE IN THE RAIN, FEELING light and elated. It was too pat to say that I'd left two years of Liz/Douglas behind in that trash room and walked away scot-free, but that's how it felt—like I'd gotten away with something and was ahead of the game.

The high lasted about two blocks—until my thoughts turned to King Carter, the president of Carter Consultants, one of my most important clients, and what the agenda of our meeting might be. That brought me down in a hurry. Aside from the twelve thousand I'd lose in commission if the account went down the tube, Briggs Drew, the agency's other executive vice president, was riding high. He'd just brought in a fat project for Bristol Myers and John Gentle, our beloved founder and president, was giving him the golden-boy treatment. I recognized it very well, though I hadn't been a golden girl for almost a year now—not since I'd brought in a new division of Baker Bank. And now to lose Carter Consultants . . . The banana-Excedrin cocktail churned in my stomach.

I told myself that I was being paranoid-alarmist. The meeting could be about something else entirely. Certainly life had been active on the Carter account lately. King was just about set to take on a new partner in California and, even more important, he'd been approached by Green Star, the British conglomerate, dangling offers of fifty million dollars-plus at him to buy Carter Consultants.

But if it were one of these issues, King would have said so. I'd known the man for almost five years and could almost hear his suave, elegantly clipped tones in scores of brief, to-the-point phone exchanges.

"Liz. I'd like to meet with you next Tuesday at eight re next year's research program."

Or: "Let's have an eight o'clock Friday re publicity on our expansion."

Our meetings were usually at eight in the morning, scheduled a couple of days in advance and they had a specific agenda which he always told me beforehand so that I'd have a chance to get my creative juices running.

The call about this meeting had been different. It had come in well after six yesterday evening.

"Please be here tomorrow morning at seven-thirty."

"Re what, King? Maybe I can do some preliminary thinking."

"Preliminary thinking won't help, I'm afraid."

"Would you like me to stay and sit in on the beginning of the partners' meeting?" The four Carter partners, each in a different city, held a regular monthly meeting in New York, and I knew one was scheduled that morning.

"No," he snapped. "No." This time more softly. "Don't be late." And he'd hung up.

Reviewing the conversation in my mind, I decided that I wasn't being a bit paranoid. I had a damned good reason to worry.

The rain hadn't let up a bit by the time I arrived at 158 East 64th Street, but even the dreary weather couldn't dim the elegance of the Manse's perfectly preserved limestone facade. New York has a diminishing number of nineteenth-century mansions left, and this was the best of the breed: a five-story twenty-five footer with a large garden. It was characteristic of Kingman Carter, connoisseur, to have picked up this prize—and on one of the city's best blocks, too. I'd heard that he'd bought it at auction fifteen years ago at a giveaway price. That was characteristic of Kingman Carter, sharp businessman. I'd always thought of King as Fred Astaire. Lanky, suave, he danced with elegant grace, always ahead and often on the backs of fallen colleagues. A malevolent Fred Astaire.

I pushed the bell to let him know that I was there, took out my key and let myself in. King had given me a key early in our relationship in case he was on the phone, as he often was, when I arrived for one of our sunrise confabs. I shook out my drenched umbrella, put it in the wrought-iron stand right inside the door and checked the alarm panel. The green light told me that the system was off.

The lofty entrance rotunda retained its original elegant marble floor—mostly white, with an intricately inlaid Greek key design in the center and a border around the edges in black. A blue and white damask sofa flanked by a mahogany end table stood against the wall to my left. Next to it was a closed panel door that led to staff offices. Ahead and slightly to the right was a gracefully curved white marble staircase with delicately carved newel posts in the shape of griffins. King had once told me that the staircase and some of the mantels had been sent in pieces from Italy.

I mounted the flight of stairs briskly. I paused briefly, my hand on the heavy brass knob of the closed door which led to King's office and the living quarters on the floors above it. Delaying wouldn't help. I turned the knob. He'd left it unlocked for me. My heels tapped across the marble until they hit the thick rose Aubusson which covered the floor of the reception area. His office door was closed. Usually he left it open when we met this early.

"King," I called softly. No answer. I knocked on the door. "King? Are you there?" Nothing. "Are you okay?" Still nothing.

I opened the door and started to walk in. I didn't get very far. King sat behind his desk, sprawled backward in his elegant Regency swivel. He was wearing a burgundy brocade robe over an open-necked white shirt. The handle of an elaborate fifteenth-century Ming Dynasty dagger, one of his most prized artifacts, stuck out of his chest at an improbably jaunty angle. His staring eyes and open mouth quelled any questions about rushing for medical help.

That knife. I could see it in King's hands, his long slender fingers caressing the intricately worked handle. He always played with it, I'd noticed, when he was about to say something scathing—something suave and succinct that made you realize just how stupid you really were. I'd been on the receiving end only a few times during the five years I'd known King, but they were enough to have provoked my own murderous fantasies. Someone's actually done it, I thought. This time, he's gone too far with someone. It didn't occur to me for a second that King had been killed by that strawman staple of the murder mysteries I devour, the casual intruder.

I'm not sure how long I stood there in the doorway. I tried to move but my feet didn't seem to work at first. When they did I ran over to King's desk and grabbed the phone. I slammed the receiver down as soon as I had picked it up. What if the killer was still somewhere in the house? The possibilities were extensive. There was Mandy's office right next to King's, the bathroom on this floor and two whole floors above, not to mention the parlor floor and the ground level.

A murder mystery buff I may be, but I'm no intrepid heroine. In fact, I'm a terrible coward. I avoided showers for two years after seeing *Psycho* and have been known to sleep with the lights on when alone in a hotel room.

I clattered down the stairs and got the hell out of that house as fast as my shaky high-heeled legs would carry me.

3

I RAN TO THE CORNER OF THIRD AVENUE AND STOOD THERE for a moment gasping and getting drenched. Of course, I'd forgotten to grab Douglas's umbrella on my way out. The street was deserted and it was too early for any shops to be open, but I spied a pay phone on the corner and dialed 911.

The operator assured me that the police would be there soon, and I huddled in a liquor store doorway to wait. I willed my mind off the horror of what had happened. If I focused on that, I'd fall apart. Instead, I tried to dope out what to do next. Unlike a normal citizen reacting to a first exposure to murder, my thoughts turned to public relations.

This death, like most deaths, had a PR component. In deaths of the nonsensational variety, the PR program is handled by the calmer family members or friends. It consists of planning the main event: the funeral, and the ancillary ones: wakes, shivahs and such, and arranging for press coverage: the obituary. This, however, was the sensational, not to say lurid, death of an important business figure, who happened to be my client. And the Gentle Group was going to have a great deal to do. I quickly returned to the phone and got Seth Frankel, one of my top aides, at his apartment.

"Steady yourself, Seth. I'm going to knock you off your chair."

"What's the matter, Liz? I was just going into the shower."

"King Carter's been murdered."

Silence.

"Look, the police'll be here any minute. I want you to go right to the office. Cancel anything you have on for today—"

"But you know I have a shrink appointment at—"

"Can it, Seth. I mean it. Get down to the office and start on a release. Keep it very straight. You know—was killed by an unknown assailant—and then get right off that onto King's prestige as a business leader and the firm's growth to the top eight and blah, blah, blah. I'll call you in an hour and a half so you can run it by me. Then you can fax it to the *Times* and the *Journal*. Let's see, Cynthia at the *Times* and, uh, Jerry at the *Journal*, do you think?"

"Yeah, I think that's the way to go, but Dr. Klingwasser will—"

"It wouldn't hurt to try and catch Jerry and Cynthia at home now and let them know what's coming. You're going to be swamped with press calls. Juggle as well as you can, but don't speculate or schmooze. Talk to you soon."

I hung up before he could *kvetch* one syllable at me. This might set Seth's therapy back six years to square one. At the moment I didn't care. I was sure Douglas would call it misplaced hostility or some such. Fuck you, Douglas.

Just then a police car rounded the corner and pulled up in front of the Manse. A man and a woman in uniforms got out.

"I'm Elizabeth Wareham," I called as I ran to them.

"I'm Officer Wong, Ms. Wareham." He was a skinny kid who didn't look a lot older than my son Scott. "This is Officer Nunez. That the house?"

"Yes. I'll let you in."

"Let us in?" asked Nunez. The black eyes in her square, coffee-colored face registered mild surprise.

I explained that the door was one that locked automatically when you closed it. I also explained why I had a key. They listened without comment.

My hand felt unsteady as I turned the key and opened the door.

As we approached King's office, I hung back in the doorway, eyes down, far from eager to take another look. Otherwise I never would have noticed it. But there it was, no more than a foot into the room, gleaming faintly in the thick green of the rug—a single earring shaped like a tiny wing in heavy matte finished gold. I recognized it instantly. Without thinking, I reached down quickly, scooped it up and put it in my blazer pocket. The motion took just a second and neither of them saw it. They were totally involved in examining King and the room and making notes on little pads as they sized up the situation.

After a few minutes, Wong said to Nunez, "Vonnie, take Ms. Wareham downstairs and get her statement while I call in the troops and take a look around."

"How do you know," I asked Nunez as we walked back down to the entrance rotunda, "that the murderer isn't still here? It's a big house."

She shrugged. "We don't. But it wouldn't be that bright for him to stick around. They usually don't unless it's family, and then they're standin' there cryin'. Besides, Tommy's a good careful cop. Don't worry."

We sat down on opposite ends of the sofa. Nunez gave the wet back of her slicker a conscientious wipe before sitting, which reminded me that my own rain-damp rear might damage the delicate fabric, but such considerations seemed dopily trivial. King was beyond caring about water-stained blue and white sofas. I felt my eyes sting with tears as the reality of his death began to sink in.

Nunez pulled out her notebook and I told her my story. She took it down, occasionally holding up a chunky little hand to slow my pace. Just as I was finishing, Wong came back down, said, "The detectives are on their way," and went outside. After a few minutes, he was back, wiping rain off his face and dripping a small puddle on the white marble floor.

"Did someone break in?" I asked.

He didn't answer. All of a sudden, the street was alive with vehicles and people. "That was fast," Nunez said, getting up

13

while Wong answered a sharp rap at the door. Three men and a woman, all in plainclothes, walked in briskly. They huddled with Nunez and Wong at the far side of the staircase. Then the woman and one of the men went upstairs and the other two men approached me. The one who seemed to be in charge called over his shoulder to Wong and Nunez, "Good job, officers. Secure the front, would you? Crime Scene Unit'll be here any minute." Then he fixed on me with intelligent brown eyes, topped by brows that resembled bent black caterpillars.

"I'm Sergeant Libuti, Ms. Wareham," he said in a pleasant Brooklyn baritone. It occurred to me that they must be giving cops lessons in feminist etiquette these days. He was a pleasant, wiry five-foot-eight and had the stained teeth and fingers of a heavy smoker. "This is Detective Remley." Remley bore a strong resemblance to a film favorite of my youth, Porky Pig.

"Connie, why don't you go upstairs and give Flo and Stan a hand. I'm gonna have a word with Ms. Wareham." Remley nodded and disappeared.

"Okay, Ms. Wareham," Libuti said, "I want you to tell me exactly what happened." As he reached for a notebook and pen, I glimpsed his gun in its shoulder holster. The sight underscored just how real all this was. He sat down, took a heavy crystal ashtray from the end table, placed it next to him on the sofa, and shook a Camel out of a half-empty pack. I took a deep breath and began run-through number two of my story.

He chain-smoked. From time to time he interrupted with questions, but not as often as his movie counterparts.

"You say you rang the doorbell first. Did it seem funny to you that Mr. Carter didn't buzz you in?"

"No, not especially. I rang just to let him know I was here. He might have been on the phone. London's five hours ahead of us. He knew I had the key. I've let myself in lots of times in the past." I heard cars pulling up and sirens. Libuti got up to admit four more men, presumably the Crime Scene Unit. After a brief confab they went upstairs. Libuti returned to me.

"What about the upstairs door?" he asked.

"That was unlocked."

"What *is* Carter Consultants?" he asked. "What's their line of business?"

"They're headhunters."

"What?" The caterpillar over his left eye rose a quarter of an inch.

"Executive search," I explained. "They're called headhunters because companies hire them to recruit top executives, and that usually means hunting up successful executives at other companies and persuading them to change jobs—you know, delivering their scalps to the client."

Libuti looked at the surroundings and said "Must be a good business."

"A very good business," I answered.

"You say Mr. Carter was spending the night here?"

"Well, I assumed so. He always did when we had an early morning meeting. And this was an extremely early one."

"And you had no idea what this meeting was about, huh?"

"That's right. As I told you, he didn't want to discuss it on the phone."

"Who else knew he'd be spending the night here?"

"I'm not sure. He often spent the night in town. His three partners are having their monthly meeting here today. Maybe they knew. Probably his wife. I guess he'd have told his assistant Mandy—Amanda Greathouse. I don't know about the rest of the staff or anyone else."

"Who else has keys to this place?" So the police didn't think it was a break-in.

"Well, lots of people do—to the front door. The staff, that's—let's see—nine of them. King's three partners, of course, and I guess Gillian—that's Mrs. Carter. But not many people have keys to the private floors upstairs—just Mandy and the partners. Sometimes they use the guest suite. Oh, and I suppose Gillian. But look, how do you know it was someone with a key? I mean, maybe King let him in, or—"

CAROL BRENNAN

Suddenly, there was a cacophony of angry voices at the front door.

"You *will* let me in here!" I knew that voice. It was Leslie Charlton. A moment later the owner of the voice stood in the arch of the reception area. With him was Mandy Greathouse.

"These people belong here," I said to Sergeant Libuti. "You have to let them in."

"I bumped into Mandy right outside and this jackass"—he glanced icily at Wong—"tried to stop us coming in. What the hell's going on?"

"It seems like Mr. Carter has been murdered, sir," Libuti said politely. Mandy's milky red-head skin went scarlet, then gray. She didn't say a word. She just stood there and looked at Libuti. And then she fainted.

4

. . . .

I TOLD PORKY REMLEY WHERE THE KITCHEN WAS, AND HE
trundled off to get a wet towel to revive Mandy. Les's long,
thin fingers clutched a furled umbrella. His knuckles were very
white. In his tightly belted trench coat and soft black felt hat
he looked androgynous. Les was a stick figure of a person,
very slim and pale skinned, but strong the way wire cable
is strong. He looked taller than his five foot eight inches or
so because his body was almost all legs. What made him
especially striking was the ice gray of his eyes and the absence
of a hair on his head. At thirty-eight he was almost totally bald
and the little hair nature had left him he kept shaved. Right
now the elongated oval face was drained of what faint color
it normally had and the furrows from his nose to the corners
of his mouth looked deep and lifeless. I felt awful for him. He
looked devastated.

"What happened?" His question was addressed neither to
me nor to Libuti, but to the room.

"We'll know more when the medical examiner gets here,
which should be in a few minutes," Libuti said. "Now who're
you, and," he looked down at Mandy who was moaning softly
under the ministration of Remley, "who's this lady?"

I answered. I was, after all, the PR representative for this
outfit.

"Sergeant, this is Leslie Charlton, Mr. Carter's partner from
Boston. And this is Mr. Carter's . . . uh, assistant." Mandy was
really more than a secretary.

She had started to come around and Remley and I helped her get up and steered her to the sofa. Her pale green eyes were wide and trancelike. She said nothing.

"You just get into town, Mr. Charlton?" asked Libuti, taking in the leather overnighter hanging from Les's shoulder.

"Yes. I got into LaGuardia just about," he looked at his watch, "half an hour ago and came right here. We're having," he stopped himself and sighed, "we were having a partners' meeting today. I guess everything's changed." He faded off at the end, as though talking at all was an effort.

"Les, why don't you sit down." I took his arm and guided him toward the sofa. He removed Libuti's ashtray to the end table and sat. "I know how horrible this is for you and for Mandy. Let me at least take some of the stuff that has to be done off your hands. I've called Seth. He's working on a release for the obit and notifying the *Times* and the *Wall Street Journal*. We'll want to deal with the business media ourselves. As far as the tabloids, TV, and radio, I think it'll be best to buck all inquiries to the police." I turned to Libuti. "Who should we refer the media to, Sergeant?"

"You can refer them to Ray Perez," he said, writing the telephone number on a piece of notepad paper. He handed it to me, then lit another Camel. The place was beginning to smell like a commuter train smoking car. "You can refer them there, but they'll wind up bugging the lieutenant like they always do."

"We can also help out on the funeral arrangements, or . . . or anything else," I added, feeling inadequate.

Mandy spoke for the first time.

"The rest of the staff will be getting here very soon." Her voice was weak, but composed.

"You're right, Mandy," I said. "I'll deal with them."

"I'm sorry, Ms. Wareham," Libuti cut in, "I'm afraid you're not going to be able to do that. I'm going to have to send you in to make an official statement. You did find the body. And the lieutenant wants to talk to you."

I was pissed. "Look, Sergeant. I've told you everything I know about this. There's a great deal to do now and I'm needed here. Les and Mandy can't do it all. I mean, there's King's wife to tell, as well as the staff, and the other partners are on their way in, and—"

"It's okay, Liz," Les cut in, "I can handle it." He turned to Libuti. "I would like to tell Mrs. Carter in person, if you don't mind. She shouldn't have to absorb this on the phone . . . or hear it from the police."

Libuti nodded. "I'll arrange to have someone take you there. Where does she live?"

"Oyster Bay," answered Les. "They have a horse farm out there. Gillian doesn't come into the city very often."

Almost never, as far as I knew. She and King led very separate lives—his focused on business and connoisseurship, with, I gathered, periodic discreet liaisons, hers devoted to her horses and what else I'd no idea. I had met her only once in passing here at the Manse, but it was enough to make clear why David Goldstone, the Chicago partner, referred to her as the Ice Queen.

"Okay, I'll go quietly," I said. And I did, holding out only for the privilege of first calling my office from the privacy of one of the staff offices. Seth read me his release draft, and I took nips and tucks, as one tends to do with any document that someone else has written. I filled Seth in on the media strategy and asked to be transferred to John Gentle, who listened without comment to my report. Then he asked his key question: "Any danger we're going to lose the account?"

5

·····················

FORTY MINUTES AFTER A PLEASANT-LOOKING YOUNG black policewoman had taken my third statement and I'd signed it, I was still waiting on a wooden slat-backed bench for my audience with the lieutenant.

Two surly youths in handcuffs were being ushered past me none too gently by a pair of weary-looking female cops, and a woman about my age was telling the desk sergeant something about her ex-husband. All in all, it looked and sounded just like every police procedural I'd ever read or watched, and I couldn't help feeling like an extra.

On my way out of the Manse, I'd looked for Douglas's umbrella, but it had vanished from the stand. The rain had seeped through both skirt and pantyhose and my bottom felt damp and cold. My temper, on the other hand, was heating up rapidly with each forward move of the big hand on the large round wall clock. Between the waves of anger and frustration, questions stimulated by thirty years of thriller-reading swam in my head. What was the motive? Money? Anger? Jealousy? That knife had to have been plunged into King's chest by someone who knew him, who'd seen him fondle it while feeling the sting of his tongue. But who?

Remley appeared and I glared at him, which perturbed him not at all. He was probably used to it.

"Come with me, miss. The lieutenant will see you now."

He led me up two flights of stairs into what I recognized must be the detectives' bullpen and around another corner to an office with a closed door. He knocked twice and a voice within said, "Right with you, come in."

He opened the door to a plain City-issue working office with two large windows.

The man sitting behind the battered mahogany desk was on the phone, his back to us. When he hung up and spun his chair around, I got my second shock of the morning involving a man behind a desk.

"Oh Jesus, it's you!" exploded out of my mouth, as my heart jumped. Ike O'Hanlon had always had that effect on me. This was all I needed.

He smiled slowly, just like I remembered, making the intense blue eyes almost disappear and turning the Irish face into all forehead, eyebrows, and chin. "Well, I'll be damned. Liz Herzog."

He turned his attention briefly to Remley who was clearly puzzled. "That's okay, Connie. You can go. Ms. Herzog—or, I guess it's Ms. Wareham—and I are old friends."

Old friends, my ass. I hadn't seen Ike since he'd ejected me from his father's Nash at two in the morning after my senior prom and made me walk the eight blocks home alone tottering on my spike heels and ready to commit mayhem.

6

....

HE LOOKED AT ME—JUST THAT NARROW BLUE IKE LOOK
that hadn't changed one bit in twenty-five years. I felt
all my pulses throb violently and was instantly furious with
myself that he could still do it to me.

"Okay, why'd you kill him?" he asked, deadpan.

"Clients don't pay their bills on time, we blow 'em away,"
I snapped.

"Sit down, Liz," he said quietly in that O'Hanlon voice with
the slightly sandy edge to it. They all had that voice quirk, all
except Rosie, but then she was only an O'Hanlon by marriage.
The kids showed their Goldenberg genes—Rosie's genes—in
other ways. "You look awful. Cup of coffee before we talk
about it?"

"Thank you. That would be fine," I said coldly, aware that
I looked awful, nettled that he'd pointed it out, and annoyed
that I cared how I looked to Ike O'Hanlon.

He picked up the battered black phone at his left hand. I
remembered irrelevantly that Ike was a southpaw like his
father—not the only resemblance between the two. "Manny,
could you promote a couple of coffees?" He looked at me
inquiringly.

"You didn't drink the stuff when you were seventeen, so I
don't know how you take it."

"Just plain. Black. No sugar."

"Both black, no sugar," he said into the phone and hung
up.

"This is going to take some time, Liz, but it's necessary. I appreciate that you have lots of PR work to do around this thing, but my work is more important, and it comes first." The voice was pleasant, but the blue look had a chill on it.

"*Jawohl, mein Oberst.*" I stuck my arm out in a Nazi salute.

"So," he ventured, "how did Liz Herzog get to be Ms. Wareham? I thought I'd heard that you were Mrs. Bernchiller, sometime back before anyone was Ms. anything."

"My name changed to Wareham in the usual way women's names change."

"Is Mr. Wareham around and about?"

"I assume he is, but not around or about me, thank God." My resolve for coldness cracked. "What the hell business is it of yours?"

"An odd question for a suspect in a murder case to ask an investigating officer. But if you mean, is my question of personal interest, of course it is. We did grow up together, after all."

"What do you mean, *suspect*? I've had as much of your supercilious—"

"Now cool down, Liz. I know you've been through a lot, and—"

"Been through a lot?" I screeched. "You don't know—" Just then the door opened and a compact young Puerto Rican cop walked in with two cardboard coffees.

"Sorry it took so long, Lieutenant," he said as he put them on the desk and left in a hurry, eager to get out of whatever he'd walked into.

I took an overlarge sip of tarrish coffee and singed my tongue. My hangover headache was making a strong comeback.

"Look, Liz, I'm not going to be the easiest person for you to deal with on this. But you *are* going to deal with me because I am in charge of this case and you have no choice. Now take a deep breath, and let's talk about what happened."

I repeated my story yet again, from King's phone call the previous day to arriving at the Manse and finding his body.

CAROL BRENNAN

Ike didn't interupt me once. When I'd finished, he looked at me hard and asked "Is that all of it?" Since he hadn't actually asked me about going back in there with the police, it was easy to not mention the earring. As I thought about it, I imagined it burning a hole in my damp cashmere pocket and dropping out right there on the threadbare tan carpet. My face flushed.

"Yes. That's all," I said. I was committed to it now.

"You mentioned you spent the night with a friend," Ike said perfectly straight, but I thought I detected a flicker of amusement and it heightened my dread of what I knew must be coming. "We'll need to reach . . . him?" The final word was a gentle question.

"Yes," I answered coldly, "him." That's all I needed in the middle of this. Douglas. I supplied Douglas's name, address, and numbers, but no further information. I could picture Ike enjoying a blow-by-blow replay of last night's Douglas-Liz melodrama and the prospect mortified me.

"May I leave now?" I asked with a pointed look at my watch. It was already twelve-forty-five. I wanted to leave that room as badly as I've ever wanted anything.

"Tell me about Carter Consultants," he said, reaching for his coffee. He drained the soggy container and picked up the phone.

"Want some more, Liz?"

"No," I answered, omitting the obligatory thank you. "Look, I went over that with Sergeant Libuti, and I'm sure by now he's got all the background he needs on the company—not only from me but from the partners and—"

"Liz," he said gently, "believe me, I know my business, and how to conduct it. I'm going to be going over the same ground again and again—not only with you but with everyone associated with Kingman Carter. Your input is especially useful not only because you found the body and worked closely with him and his partners, but because I know you."

"Used to know me," I fired back.

"And," he went on as though I'd said nothing, "I know that you're smart and observant. Besides," he flashed the O'Hanlon grin, which I wanted to kick in, "you have what sounds like an airtight alibi."

I looked at him levelly. He wanted a rundown on the company. That's what he'd get—straight from our press kit. "Carter Consultants is a twelve-year-old management consulting firm which specializes in recruiting senior executives for major American and international corporations, as well as for some of the nation's leading venture companies. Carter Consultants maintains offices in New York, Boston, Chicago, and Westport, Connecticut, and is about to open an office in San Jose, California. Kingman Carter, president of—"

"Okay," he said with a smile, but not a big one, "you can turn off the tape and send me the press kit. I'll let you go."

I didn't say anything. I'd won. He didn't speak either for a long moment. Then he said "Look, I'm going up to the Carter house and then to the Regency to interview the partners. They've taken suites there for the next few days. And then I'll be going out to see Mrs. Carter. How's this? Have dinner with me tomorrow night. By then I'll know a lot more and you'll have your PR act together and be in better shape."

I didn't answer. He'd caught me by surprise and I didn't know what to say.

"Look, Liz, seriously, I'd appreciate your help and I'd also like to see you—somewhere a little more relaxed than here. Look, I'm not saying this very well, but come to my place for dinner tomorrow night. Please."

"Your place?" I croaked. I cleared my throat. "I don't think that would be a good idea," I said unconvincingly. The thing was, I suddenly wanted to go to Ike's apartment. Besides, he wasn't bullying or teasing; he was asking.

"Hey," he said, "I won't lay a glove on you. Promise."

I was disarmed. "Okay," I said carefully. "Where do you live?"

"Sixty-six Charles Street. You know the Village, don't you?"

I nodded. I'd spent my college years in Greenwich Village, at New York University's theater department. "How about eight o'clock?" he asked.

Good behavior continues, I noted. He was asking instead of telling.

"That'll be fine," I said as I headed toward the door.

"Oh, Liz. That's *Doctor* Douglas Friedlaender, isn't it?"

"Go fuck yourself," I said as I slipped out and closed the door. But there was no heat in it.

7

I DEBATED AS I STOOD ON THE CURB WITH MY CAB HAND raised whether to head for the Regency, the Manse, or the office. When a cab pulled up and the driver asked "Where to?" I gave him my home address instead, reasoning that Les and the other partners would be tied up with the police at the Regency and there was nothing I could do at the Manse even if the police let me in, which they probably wouldn't. Anyway, the place would be lousy with six o'clock news crews, who would be all over me because I'd found the body, asking me questions I didn't know the answers to. The office could wait till I'd showered, changed to dry clothes, and grabbed an umbrella. It was still raining.

As the driver headed toward the Upper West Side, I thought about the O'Hanlons. They'd lived around the corner from us in Forest Hills, and they'd always seemed magical to me, exotic flowers in the secure safe sameness of our upper middle-class Jewish neighborhood. Captain Pat, Ike's father, had come to New York from County Mayo. The west-of-Ireland lilt of his brogue and his dashing uniform were infinitely more glamorous than my doctor father's New York accent and tweeds.

Ike's mother Rosie (nobody, including her children, ever called her anything else) was known around the neighborhood as the Wall Street Wolverine, and the other women, even my mother, half-envied her. A Jewish girl who'd kicked over the traces, married an Irish cop, and speculated like a daredevil in the market.

CAROL BRENNAN

The kids were Rebecca, Isaac, and Jacob, in that order. Rosie used to say that if they were going to be O'Hanlons they'd be Jewish O'Hanlons. In two out of three she was right. Becky was a Jap when that was still short for Japanese and Jake was a bookish kid with a good quiet sense of humor. Captain Pat used to call them his princess and his scholar. You couldn't miss how proud he was of them. Then there was Ike.

Ike was no Jewish kid. He was Irish clear through and yet, or therefore, his mother's favorite. Ike carried a sense of adventure about him that was irresistible, not only to us girls, but also to the pack of boys that were his followers. The same adventurous instincts had him in constant trouble with his father. I remember the time that Ike got the idea for a secret runaway to Jones Beach to camp out. He took Bobby Greenberg, Hank Spitz, and Mark Silverstein with him. The police found them three days later having a wonderful time. Captain Pat beat him with a belt and grounded him for the rest of the summer, but Ike used to sneak out late at night and ride his bike for hours. I saw him out my bedroom window one night when I'd woken up to go to the bathroom. I threw open the window and waved at him. He grinned up at me and waved back. Then he put his finger to his lips. He needn't have worried. I'd never have told on him. I may've been only nine but I was in love with him.

I was nudged back to the present when the cab stopped in front of 248 Central Park West. I greeted Gus, who was on the door, and headed for the elevator. As I approached my apartment, I could hear the phone. I unlocked both locks and dashed to catch it as fast as I could, given that I was suddenly calf deep in hungry cats. The kitchen phone was closest and I grabbed it.

"Hello" I said more peremptorily than I'd meant to. It was my boss, John Gentle.

"Liz, where the hell are you? The shit's hit the fan and the whole agency's a mess. Everybody's media contacts are calling, trying to wheedle inside information about your damned murder, and no one can get any work done and—"

"John," I cut in, "the police have just let me go." I didn't think it was politic to disavow ownership of the murder or to point out that he knew where I was, since he'd called me. "I stopped home for a quick change of clothes. I'm drenched. I'll be there in half an hour, forty minutes. What about you get everyone in the conference room at—" I glanced at my watch, "say three o'clock, and I'll tell them all the inside information I have, which is none. Seth and I are going to have our hands full dealing with the business aspects—and that's all we're dealing with."

"Goddamned right," he said, sounding mollified. "Who'll take over the firm?"

"Well, Rog Durand has seniority, but there's no chance. He does the lowest volume by far, and he'll be lucky if the other two don't bounce him out on his ass, now that King's gone. As between Les Charlton and Dave Goldstone . . ." The cats were now wrapped around my legs in a rubbing frenzy. "Look, John. Let me get off now so I can change and get down there. We'll talk then."

"Okay," he replied, sounding disappointed. Once John got started on business strategy the conversation could go on for hours. Discussing ins and outs of the game was the thing he enjoyed most—except making money, of course.

"See you at three o'clock," I said and hung up before he could say another word. I fed the cats, giving them a double helping of creamed kidney as a reward for who knew what. Elephi's plump gray tabby body pushed Three's more delicate Siamese one out of his way, and she was nosing in from the other side of the water dish as I went down the hall to the bedroom.

My apartment is vintage Upper West Side sprawl, with airy rooms, nine and a half foot beamed ceilings and a living-room fireplace. It's filled with squashy, comfortable modern sofas and chairs, which live happily with Shaker tables and other American antiques. There's lots of red and old brass things and books and paintings of all kinds. It's all stuff I like to be around and it goes together for that reason.

Back when Alan Bernchiller and I found the apartment, we couldn't believe our luck. It was Buckingham Palace compared to the stingy two-bedroom 1960's cookie cutter we were squeezed into with six-year-old Scott and three-year-old Sarah. I'll never forget our first look at old 8J. The kids ran straight down the hall as though they owned it already. We stood at its threshold marveling at the space and light. City roofscape views, rather than the more highly prized ones of Central Park, but great light.

I was undaunted by the peeling mauve and cream paint, the falling plaster, and the antiquated appliances. Alan was so preoccupied with his budding OB/GYN practice that he didn't notice them. I'd have killed for that apartment. Fortunately I didn't have to. My parents gave us the down payment.

The apartment became my project during the next two years. I scraped and plastered and painted and wallpapered, enthusiastically assisted by Scotty and Sarah, while Alan delivered babies. I stalked auction rooms for items such as the big, beautifully faded Orientals which covered the living-room and dining-room floors. It was the traditional division of labor, and, in its time and place, maybe not such a bad one.

I wriggled out of my soggy clothes and threw them in the general direction of the exercise bike, purchased with high hopes of taut thighs, but which in three months' time had deteriorated into a clothes tree. After a quick in-and-out hot shower, I slipped on a gray tweed knit chemise with a crew neck and a fresh pair of blessedly dry black pumps over semisheer black tights. I suspected the day would stretch into a very long one and these were as comfortable as business clothes got. I picked up the bedside phone on the mahogany table, dialed the Regency and asked for David Goldstone. He picked up on the first ring.

"Yello." He always said it that way.

"Dave, it's Liz. The police have just let me go and Lieutenant O'Hanlon's on his way to you."

"I know. Libuti's camped in the other suite with Rog waiting."

"Dave, I don't . . . I mean it's so unbelievable."

"Yeah, terrible thing," he said quickly, sounding choked. Dave was an emotional man, uncomfortable with emotional display. At thirty-nine he was still a tough smart Jewish kid from New York's Lower East Side, who had grown up in a family so poor that, as some long lost comedian used to put it, "they lived *under* the candy store." The reason I knew the facts of his early life so well was that he was aggressively up front about them: the early poverty; his scholarship to the University of Chicago and later Stanford Business School; and his devotion to his late parents, Sol and Minnie.

"I hate to lay another thing on you just now, but the business media'll be all over us about what's going to happen to the firm, who'll become president and all that. I'm going to need some time with you to discuss how to handle it."

"Yeah, it's important." He sounded weary. The murder had subdued even Dave's energy and that was not an easy thing to do. "When can you get over here?"

"I should be able to get out of the office by five or so, and by that time O'Hanlon should be done with you. Okay?"

"Sure. Come to Suite 702, that's under Rog's name."

As I hung up the phone, I noticed for the first time that the message machine on the other side of the phone was blinking a red five. I pushed the play button. The first was a hang-up. The second was from King Carter, and I gasped with shock at hearing his voice in the split second before I realized that the message was from last night. "Liz, this is King. Our meeting tomorrow morning is canceled. There's no point in involving you unless . . . I'll have to handle it another way." That was all. Three other messages played, but I barely heard them.

8

....

THE RAIN WAS STILL COMING DOWN IN DRIBS AND DRABS. While I waited under the canopy for Gus to hail me a cab, I thought about King's message. Apparently, my fears of getting fired had been unwarranted. But what could he have wanted to talk to me about, and why had he changed his mind? He'd certainly sounded strained when he'd called to arrange the meeting, and even more strained in this last message. King was not a man who strained easily.

A cab finally pulled up. Gus opened the door and helped me in with an understated flourish and a "You have a good afternoon now, Mrs. Wareham." He is the courtliest gentleman I know.

As we pulled away from the curb and drove through Central Park and downtown to my office, I pondered King's words: "handle it another way." Had he chosen to handle whatever "it" was in a way that pushed someone over the edge? Even the thought seemed melodramatic—but no more melodramatic than the sight of King with that dagger sticking crazily out of his chest.

The police seemed to believe that the killer was someone King had let in, or someone who had a key. I wondered how the earring and its owner fit in. I also knew that I should have turned that earring over to the police at once, and yet I couldn't believe—

"Hey, lady, whatcha waiting for? We're here."

It took me a second to realize he was right. As I walked

into One East 54th Street, I shifted gears into the kinds of questions that were uppermost in John Gentle's mind—the ones that affected the account. Those questions were important to me, too. What would happen to Carter Consultants now that Carter was gone? It would be quite a different firm with Les or David in the top spot. Both were smart. Maybe even as smart as King. But did either have the stature to follow a man like Kingman Carter? Well, Harry Truman had had bigger boots to fill and he'd managed.

The elevator dinged and the door opened to the eighteenth floor. The legend "The Gentle Group" in smart brushed steel greeted me from the dove gray wall. The reception area set the tone for the whole place. It was composed entirely of carefully lit soft grays—walls, velvety carpet, leather sofas. The large yellow china bowl of copper and white mums on Sharon's pearl gray reception desk was the only touch of color. As I stepped off the elevator and waved a "Hi" at Sharon, the star for whom this tony gray set had been designed entered the reception area from the direction of the conference room. He was talking animatedly to a short round man and a beige woman of indeterminate age—both dressed in what my garment center friend Joan calls "Full Cleveland."

John Gentle was a study in grays, just like the office. In other settings he looked like an unremarkable medium-tall, trim, red-faced man with thinning gray hair and dark gray eyes, dressed in a well-cut gray suit. Here on his own stage—our reception area or the conference room or his own large office, all decorated in the same artfully designed, strategically lighted grays—his hair looked silver, his eyes obsidian, and his skin healthily rosy. Bringing up the rear and beaming at John's monologue was Briggs Drew, my opposite number, Golden Boy himself.

"We're going to love working with you, Glenn," John said, beaming. "And Lurleen," he added after just a beat. "The project is really exciting. Just up our alley. And Briggs here and his people . . ." He broke off as he just missed running into me. "See, you bump into talent all over this office," he improvised seamlessly. "Say hello to Liz Wareham, our other executive vice president. Liz, meet Glenn Strader and Lurleen Spungen of Farragut Products." I shook hands and how-do-you-doed them with a correct executive smile.

So he'd put the account into Briggs's group, had he? I was furious. We'd known for the past two weeks that John had been talking to Farragut, and according to my reckoning, my group was up for the next over-the-transom account that came into the agency. Briggs had gotten the last one. No wonder John had been so evasive when I'd broached the subject of Farragut after last Monday's meeting. That bastard. I could tell that Briggs knew exactly how I was feeling by the barely contained smirk that crossed his Yale Club face. "See you at three," I tossed over my shoulder as I disappeared down the long corridor to my office.

My crew occupies the sunny southwest corner overlooking Fifth Avenue and points downtown. The corner office is mine, as befits my exalted rank. Seth Frankel's office flanks me to the north, though his perennially closed blinds admit precious little southern light. Next door to him Patti Nevins, two years removed from Wheaton, and Bruce Forsythe, three years out of Howard, share a small office and dreams of becoming account executives.

My other top aide, Angela Chappel, sits in her chic aerie to the east. Keep walking east and you hit Cormac McCafferty, budding rock star who keeps himself in guitar strings by writing damned good copy, and Kirk Aristidos, publicist *extraordinaire*.

Outside Angela's office sits Carmen Del Rio, our number two secretary. Our number one, Morley Carton, without whom my world would collapse, makes his nine-(if we're lucky) to-five (if he's lucky) home in the corner to the right of my office door.

Morley saw me and looked up from the green screen of his IBM. "Hail the conquering heroine. I thought you'd look worse." His soft Louisiana drawl made even snottiness sound caressing.

"Thanks, I think. I made a pit stop home for a shower and a change. You should have seen me before. Even one of my own cats wouldn't have bothered to drag me in."

"Seriously, Liz, are you okay?" I nodded. "The messages are on your desk, in three piles: urgent, important, and life must go on. In the last category I made an appointment for you with Agnes for a facial next Wednesday at three and Ann Marie called from Saks that the Donna Karan jacket you ordered is there. Less fun, but I guess more important, Chris at Baker Bank's been trying to get you and so has Dennis Quayle from the British Board of Trade. I gave them to Angela. Also, someone called early, before anybody was in. Sharon took the message from service. I put your mother in the urgent pile after her third call. She's already heard about it down in Florida. I told her you were okay, but I think she needs to hear it firsthand."

"You're right." When wasn't Morley right? He's the best secretary in New York, and there's very little I wouldn't do to keep him happy enough to resist the advances of would-be secretary pirates, who have, over the years, included clients. "Buzz Seth, would you, and let him know I'm here."

"Sure. He's on the phone with the *Times*, though, so he may be a few minutes. Don't worry. I'll get him to you by ten of three. I have to warn you, though, he's into deep hangdog, the 'why me?' look. You'd think the murder happened to him personally. You know, Liz, it's weird. I think of all the times you've said 'I could kill him' about King Carter. I guess someone else felt the same way—" He paused. "At least I hope it was someone else."

"Ha-Ha," I said mirthlessly, as I walked into my lair and closed the door. My office has sapphire blue carpet and chalk white walls. The sun from a windowed corner casts its south and west light on a large painting of brilliant apples nesting in an old beat-up basket. I've made sure no gray seeps into this room except, occasionally, my mood.

I hung up my coat and umbrella and dialed my mother. My chair felt somehow enveloping and reassuring. It's a full-sized

CAROL BRENNAN

space-age leather executive swivel. No matter who disagrees, I say it goes fine with the big country French table I use as a desk. I love the table and saw no reason to spend hours punishing my butt and back on uncomfortable cane just to be in period.

"Hi, Mom."

"Liz darling, I was so worried. Are you all right?"

"I'm absolutely fine. The police came right away and took care of everything." I always underplay for my mother. The alternative—to let on that I'm upset about anything—upsets her to such a degree that I end up worrying about her worrying about me and then she's worrying about me worrying about her, and on and on into Jewish familial infinity. She'd just gone down to her Boca Raton condo the week before. That was a break.

"Manhattan is so dangerous. My God, the thought of you all alone, now that Sarah's out in California—I just wish you were settled."

"I know, Mom. But I *am* settled. I have a good job, a nice apartment . . ."

"You know what I mean."

"Yeah, I know what you mean." Despite my discouraging track record, my mother wished devoutly for my remarriage.

"Would you believe the coincidence," she began, and I knew what was coming, "that Ike O'Hanlon is in charge of the case? I saw him on TV. He looked so handsome. Did you—"

"Yeah, Mom, I did. Look, I have a million calls to return and I really have to run." Suddenly, I felt like a rat. The death of my father had ended her career as a wife, and her two middle-aged daughters no longer required major mothering. She was unemployed. "Mom," I said in a different tone, "as soon as this cools, I'll fly down and see you, okay?"

"More than okay, baby. Keep in touch."

I looked through the messages in the urgent pile. Chris Maclos of Baker Bank. Baker was my group's biggest client. I'd built the account, division by division, during the past six years. Its billings were now $800,000 in annual fees, and when

Chris tooted the kazoo, I saluted. Dennis Quayle of the British Board of Trade also had called. This was my hottest new-business prospect. They'd liked our "Buy Britain" campaign proposal to sell American consumers on a new international shop-by-phone service. If the Board of Trade hired us, my halo would be back in place and Briggs Drew could start worrying for a change.

Both messages, as Morley had said, had been bucked to Angela Chappel and, if I knew Angela, handled just fine.

Roger Durand, King's Westport partner, had called and left the Regency number. The call had come in before I'd spoken to Dave Goldstone from home. By now Rog knew I'd be at the hotel in a few hours, so that could wait. Various media calls on the murder—all bucked to Seth, and at the bottom of the pile, a call from an Antony Swift. The name didn't ring a bell, but the message had come in at eight-ten that morning and the slip said he was at the Plaza Hotel. I dialed the number. When his room didn't answer, I left a message.

Just then Seth opened the door quickly, closed it behind him, and sat himself on one of the Breuer chairs opposite my desk.

Seth's hangdog look was, as expected, in place. He'd been invented by Woody Allen and plunked into my account group as a script development tactic for a new Allen opus about the agony of public relations. Seth is one of the homeliest people I've ever met, olive-skinned with large, brown, myopic eyes behind thick glasses and prominent teeth under a feeble mustache. He began without wasting time on hello, how are you, which was fine by me.

"So here's the release and the list it went to." He handed me a press list which included the *Times* and *Wall Street Journal* reporters we'd discussed, as well as the business editors of the major news services, and the top business publications: *Forbes, Fortune, Business Week*, and the like. "I talked to everyone on the list and I think we'll be fine—at least for the moment. I mean the business press will give him a good send-off and say the right stuff about Carter Consultants. But

37

after a few days they'll be at us about the future of the firm. The *Journal* has an anonymous tip about the possible Green Star buyout, and Joe at *Business Week* wanted to know if the San Jose office was a done deal or not. Of course, the first question is who's going to run the firm, and I figure we've got till Monday at the outside to answer it. Me, I'm just the schmucky publicist. They won't press me too hard 'cause they know nobody ever tells me anything. But when they get ahold of you, they're gonna lean on you."

And that's why I value Seth so much. He may whine, and he wouldn't be anyone's choice for a fun dinner date, but he's a pro in the business he says he hates, and he delivers. "Seth, you're great. You handled it just right. At the moment, I don't know any more than you do, but I'm meeting with the partners after I'm finished here, and I'll make a few calls to our best contacts tomorrow, probably not with anything definitive, just a little stroking and an idea on when they can expect some meat. Anybody hassling you to provide inside stuff about the murder itself?"

"Some, yeah, but I told them I don't know anything, which is true, and gave them the police number you gave me. I also gave the number and no other information to the Cossacks around here, in Boola Boola's group, who'd love to throw their press contacts some bread on the waters. They weren't happy."

"I'm sure not. They'll be less happy after the meeting, which is," I glanced at my watch, "now."

The conference room was filling up as Seth and I arrived. Everybody in the agency, including secretaries, clericals, and mailroom staff, had been told to be there. Even Sharon, the receptionist, had switched incoming calls to the conference-room phone and was taking messages. The long, cloud-gray room with its polished charcoal conference table was packed to beyond its capacity. It could comfortably accommodate twenty people, not fifty. The juniors and clericals lined the walls, perched on credenza and cabinet tops. I was greeted like a soldier returning from battle, with waves of camaraderie, curiosity, and concern—and a few ripples of competition.

I made my way to my accustomed seat near the far end of the table. Just then John Gentle entered, followed by Briggs Drew. I scanned the room but didn't see Angela.

John strode to the head of the table. "I called this briefing session so that we can all get back to work and you can stop whispering in the halls and looking for the inside story to feed your press contacts—or your own curiosity. I'm going to let Liz tell you what happened and the strategy she's worked out. We're all going to support that strategy so this agency doesn't look foolish and, even more important, that we keep and expand," he looked meaningfully at me, "this piece of business." John always referred to a "piece of business" as though it were a piece of steak, coincidentally or not, his favorite food. "Over to you, Liz."

"Thanks, John." I felt like I was being introduced at a rubber chicken political dinner, rather than talking to coworkers that I saw daily. "I don't have very much to say. I know that those of you who are getting leaned on by press contacts are in a tough spot, and that it's human nature to be curious, particularly about something sensational that's happened so close to home. Bluntly, I think that my so-called briefing session will be a letdown." I paused as I saw Angela appear at the doorway, looking chic and honey-skinned as usual, her tawny streaked hair smooth and satiny as it fell to her shoulders. Angela was not young—a few years older than I and (I won't say "but") beautiful in the classic long-limbed golden way that short, dark, curly persons tend to envy. Her terra-cotta de la Renta was accented with baroque pearls at her neck and ears. I caught her eye and she smiled sympathetically.

"I have very little to tell you," I said to the room. "I found King Carter dead in his office when I arrived for an early morning meeting. I called the police. Anything relating to the murder is their turf. The police information contact is Ray Perez at 580-7690. Our group is involved solely with the business side of this tragedy, and if any of your media contacts wants to discuss those aspects, they can call Seth, Patti, or me."

A knowing glance passed between Briggs and his top lieutenant, Martin Godfrey, which made it clear that they thought I was being self-important. It was equally obvious that they were licking their chops after a tasty meal of canary, namely the new Farragut Products account, and couldn't care less.

The reaction around the room ranged from disappointment to mild irritation. As soon as it was plain that there'd be no juicy inside murder story, watches were glanced at. Everyone suddenly had a great deal to do.

John stood up and the buzz quieted down. "I'm counting on each of you to be a cooperating member of this team—to be discreet and to keep your mouths shut. They used to say back in my war, which you're all too young to remember," he said ignoring Irving Kleinfeld and Dolly McQuade, who were quite old enough to have vivid recollections of World War II, "loose lips sink ships. Anyone who sinks our ship, or even springs a little leak," he continued with a vintage John Gentle smile on his wide thin mouth, "is fired."

9

....

"CHRIS WANTED TO SET UP A MEETING ON THE 'Baker Bank Targets the World' seminars. I set one up for next Tuesday at eleven o'clock down there. I put it on your calendar. Dennis wants you to call him back. He also wanted to know when he can expect the events budget for our proposal. I'll have it finished by tomorrow, and I'll—"

She stopped in mid-syllable as I put the earring on the desk.

"Okay, Angela, what about it?"

She stared at it and I stared at her. Nobody said a word. As she looked up at me finally, her face colored, the rising coral in her cheeks making her look, ironically, even more delectable. "I . . . I . . . guess I lost it," she said as she reached for it. "Thanks."

"I guess you did." I responded in kind by closing my hand over it. "Do you have any idea where?"

"N—No, actually, I . . . uh . . ."

"Angela, cut it right now. I've gone out on a long long limb for you. I've taken evidence from the scene of a murder. They could put me in jail for ninety years or something. I have done this because you are my coworker and my friend and I believe in you. Now, dammit, talk to me."

The coral cheeks drained to ivory and Angela looked every minute of her forty-six years.

"I was there last night," she said in a soft voice.

I waited for her to continue, but she didn't. "I know *that*. You wore those earrings yesterday," I said. "I need to know

41

the rest. When exactly were you there? Was he dead? Was he alive? Hell, I didn't even know that you and he saw each other."

Angela had met King Carter last year when Seth was home sick and she'd helped me out on the Carter Consultants Leadership Conference. I did not know that she and King had ever laid eyes on each other again.

"Okay," she said and took a deep breath. Some of the color returned to her face. "I do owe you an explanation. First of all, King was very much alive when I left him last night. We were together till, oh, I don't know, twelve-forty-five or so. I took a cab right home and watched *They Died With Their Boots On.* That started at one and I caught the opening credits. For the rest, I'll have to go back to last October, because it won't make much sense otherwise. You remember I met King during that conference and we kind of noticed each other. His combination of elegance plus power was very sexy to me. But it was also a lot more. I think we each recognized a kindred spirit."

"Kindred spirit!" I cut in. "King was a shark, and you're . . . you're . . ." Suddenly I realized that apart from her charm, general friendliness, and skill at public relations, I knew very little about Angela Chappel. I knew that she was seriously rich—her mother had been a Frost of the Frost Cereal family. I knew she was separated from her second husband, Barney Seever, the tennis player. I knew she owned a wonderful Fifth Avenue penthouse, which I had visited, and a Southampton weekend place, which I had not. I didn't have a clue to what she was really about, including why she chose to work extremely hard at a PR agency that she could buy and sell several times over.

"I guess I don't know you very well, Angela," I said quietly. To myself I added, "Then how do I know you didn't kill him?"

The question must have registered on my face. I lowered my eyes to the earring on the desk.

"Liz, look at me. I didn't kill King. You have to believe that. You *do* know me . . . in the important ways. You work with me every day. Don't you know I couldn't kill anyone?"

I didn't answer.

"You *must* know that. If you had any doubt about it, you'd have given that earring to the police."

She had me there. What I knew damned well was that I *should* have given it to the police, no matter what I believed. I looked at her as I gnawed my thumbnail, a nervous habit I've not been able to break since age three. "I believe you didn't kill him," I said. "And I interrupted what you were telling me. Please go on."

"When I say kindred spirit," Angela continued, "I don't mean that we were alike, I mean that we suited each other. We saw a great many things the same way. We . . . this may sound odd, considering what you think . . . thought . . . of King, but we instinctively trusted each other."

"Are you saying that you were in love?"

"Not in the way you mean, Liz. Not in the way most people mean. We saw each other sporadically; went away for a few weekends. Sex was good. King was quite accomplished—as he was in everything he did. But it wasn't the main event for us. Also, there was never that possessiveness, that kind of exclusivity that goes with being in love. Neither of us wanted to see the other all the time or arrange our lives to be together. When we did see each other, though, there was this thing. It's hard to explain. We could talk about anything with no disclaimers that this or that was confidential. We just . . ."

She couldn't go on. The tears had started to run down her face. I got up from behind the desk, walked around to the other side, and put my arm around her shoulder. While she cried soundlessly, I felt my own tears start, the first I'd shed for this man who'd been my client for four years. I hadn't liked him, but I had admired him. And now he was dead. After a few minutes I fetched the Kleenex box from my bottom desk drawer and we helped ourselves.

Angela took a deep breath and wiped her nose and eyes. How come, I wondered, she looks wonderful when she cries— no shiny red nose, no swollen eyes. I put it down to genes. She started to talk and I clamped my teeth shut, determined not to say another word or move a muscle until she was finished.

"Anyway, it was very spur of the moment—last night's get-together with King, I mean. He called about eight o'clock or so. Almost didn't catch me in because I was just leaving to meet some people for dinner at Mortimer's. He said he needed to see me and I didn't question it. If he said 'needed' he meant needed, not wanted, so I left word at Mortimer's that something had come up and I went right down to the Manse. It had been more than five months since we'd last seen each other and I didn't realize how much I'd missed him until I went upstairs and saw him at the door of his office. He was in shirt sleeves, an open-necked white business shirt—no tie or ascot. That was unusual for King. He always wore one or the other. And he looked so pale and worried. He asked if I minded staying in, rather than going out to dinner, which of course I didn't. I always loved being there with him.

"We settled into the sofa and had a couple of scotches and some smoked salmon he'd had sent in. And we talked—really about nothing—while we ate and drank. Of course I wondered what it was all about, but I didn't ask. He obviously had something important to say and would do it in his own way. We never pushed each other. I remember when I wanted to end my marriage to Seever. I was so upset about whether to do it and how to handle it. It was shortly after I'd met King but I invited him to dinner, because somehow he was the only one I wanted to talk to about it. I never raised the subject till we were finishing coffee, and he never asked. When I did get around to it, his advice was right on target and I followed it.

"Anyway, back to last night. When we were well into coffee and brandy, he looked at me and I knew he was ready. I remember exactly what he said: 'Angela, there's some trouble and I don't want to lay it at your doorstep, if there's no need. But there may *be* a need, and frankly I'm not sure who else I can trust.' He said he believed he could handle it and that it might be over after tomorrow, but he couldn't be sure. I remember he sort of half-smiled and said that even a supreme egoist shouldn't overestimate himself. Then he got very serious and took my hand and said—" She paused. "It gives me the chills just to think about it, Liz. He said, 'If anything happens to me, there's certain information I want you to have. You'll know what to do with it.' He told me he'd leave it in the house for me and where. Then he said that if anything did happen to him I was to go and get it personally and decide what to do. He repeated 'personally' and said that meant me and me alone.

"Then he said, 'That's that,' and didn't mention another word about it. He seemed to feel in a much better mood. I was awfully worried about him by then, but I couldn't say anything, you see, the conversation was over. We made love on the sofa and I guess that's when I lost the earring. Then I went home."

"God," I began and realized that my voice came out hoarse with tension. I cleared my throat. "I'm . . . I guess *amazed* is the word. Your lover . . . your friend's been murdered and you're supposed to go get some mysterious piece of paper and know what to do. And here you are looking like the cover of *Vogue*, putting a budget together for London and making appointments about bank seminars. How do you do it? And why?"

She smiled wanly. "I'm used to hiding my feelings, Liz. I'm very, very good at it. My training started young. Believe me, it's a skill that has its uses."

"Angela, why didn't King go to the police if he thought his life was in danger?"

"He had his reasons. He always had his reasons."

I thought about the King I knew, the ways I'd seen him operate, and agreed that she had a point. "You're going to have to tell the police about this, Angela."

"Perhaps."

"What the hell do you mean, 'perhaps'?"

"Just what I said, Liz." Her face hardened. "Perhaps. I will wait until the police are out of the Manse. That shouldn't be more than a few days. And then I'll go and get what King left for me and after I see what it is, perhaps I will go to them."

"Angela, you *will* go to the police," I said, my voice sounding harsher than I meant to my own ear. "If you don't I will. This isn't a game. We're dealing with—"

"What do you mean, we?" Angela cut in. "This has to do with King and me, not you. If you go to the police, I'll just deny everything."

"Now you listen to me." I was suddenly furious and I lowered my voice to a near-whisper to keep from screaming. "It *is* 'we' now. You can damned well say that if I hadn't found your earring you wouldn't have told me, but the fact is I *did* find your earring and you did tell me." I stopped and waited for her to say something. She didn't. "Actually, after hearing you, my guess is that King had intended to discuss this mystery with *me* and then changed his mind." She was startled.

"Yes," I continued, "he called late Monday afternoon to set up an early morning meeting the next day, and he wouldn't say about what. Then he left a later message on my home phone, which I didn't get because I didn't sleep at home, canceling the meeting and saying he'd 'handle it another way.' I guess you were the other way."

She looked unsure, but didn't speak.

"Look, Angela. King trusted you. You can trust me. Don't go into that house alone. I'll . . . I'll come with you." Was I nuts? "You'll see whatever it was King wanted you to see, and then you'll decide. But I'll be there to—uh—well, I'll be there if you need me."

She looked at me, her lips compressed. I thought she'd say no, and I had no idea what I could do about it—maybe just be relieved. Then her velvet brown eyes flickered. "Okay," she said.

The phone buzzed and I picked it up. Morley's voice brought me back to what felt like the real world. "Liz, I know you didn't want to be disturbed, but it's ten past five. I'm leaving and I think the partners are expecting you at the Regency."

"You're right. Would you give a call before you go and say I'm on my way?"

"Sure thing. See you tomorrow." He hung up.

"Angela, I've got to go now. King's partners are expecting me at the Regency and I'm already late. Let's sleep on it. Nothing we can do now anyway. Try to get some rest, huh?"

"I will," she said, attempting a smile. "You too."

I turned to get my coat off its hook.

"Liz?"

"Umm?"

"Can I have my earring?"

I hesitated. If I gave it to her, could she turn her back on our agreement? Pretend this conversation had never happened? Damned right she could. Should I just hand it over? If I was wrong about Angela and I gave it back, it was only my word against hers that she'd ever been at the murder scene.

"Liz, if we trust each other, we trust each other. I give you my word, I won't go into the Manse without you."

I reached into my wallet where I'd put the earring. As I gave it to her, I said a silent prayer that I was doing the right thing and, right or wrong, that Ike O'Hanlon would never find out about it.

10

....

Roger Durand opened the door of suite 803. His swan white hair wasn't one bit rumpled, but his face uncharacteristically was. It was the kind of mid-fifties face one saw on television anchoring network coverage of the Republican National Convention or above a white coat, advising authoritatively how to care for your hemorrhoids.

"Liz. Glad you're here at last."

The resonant voice matched the face. I'd always thought that if Roger had a brain he could take over the world. As it was, the danger didn't arise.

"Hi, Rog. I made it as soon as I could. O'Hanlon kept me forever." I saw no reason to mention any previous relationship I'd had with Ike O'Hanlon. It would only give the partners the misguided idea that I had some pull there, which would be asking for trouble. "I've just come from the office," I continued, "I didn't get back to you—" I stopped abruptly as Rog almost imperceptibly shook his head. I went on, covering as smoothly as I could. "The press has been all over us, as you can imagine." Why didn't he want me to mention his phone call?

I walked past him into the suite's living room, which attempted English Drawing Room and, on the whole, didn't fare too badly. Dave Goldstone was sprawled on a flowered chintz sofa, cradling an ivory phone in one big paw and stubbing out a filtered cigarette in a heavy glass ashtray with the other. Les Charlton, seated in a slender cane-backed chair, was bent over a replica of a Sheraton desk making notes on a large yellow pad. A coffee service tray which had long since done its job lay on top of a credenza, along with plates of mostly eaten sandwiches and a couple of Dave's used ashtrays.

Dave waved his free hand at me in greeting and Les looked up from his pad. Both had their suit coats off and ties loosened. Only Roger was jacketed and tied, as though he couldn't risk removing his armor before dangerous adversaries.

"Hi guys," I said as I took off my raincoat and stowed it in the closet.

I parked myself on a wing chair and fished a pad and pen out of my bag. Les looked up. Though his face was still paper white, it had recovered its characteristic look of cool authority. He was a natural leader, also a great client—most of the time: smart, receptive, never churlish. Occasionally he'd veto something I proposed, and when he did he was immovable. But if he were perfect he wouldn't be a client. He was also the only one of the partners whom I'd never heard King put down. Of course, I wasn't around all the time. Personally, Les was an enigma. He lived alone and, so far as I knew, had never been married. His private life was just that, and I had no idea whether it included women, men, or sheep.

"O'Hanlon left here just about an hour ago," he said, "so we haven't had much time to get things sorted out, but we've come to a few . . ." He stopped as Dave hung up the phone and strode over to my chair. Dave was a big man with dark hair and eyes and olive skin. At thirty-nine he could have been an ex-football player gone slightly to seed. Though far from fat, it was apparent that he ought to watch the odd french fry more carefully than he did.

"Hi, kiddo. Terrible thing," he said, squeezing my shoulder. I put my hand on his and squeezed back. Dave was the only one of the partners that I was on comfortable touching terms with.

"God, yeah," I said. We'd both said approximately the same things on the phone earlier, but that didn't matter. It's just part of the death ritual. People keep saying the same things over and over until they absorb the fact of what's happened. I remembered this vividly from my father's funeral and shivah.

"You know, when I stopped home to change clothes this afternoon there was a message from King on my machine." Three startled faces turned to me. "From last night, of course," I said quickly, "but it had the same effect on me, hearing his voice—just unbelievable." There was silence as we all reflected on this. Dave broke it.

"I'm about ready for a drink," he said as he crossed into the alcove where the portable bar was. "Anybody else feel the need for a belt of something?" Everybody did. I got up and helped, pouring a Tanqueray with Perrier on the side for Les and a Chivas and soda for Rog. Dave built himself a hefty Wild Turkey on the rocks and I let desire overcome discretion and accepted some Dewars straight—dangerous because I hadn't had a thing to eat since the early morning banana. I spied a packet of smokehouse almonds and took them back to my chair along with the drink in hopes that a munch or two would forestall getting smashed.

Dave took a gulp of his bourbon and returned to the sofa, where he sat with his legs apart, with a hand on each thigh and his top half leaning forward. I knew that posture. He was ready for business. Les took the cue and began after taking a delicate sip—first of the gin and then of the Perrier.

"To answer what's no doubt your first question, we've decided that Dave should become the new president of Carter Consultants."

Rog's face flashed anguish as fleetingly as the Times Square digital display sign. The expression was replaced immediately by a perfunctory smile as stiff as his upper lip. "We thought," he said like an announcer with a too-tight collar, "all things considered, that David would be the best choice." He paused. A flicker of distaste tightened his mouth. Rog had always looked down his patrician nose at Dave. The fact that Dave outperformed him by the proverbial country mile—the Chicago office did four times the business of Rog's Westport operation—added salt to the wound. Rog cleared his throat and continued. "Though I have seniority I, uh . . . at this time . . ." He ran out of steam very quickly hearing his own words, realizing perhaps that even I might recognize unadulterated bullshit when I heard it.

"I certainly understand, Rog," I said in a cameo appearance as Florence Nightingale, "the three of you had to come to the decision that made the most sense on balance." I looked straight ahead, afraid that if I caught Dave's or Les's eye I'd giggle. That signaled to me that the scotch was taking effect and I'd better watch it. I reached for a handful of the almonds.

"Look," Dave cut in, "the circumstances are lousy. Much as you want to be Number One, who'd want to make it this way?" Who indeed? I thought and brushed that thought under my mental rug real fast.

"I know," I said, "but congratulations, anyway. You'll do a great job."

"We know he will," said Les, with the semblance of a smile, "and Rog and I'll take on whatever extras we have to to make things go smoothly." Roger nodded, happy to be included by Les, whose elegance he admired in the way he'd admired King's. I wondered what had been the deciding factor—why Dave rather than Les? The media, at least *Forbes* and the *Journal*, were going to wonder the same thing, so I asked the question. Dave and Les exchanged glances that must have been meaningful to them, though not to me. Les said, "As you know, it wasn't volume of business, Liz; Dave and I run about neck and neck on that score. But I think he's stronger on administration and management than I am, and very frankly, he's a more dynamic presence." Dave started to interrupt, but Les held up a thin white hand. "No, I mean it. David Goldstone isn't King Carter, but that's not the point. He's the right person to take this firm where it needs to go now. And that *is* the point. I think that's what you need to tell the press—and anyone else."

Dave said "Thanks for the vote of confidence. Now all I have to do is live up to it." He grinned ironically. Rare for him. Dave wasn't long on irony. I wrote Les's quote down. It was a good one.

"What about the New York headquarters?" I asked. This was important. A great deal of King's business had been on Wall Street and there was no way to move the firm's center of operations to Chicago without a major client hemorrhage.

"That's the bitch of it," Dave said with a frown that deepened his facial crags. "I'm going to have to move here—no way around it—and Shelly's going to hate that, not to mention the kids."

"Yeah," I responded, "I know it's a pain to uproot them, but Shelly'll feel at home in Scarsdale or Great Neck in no time, and the schools . . ."

"Sure. You're telling me just what I tell candidates I'm trying to convince to relocate: 'it'll be great, no sweat at all for the wife and kids.' Only now it's me I'm talking about and *my* wife and kids, and it doesn't seem so easy." He took another swig of bourbon. "Ahh, we'll work it out."

"What about the Chicago operation?" I asked. "Are you going to take on a new partner?"

"No—at least not now. Art Sharpe's been my strongest performer for the last two years. He's a good team player. I'm going to give him a shot at running things and see how he does. If it works out, I think all of us would feel good about some kind of partnership for him down the line. I haven't talked to Art yet, of course, but I'll fly him in next week to sit down with us. Meantime, that part of it isn't for anybody else's ears yet—understood?"

"Sure." I made a note and looked up. "Why not just tell me all of it? Then we'll decide what to go public with, and when—okay?"

"Sounds good," Les said. The others nodded.

"By the way," said Dave, "I'll be leaning pretty heavily on Charlie Kaye in New York, at least for starters." If the distaste Rog had shown for Dave was a flicker, what he exhibited for Charlie Kaye was a paroxysm. It figured— both that Dave liked Charlie and that Rog loathed him. Les seemed oblivious to him, which wasn't easy. Charlie was an extremely bright young man who'd been with King a little over a year, and in that short time had become the office star. He'd come from Korn Ferry, the world's largest search firm, and had brought with him a few high-tech clients and, more important, several major financial institutions, including my own client, Baker Bank. To call Charlie Kaye ambitious was to call Schwarzenegger strong.

Accordingly he'd made enemies, colleagues some of whom were still rubbing his footprints off their backs. He loved seeing his name in print and he bombarded Seth and me with story ideas, some of them not bad. When I'd heard Charlie was dating Mandy Greathouse, I'd hoped he wasn't just using her because of her closeness to King. Mandy had always seemed a vulnerable sort. Maybe it was just that milky pale redheadedness. Now that King was gone, I put it at about even money that Charlie would drop Mandy. My own instincts said Charlie Kaye was a determined piece of work who didn't always play nice, and that even a smart tough article like Dave had better watch his back.

I popped another almond and yielded to the temptation of another sip of scotch. "What about the California office?" I asked. A slight pause. "That's on hold," said Dave quietly. So that was part of the deal. Dave had strongly advocated taking on a new partner to open an office in Silicon Valley to capture a larger share of the region's high-tech search business. Les had just as strongly opposed it—and for good reason. As it was, Les handled all Carter's high-tech business from his base on Boston's Route 128 high-tech corridor. He wanted to open a Silicon Valley satellite of his own and commute between the two. King had sided with Dave on this issue, and had gone as far as cutting a preliminary deal with a prospective West Coast partner. But King was gone. My guess was that Dave's presidency was a trade-off for dumping the California partner idea.

"Of course, it'll be tough to get any work done," Dave continued. "O'Hanlon and his people are going to be all over us until they find their man." He snorted. "If it *is* a man."

"What's that supposed to mean?" asked Les. His voice was soft, but not his face.

"You know damn well what I mean. King was ready to give the Ice Queen the chop. No more Oyster Bay for her. No more horses. With her screwing around, she'd have been lucky to—"

"That's enough," Les said. He still didn't raise his voice, but his tone stopped Dave cold. "The lady happens to be a friend of mine. More to the point, she was out of town when it happened, as you well know."

"So she says. Anyway, she could have jobbed it out," Dave said. Les looked at him but didn't answer. Dave held up his hand. "Okay, I'll back off. The last thing we all need is for you and me to fight."

The tension in the room broke, and Les's face relaxed. I was fascinated. So, it seemed, was Rog. It crossed my mind that, from a PR standpoint, Gillian Carter would be an ideal murderess—no taint on the firm at all. Maybe Dave's outburst had been brought on by the same kind of wishful thinking.

"I was thinking more along the lines of Gerry Klose," said Les.

"Who's Gerry Klose?" I asked.

"You don't know about that?" Les seemed mildly surprised. "Gerry Klose was in line for the top spot at Seagrave Bank. Ollie McCabe had been grooming Gerry as his successor and everybody thought it was a done deal as soon as Ollie retired. The Board of Directors hired King to present a slate of candidates—just pro forma. Well, King didn't give Gerry an exactly glowing review and, as an alternative, turned up a real winner from Chase. The rest is history—including the fact that the only job Klose is doing now is drowning himself in bourbon."

I turned to a new subject. "A couple of our media contacts seem to have gotten a whiff of the Green Star deal. I know there's no way to know yet, but how do you think it's going to go?" Three faces shut down and none of them said a word.

Just then the phone rang and I jumped slightly. Dave reached over and got it. "Yello. Yes, she's here." He handed me the phone as he said, "For you."

"Hello," I said cautiously. "Hold on, please," an unfamiliar woman's voice said. Then Ike O'Hanlon's voice startled me. "I'm downstairs in the lobby. Come on down. We have to talk."

For a wild two seconds I fantasized that he couldn't wait one more minute to tell me after twenty-five years how sorry he was for having dumped me after the prom. Shouldn't have had the last sip of scotch.

"We're in the middle of a meeting here," I said coldly. "Can't it wait till tomorrow?"

"I'm afraid it can't. Don't ask me any questions now. Be down here in five minutes. Make some plausible excuse and don't say you're meeting me. You used to be an actress. Act." He hung up.

11

·····················

WHEN I LEFT THE SUITE, ROG DURAND WALKED OUT with me. As soon as the door closed behind us, he said, "I need to talk to you alone." That was no surprise, considering how insistently he'd cut off my mention of his phone call.

"What about, Rog?"

He clutched my shoulder and propelled us to the end of the hall. Then he said, "They're going to try to pin it on me."

"What?" I really wasn't sure I was hearing what I was hearing. "Who's going to try to pin it on you?"

"*They* are. Goldstone and Kaye. You know how they stick—" He broke off, remembering, by the embarrassed look on his face, that I was Jewish, too. I decided the point didn't need reinforcement.

"Look, Rog, I think you're just upset. Dave said he thinks Gillian Carter arranged the murder. And Les thinks it was this guy Gerry Klose. Charlie Kaye, as far as I know, hasn't expressed any opinion." As I talked, I began to wonder whether Rog's apprehensions might be based on more than paranoia about Jewish conspiracies. Maybe he was afraid for some good reason—like he did it.

"Why should anyone think you killed King?" I asked carefully.

"I . . . I . . ." A rising red tide suffused his face and, just as quickly, was gone—like Donald Duck. "No reason. I was deeply fond of King. You know that." He waited for my acknowledgment. I nodded. "Do you . . . do you know why he wanted to see you this morning?"

"No idea. Anyway, he decided he didn't want to see me after all."

"Yes," he said distractedly. His head bent down toward me in a new thrust. "I'd watch Kaye. Something going on there." He added proudly, "I told O'Hanlon that."

"Do you *know* that, Rog?"

"I do," he tapped his chest, "in here."

Oh Jesus! "I wouldn't say any more," I responded gravely, tapping my forehead, "till it gets up here."

Ike was standing not far from the reception desk when I came down. He was standing still but looked as though he were pacing anyway. I remembered that he never could bear to be kept waiting.

"I asked you to come right down," he said.

"You *told* me to come right down," I corrected. "I couldn't. We were in the middle of a meeting, and I couldn't plausibly bolt and run in five minutes. Besides, though you'll probably find this hard to believe, we were discussing fairly important things."

I'd figured that it was a pretty safe bet he wouldn't come up to the suite after me. I'd also resented his peremptory summons, so I'd just gone ahead with the meeting, discussing such things as the funeral, which was to be the day after tomorrow; and which reporters Dave should talk with over the next couple of days and when he'd be available. None of them wanted to talk about the Green Star merger. That was understandable. Until they heard from Sir Brian Salter, they wouldn't know which way the wind blew.

Les would be going back to Boston right after the funeral and Rog was returning to Westport tonight, since it was only an hour away. Dave's wife would be flying in from Chicago for the funeral and bringing clothes with her to see Dave through another week or so in New York. Meantime, Mandy had had Saks send some emergency shirts, socks, and underwear up to the hotel.

"Who was the woman on the phone?" I asked.

"Officer Nunez. I use her as a beard all the time," Ike answered as he took my arm none too gently. "Come on, we've got to talk."

"Hey," I said, "I thought we were going to talk tomorrow night, remember? I'm exhausted now—and hungry. I haven't had a damned thing to eat all day except two handfuls of almonds and a belt of scotch. Besides, I've got to go home and call my kids. They'll—"

"What do you feel like eating?" He steered me out of the hotel toward the curb where a charcoal gray Volvo sporting a police shield on its dashboard was illegally parked.

"Now I know who screws up the traffic in New York," I said. "You ought to be ashamed of yourself." He opened the passenger door and helped me into the car, in the manner of a Boy Scout helping a lady who doesn't really want to go across the street. He got in the car and started it.

"What do you feel like eating?" he repeated.

I knew when I was outvoted. "Comfort food—noodles, pasta," I replied unenthusiastically.

"You got it," he said as he turned west on 57th Street.

"Are you going to tell me what the hell this is about? You rout me out of a meeting. You throw me into your car." I turned to look at him. "Someone else been murdered, perhaps?" I asked sarcastically.

"Yes."

I did what must have been a traditional movie double take and felt my head go light and funny.

"You wouldn't joke about something like that?" My voice sounded distant in my own ears.

"No." I waited a couple of seconds for him to say more, but he didn't. Very few people answer momentous questions with a simple yes or no, unadorned. But Ike always had, especially in cases when I urgently wanted to hear more.

"What are we going to do, play twenty questions? I start naming people and you tell me when I've hit the right victim?"

"Hang on. We'll get a bite or two of comfort food into you and then we'll talk."

I knew it would be useless to try to get any more out of him until he was ready. I hadn't paid any attention to where we were headed, but I looked out the window now and saw that we were turning back east off Tenth Avenue onto Fifty-second Street. We pulled up just a few doors from the corner in front of an almost unnoticeable storefront that had its windows covered by red curtains and a small sign in the lower left corner of one window that read "Costanza's." Ike got out of the car, came briskly around to my side, and opened the door.

He reached for my hand and I was surprised—on two counts. First, that I gave it to him and second that it felt so natural and good when he grabbed it in his bigger and far warmer one.

"You're a one-man parking-violation crime wave, aren't you?" I said to break the romantic stirrings I was beginning to feel. I'll be reading Barbara Cartland regencies next, I thought as he led me toward the storefront. This bastard that I haven't seen in twenty-five years practically kidnaps me, throws me into his car, and tells me someone's been murdered, and I get all mushy-headed when he touches my hand.

"One of the perks of the job," he said and it took me a moment to realize that he was responding to the crack about parking. He opened the door. That was another surprise. The restaurant was small and rather narrow with stripped brick walls—one of them with a fireplace in which a smallish fire cast wonderful shadows about the room. The tables—seven in all—were candlelit. At the back of the room was a polished mahogany service bar; a door behind it must have led to the kitchen from which mingled perfumes of olive oil, butter, garlic, lemon and other deliciousness issued forth. Even though it was only seven-thirty, a tad early for New York dinner, five of the tables were occupied with smart-looking people of various ages, all of whom had somehow a Continental flavor about them.

A distinguished-looking, silver-haired man in his sixties rushed from behind the bar to greet us. He clapped Ike on the back as they began an animated conversation in Italian. I always feel awed by people who can language hop skillfully, and I was astonished that Ike O'Hanlon had become one of them. All I caught were the mutual *come sta*'s and many *buono*'s and *bene*'s, which testifies to my virtual illiteracy in any language but English—and sometimes I'm not too sure about that one. I felt transported to "a little place that the tourists don't know about" in Rome and, despite everything, I was charmed. Ike still held my hand and he squeezed it slightly as he introduced me. I managed a smile, a *come sta* and a *grazie* exhausting an entire third of my Italian vocabulary. They switched to English for my benefit.

"Liz, this is my friend, Alberto. He and his wife Costanza own this place. You don't know it yet, but her pasta is about to spoil you for any other this side of the Atlantic."

"Ike exaggerates, of course, but not a lot," Alberto said with a very white smile. "I am very pleased to meet you, Liz." His wonderful accent caressed my name, making me remember fleetingly a couple of long-gone delicious encounters with a dashing Italian.

Alberto showed us to a table along the wall opposite the fireplace and questioned Ike in Italian about our drink order.

"Want to continue with scotch, Liz, or would you rather have some wine?"

"I'm in your hands," I answered, wishing I were and feeling like Alice through the looking glass. I gave myself a quick mental rap on the knuckles and instructions to cool down.

Brunellos and Bardolinos were seriously discussed by Alberto and Ike. Evidently the Brunello won out because Alberto hurried away and returned with it after a few minutes, during which neither of us said a word. After wine was poured and a basket of fragrant hot bread was set down between us, Alberto left us to our own devices. Ike looked straight at me.

"Who's Antony Swift?" he asked blandly.

"Who?"

"Antony Swift. Who is he and how do you know him?"

"I haven't the faintest idea, and I *don't* know him," I answered, mystified and annoyed. The surreal quality of the evening and Ike's tactics were getting to me.

"He was strangled with a pair of pantyhose in his room at the Plaza, and he had a telephone message from you." His voice was still bland, but there was an edge to it.

A cartoon light bulb went on in my head.

"Oh my God." I let it sink in. "Ike, I have no idea who the man is. I never spoke to him. When I got to my office this afternoon, he was in my pile of urgent messages and I tried to return his call. His room didn't answer."

"I'm sure it didn't. He was murdered sometime this morning."

I reached for my glass and took a healthy sip of the wine. It warmed me all the way down, which was what I badly needed since I felt myself shivering.

"What time did he call you?"

"I think the message slip said something like, um, ten after eight. Our receptionist took the call because it was before Morley—he's my secretary—got in."

"And you have no idea who he is, Liz."

I shook my head slowly, certain, as I searched my memory, that I'd never heard the name before in my life. I took another sip of wine and decided I was probably getting drunk—and didn't care.

"Swift was British," Ike pursued. "That ring any bells?"

"Look, Ike, stop toying with me, okay? I don't know who Antony Swift is, but I'm sure you do. I'm also pretty sure it's more than coincidence that shortly after my client is killed, some other guy who tried to call me is also killed. So let's skip the cat and mouse police interrogation, and I'll help you if I can."

"All right," he said with what looked like a real smile. "Guilty as charged—an occupational hazard. Antony Swift was a British private investigator. Scotland Yard says he was a one-man, veddy, veddy high-level operation—executive vetting, fraud in high places, the occasional checking out of a prospective mate for an upper upper family—that kind of thing. We don't know who his clients were and that may be tough to find out. All his work was highly confidential. Scotland Yard's helping us out over there. Whoever killed him took his wallet, cards, and, I guess, anything resembling a diary. I'm assuming that somebody at Carter Consultants was either his subject or his client. Any ideas?"

I had some ideas, all right, but I wasn't at all sure what to do about them. Fortunately, Alberto bought me a little time to think. He came over to discuss serious stuff—food— with Ike, while I pondered the ethical considerations of client confidentiality and its appropriate place in a case of murder. I decided fairly fast that the murder took precedence.

"Well," Ike said, giving me his clear blue look.

I met his eyes for a second and then jumped in. "I'm going to tell you some confidential things and I'd appreciate your handling them that way," I said, feeling suddenly formal. He nodded.

"Let me tell you first that Carter Consultants—especially King—does a lot of business in England, so I'm sure there are all kinds of British relationships that I know nothing about. But there is one I *do* know about. For the last, oh, three months or so King's been talking with Sir Brian Salter, the head of Green Star Industries, about a merger." I paused, feeling uncomfortable with the unaccustomed task of sorting my client's laundry in front of the police. Ike prodded me along.

"What's Green Star Industries?"

"A British conglomerate. They own employment agencies, computer companies, and God knows what else all over England and Scotland. The company went public a few years ago and the stock took off like a rocket. It's been a little shakier recently. Salter's trying to take Green Star international and he's targeted executive search acquisitions as the way to go because they have high profit margins. Also, access to their clients can be a useful springboard to get into other businesses. Last year he bought Beaulieu LaSalle—that's a French headhunter—and it seems to have been a good move. He wants to buy Carter Consultants, as I get it, for two reasons: one, to get a high-level foothold in the U.S. and two, to use the Carter name to get into executive search in England."

"Hmm." Ike was puzzled. "Why does this Brit with a 'sir' before his name and deep pockets need a bunch of Americans to open a British headhunting firm for him?"

"Image."

"Well, you're the image maven. Spell it out for me."

I failed to continue immediately because two heaping plates arrived. The smell was celestial.

"Fettucini carbonara," Alberto announced with quiet pride, and was gone. He did not return with the oversized pepper mill which has become standard in any American restaurant that serves entrees at double-digit prices, nor with the grated parmesan that most Italian restaurants offer with any and all pasta dishes. I guessed that Costanza had definite ideas about the food she prepared and figured that if she hadn't included the ingredient, it shouldn't be there. She was right. The fettucini, gilded with its rich sauce of egg and cheese, heavily laced with smoked bacon, was perfection. I savored it, sipped some Brunello, and ate another forkful. Ike said nothing, since he was similarly occupied.

"I guess you still want to know about images, huh?"

" 'Fraid so."

"Okay. You see, to be really successful in headhunting, you have to convey the image of a top management consultant, not of an employment agency."

"There's that much of a difference?" he asked.

"All the difference in the world. It's true that a headhunter fills jobs, but he's one hundred eighty degrees opposite to an employment agency, which basically finds jobs for people who are out of work or unhappy where they are. The agency works on spec and gets a commission if there's a hire. The headhunter, on the other hand, finds executives for his client companies and, believe me, he's not interested in the unemployed or the unhappy. In fact, when headhunters get unsolicited resumes in the mail they mostly ignore them, and if you're out of work, don't bother to try to get through to a headhunter on the phone. You won't."

"So if you want a job, they don't want you—like Groucho Marx, who wouldn't join a club that'd have him as a member."

"Exactly. The headhunter raids other companies to find successful executives who're happy where they are and persuades them they'll be happier and more successful working for his client."

"Pretty predatory stuff," Ike said. "Sounds like the headhunters back in the bush have a better set of ethics."

"Well, I'll admit that there are those who chuckle at the use of 'ethics' and 'headhunter' in the same sentence. Then there's the joke about the shipwrecked headhunter swimming to safety between two rows of hungry sharks who let him through on grounds of professional courtesy."

"I thought that was lawyers," Ike said. "Or reporters . . . or was it PR types?"

"Touché," I said with a grin. "Anyhow," I continued, "the business in fact does have its own ethical code."

"Yeah? What?"

"Well, you never poach on your own client's preserve. I mean, if First Boston were your client, you wouldn't try to lure one of their investment bankers to Morgan Stanley, who might also be your client. That's why smart headhunters won't take lots of major companies in the same industry. Where would they hunt?"

"I see," he nodded.

"Executive headhunters are also strong on confidentiality. If they didn't protect their candidates, the heads they were hunting would be afraid to talk with them, and the headhunters would be out of business. Also, by the nature of what they do, headhunters hear a lot of proprietary information—inside stuff about individual companies, trade secrets.

"In fact, though it's not exactly kosher, sometimes a company will order a search when they have no intention of making a hire, just so the headhunter can talk to candidates and provide feedback on what the competition's up to."

"Where I come from they call that spying—"

"Well, it's, shall we say, a fine line," I said, twirling fettucini around my fork and popping it into my mouth.

"Hah," he replied.

"Oh, I should mention that top headhunters don't work on spec, the way employment agencies do. They get paid whether or not they fill the job. That's so they won't be tempted to palm off an unsuitable candidate to get a commission. Of course, if the headhunter can't come up with the right scalp, even though he'll get paid for that assignment, chances are he'll lose the client."

"So how much do these ethical sharks *make*, actually?"

"For a single high-level search, we can be talking well into six figures for the headhunter."

"More than your humble civil servant can possibly imagine." He widened his eyes in exaggerated innocence. "So Green Star with its string of mere employment agencies would be in a lousy position to open up shop as a headhunter, especially in its own country."

"You got it," I said. "And the Carter name is as high prestige as you get in the industry. Korn Ferry and Russell Reynolds are many times bigger, but Carter is the eighth largest in the country in sales, and that's with only four partners." I stopped. "Three now, I keep forgetting."

"Sounds like Carter would be a pretty valuable catch for Green Star. Had Salter gotten around to naming a price?"

"They were talking in the fifty million dollar range." Ike pursed his lips in a soundless whistle. "I got that from Dave Goldstone," I added. "He's the most open of the partners—at least with me."

"Will Carter Consultants be worth anything like that without King Carter?" Ike asked. It was a good question. I shrugged, palms open.

"I honestly don't know. My guess would be probably nothing like fifty million. King was not only Carter's president and biggest producer, he had the most British contacts, though Les Charlton is the one who graduated from the London School of Economics."

"I gather all the partners were bullish on the merger?"

"Wouldn't you be? Even though it was structured so that King got the largest share, the others stood to gain some pretty heavy bucks. Even poor Rog Durand would have gotten five or more million."

"Poor Rog?"

"Well, Roger isn't exactly what you'd call a Rhodes scholar, which proves that an MBA from Harvard isn't a foolproof credential."

"I could have told you that," Ike said, lifting his last forkful of fettucini to his lips.

"I'd take anything Rog said—like about Charlie Kaye—with a generous helping of salt." He raised his eyebrows inquiringly. I continued: "From what he told me, all Rog can accuse Charlie of is pushiness, and he's certainly guilty as hell of that."

"Durand seems a touch nervous. Any idea why?"

"Without King, Rog may be scared that the other two will cut him loose.

"Rog and King knew each other back at Harvard, and he was King's first partner. It was a good few years before Dave came, and then Les. It was one thing to be eclipsed by King—almost anyone would be—but Dave and Les left Rog at the starting gate pretty fast, and he's not so dumb he doesn't feel embarrassed. Also, his office had an especially tough year this year. I guess the money from the Green Star deal would be really important to him."

"The deal could still happen, though?"

"I would think so. Dave's going to head Carter and move to New York. That's what we were meeting about. His style's totally different from King's, of course, but he's smart and effective and has more energy and ambition than anyone I know. Salter would make a big mistake to turn away from Carter Consultants because King's gone."

Alberto appeared and filled our glasses with the last of the Brunello and cleared our empty plates.

"Ike didn't exaggerate one bit, Alberto," I said. "My compliments to Costanza."

"*Gràzie tante*," he replied with a slight bow, assuming that even I would understand that. "I will bring you a light salad for refreshment," he added as he disappeared behind the bar.

"What do the partners think is going to happen?"

"I don't think they know what's going on with Green Star at this point. I asked them just before you called and none of them had a word to say." I paused. "So if we assume that this detective was killed because of something connected to the Green Star–Carter deal, the question is, was he investigating Carter, or did King hire him to look into Green Star?"

Ike looked at me poker-faced. "That certainly is the question," he said.

Alberto arrived with the salads, this time with a large pepper mill under his arm. He served us, ground out the pepper that we asked for, and left.

Ike looked at me hard. "Liz, I don't want you to say anything to the partners—or to anyone else about Antony Swift or about the fact that he tried to contact you, okay?" I nodded. "Good," he said. "Now let's talk about something else."

"I've got something else," I said, relieved at the prospect of a subject change. "Where did you learn to speak Italian so well?"

"*Della mia sorella, la principessa*," he replied.

"Your sister, the princess? Becky was always the ultimate princess, but what's that got to do with it?"

"So you don't know. I figured Roo would have told you. I know she's in touch with my brother Jake." But my sister hadn't told me whatever it was Ike was talking about, or anything else about the O'Hanlons simply because through the years I switched topics every time she brought them up.

"No, she didn't," I said.

"Well, Becky is a *real* princess now. She married Prince Gaetano d'Allessandro about twenty years ago. God, she was born for it, and it's worked out really well. Tano's a good guy besides being megarich, and he still thinks that Becky O'Hanlon of Forest Hills is the greatest thing that ever happened to him. Anyway, she has villas all over the place and I've spent a lot of time over there, especially after—" He compressed his lips. For a split second his expression darkened. Then he smiled and said, "Not important."

The words were out before I thought about them: "Especially after what?" For some reason it seemed terribly important for me to know.

"After my divorce," he said, looking straight at me with an expression I couldn't read. I was surprised, though I shouldn't have been—and instantly jealous. Ike was so damned attractive, it would have been surprising if he'd gotten to be forty-five *without* ever marrying. What did I think he'd been doing all these years, waiting for *me*? "I wasn't good at being married," he said with a faint smile.

"I wasn't either," I said softly, "in spades. I tried it twice, after all." He reached across the table and took my hand.

"Maybe we're just impossible enough for each other." The tone was light, but his hand on mine wasn't. I stayed very still, locked into those blue eyes. I felt my nipples stand up like little volunteers. If I looked at his face one more second, I'd be in thrall forever. Instead, I concentrated on his red paisley tie, which changed before my eyes into a flowered pattern I remembered from a long time ago. The overstuffed sofa in the O'Hanlons' living room. His family away for the weekend. Ike and me naked—burrowing, rolling, tonguing, flying. Liz Herzog deflowered on a red flowered sofa. I was seventeen. I've had lots of sex since then. It's been fancier, but it's never been better.

My heart was beating crazily, skipping a few, as it tends to do when I'm too excited. I had to stop. It was too scary. I withdrew my hand and busily wiped my mouth with the large linen napkin.

Mercifully, Alberto arrived and removed the empty salad plates and Ike ordered espresso and brandy. I watched

Alberto's pin-striped back walk to the bar.

"He looks more like a banker than a restaurateur."

"Good guess," Ike said. "He was an almost innocent bystander in the Banco Ambrosiano business. Lucky to get out of Italy with a few bucks and no holes in his skin. Also lucky that Connie liked to play with the servants when she was a kid and learned how to cook."

12

....

I WAS FLYING SO HIGH I ALMOST DIDN'T NEED THE ELE-
vator to get up to my apartment. When Ike delivered me
home I ached to ask him up. But I didn't do it. The evening,
not to mention the day, had been such a rich stew of tragedy,
excitement, and, at its end, exhilaration, that I needed digestion
time. He said he understood. I believed him, since Ike never
did use "I understand" as perfunctory politeness.

We held each other and kissed long and searchingly. Twenty-
five years was quite a chunk of time to catch up on, but we got
a jump start and exchanged unspoken but clear promises for
tomorrow night. Here I go again, I thought, when I came up
for air. I was leaving myself wide open, but at the moment it
felt well worth the risk of getting clobbered.

I let myself in and responded with edible offerings to the
blandishments of my two furry roommates. As I held the cat
food can under the electric opener, I absently sponged the
white formica counter. Good thing it was Freddie's day to
clean tomorrow. Things were definitely getting a bit grungy.

I glanced up at the black kitchen clock above the fridge.
The red hands told me the time was ten-thirty-five—probably
a little early to reach Sarah in her Stanford dorm room, what
with the three-hour time difference, but I might have a shot
at catching Scotty home in Providence. I headed down the
hall for the bedroom where I stripped off everything, climbed
into my somewhat tattered thick white terry robe, and pulled
it tight around my waist. I lay down on the bed, with three

pillows plumped behind my head. I was feeling surprisingly sexy and sybaritic, and allowed myself to revel in the feeling for a moment before doing anything.

As I picked up the phone to dial, my eyes lit on the framed photos of both kids on the dressing table across the room. Scott, the charmer, with a head full of my curls and his father's large brown eyes, smiled at me with warm confidence. Sarah, the achiever, looked at me with a serious dark blue gaze and the faintest of smiles, straight, wheat-colored hair framing a face reminiscent of my own in its slightly feline aspect.

Scotty wasn't in. I left a message on his machine. As I hung up, I glanced at my own machine, which showed three new messages. I reached for my phone-side pad and pen and pressed "Play." When I heard King Carter's voice begin last night's message I realized that I had totally forgotten to mention King's message to Ike. I decided it could wait till tomorrow. After all, all it said was that King had decided to cancel his early morning meeting with me and was going to "handle it another way," which was not informative. I'd simply bring the tape with me to his house tomorrow night.

The first new message was from Douglas: "I was sorry to hear about your situation. I spoke with the police, of course—very pleasant fellow. O'Hanlon, I think his name was. If I can help in any other way, I'd be glad to." Fuck you, Douglas, I thought for the second time that day. I wondered what he'd actually said to Ike and realized that I'd probably never know. If I were an animal, I'd be the cat that curiosity killed, at least that's what my mother used to say.

The second message was from Barbara Garment, my best friend. We'd met as Central Park playground mommies. Eight years ago, Barbara had shed mild-mannered Art and become a writer on such topics as *In the Enemy Camp: Living with Men Who Can't Love*, her latest book.

"Heard about it on the six o'clock news. By the way, was the cop on TV *the* Ike O'Hanlon, he of your checkered past? If so, watch it, Liz. Give me a call."

The last message was from Mandy Greathouse who asked that I call her at home whatever time I got in. I reached for the phone and dialed. She answered before the first ring was over.

"Hi, it's Liz. You must have been sitting with your hand on the phone."

"Yes, I . . . uh . . . Thanks for getting back to me."

"That's okay. I'm glad you called, actually. I wondered how you were."

"I'm all right," she said, not sounding all right. "I, uh, wondered, what was it that you and King were supposed to meet about?" She paused and went on rapidly, sounding uncomfortable and apologetic. "I mean, I usually know these things . . . uh, King always—" She stopped.

"Mandy?" No answer. "Mandy?"

"I'm sorry, Liz. I feel like such an ass. Look, somebody asked me what the meeting was about and I . . . I don't really know why . . . maybe I was just upset, or I felt like a fool because I didn't know, but I answered that it was confidential and I couldn't discuss it. I . . . I'm not used to lying and I . . . oh that's my call waiting beeping. Hang on, will you?"

I hung on and in a second she was back.

"Mandy," I said, "I can't really help you. King wouldn't tell me why we were meeting. Actually he changed his mind about the meeting altogether. I didn't sleep at home last night or I'd have gotten his message on my machine canceling it."

"Oh." Her voice sounded small. "I, uh, have someone hanging on, Liz. I have to go now. I'll call you tomorrow." Before I could say okay, she'd hung up.

I picked up the TV remote and clicked it on and over to Channel Two, turning the sound off. Seven minutes to eleven. Enough time to give Sarah a try before the eleven o'clock news. Maybe she'd be in after all. I was about ready to hang up after the fifth ring when she picked up. Her voice was breathless from running.

"Hi, Mom. I was next door and thought I heard it ringing. How are you?"

"I'm fine, honey. Things going well?"

"Great! I think Debbie and I are going to be fine as roommates. I know it's less than a month, but you can tell. I've got this job in the registrar's office." She anticipated my question and cut it off. "Don't worry, it's not that many hours and it won't cut into my studying. Also, it'll give me as much spending money as I need."

I love that girl. Sarah would never in her life be pushed out of someone's car at two A.M. and left standing in her high-heeled sandals on the sidewalk, crying.

"You are *some* kid," I said. It seemed a shame to break in with my news of the murder, but I figured I'd better, and I did.

"Wow," she responded softly. "You sure you're going to be okay, Mom? I mean, what if one of these people you work with killed this guy? Grandma would tell you 'don't mix in.' I'm telling you the same thing."

She was quick off the mark, and I hadn't even told her the half of it. I hadn't mentioned Antony Swift or anything about Angela and her earring—or Ike.

"Honey, I'm fine, really—and I will be. My whole role now is to write press releases and help build a reputation for the firm's new president." I wasn't sure she believed me. After all, she'd known me a long time. We said mutual "love you's" and hung up.

I turned up the sound on the TV just in time to hear Tom Bradley leading into King's murder. The scene switched to the front of the Manse and a shot of Sally Fiorella, the WCBS reporter who was covering.

"I'm standing in front of 158 East 64th Street, the house where millionaire businessman Kingman Carter was found murdered—stabbed to death with his own antique dagger early this morning."

A photo of King, very much alive, a phone held to his ear, flashed on the screen. I recognized it as one taken for a new brochure we were preparing. I knew Seth hadn't provided it, so somebody at the agency must have snitched a copy to make points with Sally. "Carter was the president of Carter Consultants, an executive-search firm which was headquartered in this house. He had also served as a dollar-a-year Presidential adviser and on several corporate boards of directors. His body was discovered by Elizabeth Wareham, his public-relations advisor, when she arrived for a before-hours meeting this morning." The front of the house again filled the screen. The front door opened and Ike appeared, looking telegenic as hell. Sally promptly nabbed him. "Lieutenant Isaac 'Ike' O'Hanlon is in charge of the case. Lieutenant, have the police found anything that might lead to an early arrest?"

"We hope to be able to crack this case quickly, Sally, but if by 'early' you mean in the next ten minutes," he gave her a modified O'Hanlon grin, which defused his sarcasm—though not entirely—"I think that's unlikely."

"Had the house been broken into?"

"We've found no sign of that."

"Then the murderer was let in by Mr. Carter, or let himself in with a key?"

"I can't say that yet for sure."

"But . . ." She was a persistent twerp with a know-it-all manner. I didn't know which irritated me more, that, or the fact that she was so darkly pretty that I was scared that my Italophile might find her tempting. He cut her off at the pass.

"I didn't say it *wasn't* a break-in. I said we had found no sign of one so far. We would be misleading your viewers to speculate at this point." Good touch, that "we." I prep clients for interviews all the time, and Ike was a pro. Cooperative but firm, not to mention charming.

Sally persisted. "How did Elizabeth Wareham get into the house?"

"Ms. Wareham had a key," Ike replied casually. Sally opened her mouth to speak, but he continued before she could utter a syllable, "as did many people associated with Carter Consultants." I mentally blew him a kiss. He continued. "We'd like to ask anybody who has information, or who may have seen anyone entering or leaving this house last night or very early in the morning to call this special police number." The number flashed on the screen, while Ike assured viewers that calls would be kept confidential.

He started toward his car, signifying that the interview was over.

"Thank you, Lieutenant O'Hanlon." The camera panned back for her closing shot. "At the house where King Carter was murdered, this is Sally Fiorella for Channel Two News." I clicked her off and closed my eyes. This day had been a month long. I felt so revved up, I knew I would be awake all night. That was the last thought I had before I fell asleep.

The phone rang me out of a dreamless oblivion at seven-fifteen. I nudged Three's backside off my shoulder and reached for the receiver. The voice on the other end was even more comforting than sleep: Sam Boyd. The government agencies and companies who pay Sam fat retainers depend on his management consulting to make their organizations run better. I depend on his friendship to make my life run better, and on occasion to keep it from falling apart.

"Hi, lovely. Knew I'd probably wake you, but I just got in on the red-eye from San Francisco. I'm out at Kennedy. I heard about King, of course. You okay?"

"Better after hearing you, Sammy. What a rotten mess! Yeah, I'm all right, but . . ." There was a lot to say, but, between what I was sworn to secrecy about and what was too complicated to go into on the phone, I found myself unable to finish the sentence.

"You don't sound too terrific. Where's the Good Doctor? Actually, I half-expected you'd be at his place."

"Dr. Douglas and I are finished, as of yesterday morning."

"You mean you found King murdered and decided to dump Douglas? I don't see the connection."

"No, Douglas decided to dump me and then I found King. And there is no connection."

"You certainly had an eventful day. Am I supposed to say 'sorry' or 'good'—about Douglas, I mean?"

"What do you feel like saying?"

"Good. He was a nerd. No, I'm not being precise enough. He was a *pompous* nerd. I was in a meeting over at Robotrac in Silicon Valley when I found out about King. Shep Bloom walked in late with the news. God, you should have seen the faces. Some pretty interesting reactions."

"Interesting? How do you mean?"

"Look, lovely, no time to go into it now. Have to catch a cab and get to a breakfast meeting, then I'm scooting right back to Washington on the first shuttle I can make. I have to be back in New York Monday though. When's the funeral?"

"Thursday at two. Frank E. Campbell . . . Madison and 81st. You coming?"

"Maybe. Can't say I liked King all that much, but I have worked with him, and with Les, from time to time. In fact, I may—"

At that point a recording broke in to tell us that our time was up and if another five cents wasn't forthcoming the call would be "terminated," which always had an ominous sound. "Look," Sam said quickly, "I *will* come in for the funeral. I have to be in New York Friday anyway. Dinner Friday night?"

"Great," I was able to get in before the phone company did its worst.

13

....

"BUT HE'S SO UGLY."

"Okay, John," I responded, "so he's ugly. We're talking about a spokesman to catch flak from the TV reporters, not a movie star. Besides, I've already set it up."

"We are in the image business, Liz," John explained with exaggerated patience. "Millions of people, including clients and potential clients, are going to see that face on the tube identified as Seth Frankel of the Gentle Group, and that'll be their image of this agency. Would you hire an agency that looked like Seth Frankel?"

If he thought I was going to answer that question, he was smoking his socks.

"Look, John, we've been over this. *I* can't do it. The sharks would get into the whole business of my finding King's body. I mean, look at those headlines." I pointed to the pages on his desk. HEADHUNTER SLAIN, the *News* shouted in 144-point type. HEADHUNT FOR KING'S KILLER, the *Post* screamed back. "We want to defuse the sensationalism as much as we can. Seth's perfect for that. He has no inside information, and everyone knows it. If he needs to contact the partners, they're comfortable with him. He's worked on the account for three years—and done a first-rate job, I might add."

"I wasn't suggesting that *you* should do it. How about Patti?"

I shook my head. "Too inexperienced and anxious to please the media."

"Can't you use Angela? Now to have *her* on TV representing the agency would be—"

He was really warming to that idea and I had to head it off fast. Tactical warfare was called for.

"Well, I *could* use Angela, of course, but that would take her off the Baker Bank event at a crucial time," I mused disingenuously. "I guess I could bring Kenny in to do Baker on a freelance basis."

Kenny Abbott had quit the agency recently to write a book on the soft underbelly of American banking. "Let's see," I figured, a finger on my lower lip, "he's charging five hundred dollars a day. We shouldn't need him more than . . . oh, I guess twelve days or so, what with having to brief him on Baker and get Angela up to speed on Carter . . ." I was bluffing. Kenny could take on that seminar blindfolded, and Angela probably knew more about Carter Consultants at this point than anyone in the agency, including me. The bluff worked.

"Yeah, I see what you mean. I suppose Seth will be all right. But for God's sake, don't use him any more than you have to."

Agency lore had it that John's grandmother had been a Parisian landlady. I couldn't confirm the story, but whether I had nature or nurture to thank for it, his cheapness had won out. He couldn't stomach an extra six thousand dollars—even for agency image.

John's phone bleeped just then. It was a call for me from Dennis Quayle at the British Board of Trade. I said I'd take it in my office.

As I ran down the corridor to catch the call, I almost collided with Morley coming around the other way, unwinding his nine-foot silk aviator's scarf.

"A gracious good morning to you, Liz. Feel better?"

He made a graceful, salaam-type bow. Sirpan (formerly Alvin), Morley's roommate, had recently converted to one of the currently fashionable Eastern religions.

"A GGM to you, too," I answered on the run. "I've got to catch this call—Quayle. I'd kill for a cup of coffee."

"So that's why you keep me around," he called after me. "You wouldn't dare ask a female secretary to bring you coffee."

I grabbed the phone before my bottom hit the chair.

"Hello, Dennis. I was just about to call you. Sorry I didn't get back to you yesterday, but I guess you've heard."

"About King Carter? Yes, I'm afraid so. Bad news travels quickly." He paused and continued in an abashed-sounding voice. "Liz, I'm afraid I owe you an apology. Late last week I suggested someone ring you and I never got round to ringing you myself to let you know."

"Well, that's okay, Dennis. I'll be delighted to talk with anyone you've sent my way." A potential client, maybe?

"But you see it's a bit more complicated. This chap—we were at school together—is a private investigator of sorts. He was interested in something to do with Carter Consultants. I didn't ask what. One doesn't with Antony. I couldn't help him, but I gave him your name, especially as he said he was going to New York. I hope I haven't put you in an awkward spot."

I swallowed. "Uh, no. No, of course not. I'll be, uh, happy to talk with him," I said, feeling like a liar and a fool, and unsure which I disliked more. Mercifully, Morley set out a large white mug of black coffee in front of me. A whiff and a sip helped.

"You haven't heard from him yet then?"

"No, I haven't," I said. "What sort of information was . . . will he be looking for?" If I was going to play detective I'd have to get the tenses right at least.

"I haven't the foggiest, except that he did use the word 'sensitive.' In any case, I do apologize for not getting to you immediately. It could have been a difficult situation for you."

You don't know the half of it, friend.

I assured Dennis that he hadn't made a serious gaffe and then turned the conversation to our proposal to the Board of Trade and assured him he'd have the rest of the package before the week was out. We bid each other cordial good-byes.

CAROL BRENNAN

I let it sink in. So Antony Swift had been investigating Carter Consultants. For Green Star? That seemed a good bet. But maybe not. Green Star was the only British factor I knew of that might want to investigate Carter. But my knowledge was limited entirely to what the partners told me and what I picked up in scuttlebutt from reporters and from Sam Boyd, who always knew everything. Still . . .

I decided to call Ike right away with this new information—balancing the books, perhaps, for my deceit about the earring, not to mention the enormity of what I was about to commit by sneaking into the Manse some night soon with Angela.

I was put through to Ike right away.

"Good morning, Liz." I thought he sounded crisply formal and I responded in kind.

"Look, I just got off the phone with an Englishman I have some business with. He called to tell me that he had suggested that Antony Swift call me. They were old school friends. He told me that Swift was investigating Carter Consultants. I thought you'd want to know that right away."

"Bet I do. Thanks. Name?"

"What?"

"The name of your British contact."

"I don't want you to call him right now."

"What are you talking about?" A belligerent tone. I could picture that chin jutting out.

"He doesn't know that Swift is dead, and I pretended I didn't know, so it would be really tough for me if he got a call from the New York police five minutes after we got off the phone. Besides, he doesn't know any more than I've already told you. I asked him." I was beginning to be sorry I'd called Ike. Let him get his own information.

I'd been swiveled around with my back to the door. As I swung back to the desk for a sip of coffee, I saw Angela standing there and just about jumped out of the chair. I had no idea how long she'd been there or what she'd heard. I was angry at her and Ike and me.

"I've got to go now," I said coldly into the phone.

"I'll see you later," he said.

"Maybe not," I answered, but he'd already hung up.

"How long have you been standing there? Why the hell didn't you cough or knock or something?"

"Liz, you close your door when you don't want to be disturbed. I did what I always do when your door is open and you're on the phone. I came in and waited for you to finish." Calm, reasonable, and blameless.

I felt myself blush with shame. She was right.

"I'm sorry. I guess I'm just jumpy. How much did you hear?"

"Just the last part, where you said someone didn't know Swift was dead."

"Angela, I need your word that you won't repeat the conversation to anyone."

"Okay." She didn't even ask any questions. It must be comfortable to be that incurious. Or maybe she didn't have to ask questions. Maybe she knew all about it.

I, on the other hand, had lots of questions. I picked up the *Times* and took another look at its coverage, just in case I'd missed something useful in my initial early morning scan. The story had made the lower left front page. A gentlemanly EXECUTIVE RECRUITER MURDERED headlined a comparatively staid, though comprehensive, rundown.

It told me a few things I hadn't known: that, according to the medical examiner, King had died instantly of a single stab wound to the heart some time between four and five A.M.; that Gillian Carter (formerly Sprague), forty-one, had been a secretary at the U.S. Embassy in London before marrying King six years ago; and that she'd been out of town while her husband was being murdered.

I looked up. Angela was waiting patiently to start our meeting.

"Angela, was King disenchanted with the fair Gillian?"

"To put it mildly. Disgusted is more like it. He would have ended the marriage if—" Her eyes moistened. She composed herself. "If he hadn't been killed, he'd have divorced her.

She'd have had to get off her horse and go back to work."

"You don't divorce a millionaire and wind up in the typing pool. Especially if *he* does the divorcing."

"Maybe not, but she's a great deal better off financially with a third of his estate than she would have been after a divorce. When she wasn't in the saddle, she was in the sack. After King's lawyers finished with her, all she'd have gotten was what he'd have felt generous enough to give. And he wasn't feeling generous."

"How do you know she'll get a third of the estate?"

"New York State law. The spouse gets at least a third, no matter what the will says. But she couldn't have killed him, could she? The papers said she was out of town."

"I guess not," I answered, nibbling my thumbnail.

The rest of the day flew by. Angela and I chewed over the Board of Trade proposal, then I spent hours on the phone to the media breaking the news of Dave's taking over the presidency of Carter.

Over my BLT desk lunch—everything cold but the tomato—I browsed through the *Wall Street Journal*. Their coverage of King's murder virtually duplicated that of the *Times*. When I turned to the jump page, another headline caught my eye: GRIMM LEAVES ROBOTRAC. That was a surprise. Les had placed Marcella Grimm in the number two spot at Robotrac not quite a year ago, and we'd hyped the hell out of it—"Dynamic Young Woman Becomes Chief Operating Officer of One of the Country's Hot High-Tech Firms, the Leader in Robotics." It was a natural. We'd scored with *Forbes, Fortune, Business Week*, the *Journal*, everybody. Today's story didn't say much, just that she was leaving to start her own consulting business, which I took to mean she'd been fired. Wow, that was quick! She must have really screwed up.

Robotrac was one of Les's mainstay clients. He'd have to do some fancy footwork to smooth things over. They'd paid him a hefty fee to find Marcella and they were going to want a solid replacement in a hell of a hurry. This was all he needed on top of his partner's murder.

As I crumpled the remains of the sandwich in its wrapping and threw it into my wastebasket, I recalled that Sam Boyd had said he'd been at a meeting at Robotrac when he heard about King's murder. He'd be able to tell me what was going on.

I was getting Seth prepped to be thrown to the TV wolves, when Angela appeared at my door, this time with a pointed knock on the frame, and announced that it was four and time to leave for a meeting with Baker Bank at the Hayden Planetarium, where the "Baker Targets the World" seminar was to be held in three weeks.

The meeting took two painful hours. Chris Maclos had cavils with everything from the draft of her introductory speech ("too soft sell") to the lighting ("not bright enough"). I switched myself into the psychiatric-nurse mode I adopt when clients get crazy: cheerfully accommodating on the points that don't matter, and cheerfully firm on those that do. By six P.M. we wrapped it up.

The Planetarium is at Central Park West and 81st Street, only five blocks from my apartment. It was good to breathe fresh air, even for the few minutes it took to walk home. When I opened the apartment door, my spirits perked up at the wonderfully clean smell that the place had after a day of Freddie's ministrations—a delicious amalgam of lemon furniture oil, Windex, newly vacuumed rug, and drier-warmed clean clothes. Some entrepreneur should bottle it and sell it to inept homemakers to sprinkle around the house whenever they need a lift. Instantmaid Unlimited. Maybe I'd quit public relations and start the company myself.

Freddie and I had a relationship that was strange in some ways, but it worked for us. I grew up with household help. I'd had a cleaning woman while the kids were growing up. And I hadn't thought about it twice, except to be glad that I didn't have to do the work myself. But here was Freddie, only a few years older than Scott, and a talented dancer. The prospect of her cleaning my toilets had made me uneasy—guilty.

I'd summoned up my courage and told Freddie how I felt. She was smart, I argued. She had two years of college. She could do something else, something better. "Would she be my maid if she were white?" I asked. She'd looked me straight in the eye and told me that she was *not* a maid, that she was a dancer who made her money cleaning houses, for the time being. She said she preferred her "cleaning contracts" to waitressing, which was what her white dancer friends did, and that I was the same kind of "1950s half-assed liberal" as her mother, who was a schoolteacher. I'd thought it over and decided I could live with it if she could. And we both have, except that she thinks I eat and drink unwisely, and I think she doesn't sleep enough.

I went into the kitchen to feed the ubiquitous cats and saw Freddie's note propped up against the Cuisinart.

Dear Liz,
I heard about that murder on the TV. Are you okay? We're out of Mr. Clean, vacuum-cleaner bags, and silver polish. Also you should get some vitamin C and B12. The fridge doesn't look like you're eating right with Sarah gone. The phone man was here and everything is working fine now.

—Freddie Mae

The phone man? I shrugged and went back to the bedroom. The answering machine registered one new message. I pressed "play" and heard my sister Roo saying that it was Wednesday at six P.M., and asking how was I managing with all this craziness, and would I give her a call.

My knees went weak and my heart started to pound. It wasn't the message from Roo. That was innocuous enough. But all of yesterday's messages, including the one from King, which I'd carefully saved, had been erased.

14

....

I SEARCHED FOR OTHER POSSIBLE EXPLANATIONS. IT COULD have been a legitimate repairman, who got the apartment number or the address wrong. But no way did anyone erase those messages by mistake. It wasn't that easy. You had to lift up a little plastic door and simultaneously press two buttons a handspan apart, to erase.

I found I was sweating. I thought back. Who knew about that message from King? I remembered that I'd mentioned it to the partners at last night's meeting. I'd told Angela about it during yesterday's earring revelations, and I thought I'd said something to Mandy late last night on the phone. But the idea of any of those people masquerading into my apartment to erase a phone message was bizarre. Two of the five were ruled out, anyway. Freddie's note had said "the phone *man*." That left the partners. I felt sick and scared. I bit my thumb and willed myself to calm down and think.

No, it didn't have to be one of the partners. Any of those five people could have told others about the message. Still, why would someone want to go to the trouble and the risk of erasing it when it didn't say a damned thing? But none of them had known exactly what King had said.

I reached for the phone and dialed Freddie's number. After eleven rings I was about to give up when she answered out of breath.

"Freddie, I'm so glad I got you."

"Just got in from the health food store. I invented a new step.

I'm calling it the *jeté en l'air* with two bags. The Tiger's milk and molasses fell out, but who's perfect? Did you see my note about the vitamins and cleaning stuff?"

"Yes. Yes, I did. That's, uh, why I'm calling. I just need to ask you a couple of questions—about the phone man."

"Yeah, I was surprised to see him, because you didn't leave a note, but he had this repair order form and—"

"What did he look like?"

"Look like? Let's see," she thought for a second. "White man. Sort of medium size, khaki shirt and pants, brown leather jacket—kinda baggy. He had longish brown hair and a mustache. Oh yeah, and a green cap with like a bill in front and glasses, a little tinted."

Didn't sound like anyone I knew. A hired hand, maybe.

"What did he actually do, Freddie?"

"Well, he asked where all the phones were, and I showed him. Then he went into the bedroom. I stayed close by in your bathroom. To keep an eye on him. I was cleaning in there anyway. I heard him play the message machine and after the first few I went in and asked him why he needed to listen to your messages to fix the phone. He said that sometimes the message machine screws up the phone and he needed to test it, but he said he'd heard enough to know yours was okay. A couple of minutes later he peeked his head in and said that everything was fixed and would I sign the order." I found myself admiring that touch. Sign the order indeed! "Then he left. Why you asking me all this, Liz? The phone still not right?"

"No, no, Freddie, it's fine." No point in upsetting her. I'd just leave her a note next week that I wasn't expecting anyone and she shouldn't let anyone into the apartment. I'd have to have a word with the doorman, too.

"Liz, while I have you. Is it okay if I stay over next Monday? We're doing a showcase and I have a late rehearsal. It's gonna be a killer." I shuddered involuntarily at the word. "If I can get through cleaning Barbara's place fast, I might even stop by and catch a few Z's before it starts."

Freddie stayed the night in Scott's room from time to time when she had a late-night something or other in Manhattan. It was a matter of convenience, rather than fear of a two A.M. subway ride to the Clinton Hill section of Brooklyn where she lived with two other dancers, or the six block walk from the station to her apartment. Nothing scared Freddie. Almost six feet tall and ebony, she carried herself like an Egyptian queen—her beautifully modeled, close-cropped head held high on a long dancer's neck. Maybe her karate black belt helped her confidence, too. I told her next Monday was fine, urged the pre-rehearsal nap and promised, fingers crossed, that I'd get the vitamins.

The phone call had taken the edge off my panic. At least the bogus repairman had heard King's message and could report back to his employer that it and I were no threat.

15

....

THE CAB WENT STRAIGHT DOWN COLUMBUS AVENUE, which becomes Ninth Avenue, not a picturesque route, but by far the fastest from the Upper West Side to the Village for my evening with Ike. Whatever romantic cloud I'd been floating on last night had blown away with today's events and dropped me rudely on my ass, feeling mad, scared, and decidedly unerotic. I'd forced myself to shower, which I accomplished with only two peeks out the side of the curtain for a possible bathroom bogeyman. By the time I'd dressed in black jeans and a big black turtleneck, it was time to leave. I'd debated briefly whether to put in my diaphragm, just in case my mood changed, but I couldn't bring myself to do it. I'd petted the cats good-bye and had the front door open when I decided "you never know" and ran back to the bedroom and popped it into my purse.

As we passed Lincoln Center, it occurred to me that Ike might chew me out for not having turned the tape with King's message over to him immediately. If he did we'd surely have a battle, because the last thing I felt like was taking any shit from him. I shut my head down for the rest of the ride and listened to the "beautiful music" station the driver had selected. Thank God he wasn't a talker.

In the middle of "These Foolish Things Remind Me of You" we pulled up in front of a small antique firehouse on Charles Street near West Fourth. Its facade was brick with decorative cement work crowning the high arch of a garage door, which was flanked by twin weathered oak entrance doors. The lefthand one sported a large brass knocker. I banged it a couple of times and stepped back to get a better look at the house. It was charming and perfectly preserved. I wondered how Ike could afford to live here on a cop's pay. Maybe the developer had broken the house up into small flats and Ike had some good stabilized rent deal or . . . I heard quick footsteps and the door opened to reveal Ike looking trim and handsome in well-worn jeans and blue and black buffalo-checked shirt. He took my hand.

"Must be colder out than it seems. Your hand's icy. Come on in." We were standing in a small vestibule painted deep red with white trim. About twelve feet inside was a flight of stairs with matching red carpet treads and polished wood banisters. I followed him up the stairs and found myself in a large, high ceilinged room—maybe twenty by fifty with a dark wood-surrounded fireplace at each end. The walls were white and the floors stripped waxed pine. At one end of the room big windows looked out on Charles Street; at the other, sliding glass doors opened onto a landscaped deck. The window end had an open kitchen built against the wall and a long, old refectory table and chairs in front of the fireplace. The end nearest the deck had a seating arrangement of comfortable-looking black leather sofas around its fireplace. In the corner near the doors to the deck was a Steinway grand piano. Oriental rugs in reds, blues, and cream broke up the expanse of pine floor. Behind the long sofa was a staircase which obviously led to a second floor. I took it all in in an instant and was astonished. Clearly no small flat. This was Ike's house and it was a knockout.

"Ike, it's . . . it's perfect."

He flashed the O'Hanlon grin. "I know what you're thinking. No, I'm not on the take and I don't deal dope on the side. Internal Affairs has spent plenty of taxpayer bucks looking into Lieutenant I. R. O'Hanlon. I come up squeaky clean." He walked to a polished walnut cabinet—eighteenth-century English to my eye—on which sat assorted bottles and glasses and a heavy brass ice bucket. "What to drink?"

"Scotch, please."

"You a single malt fan? I've got Glenfiddich."

I nodded, my manners fighting with my curiosity about how Ike managed to live in such a place, and to own a Volvo, come to think of it. My manners were losing.

"Okay, I'll bite. No take, no dope. A legacy from a newly discovered rich relative?"

"Ice?"

"No thanks, just water on the side."

He handed me a glass of water and carried our scotches over to the sofas, which formed a ninety-degree angle with a copper-topped coffee table in the L. We sat, each on a different sofa.

"No, no legacy. I made the money quite honestly. It seems I'm a pretty good investor, which shouldn't be too surprising. After all, I *am* Rosie's son as well as Pat's."

"Well then, why, uh, why, if you can . . ." My tongue was tangling around what I wanted to ask, but Ike anticipated the question. I guess he'd heard it before.

"You want to know why I bother with this often frustrating, low-paying job when I'm, shall we say, independently wealthy."

"Well, yes." I hastened to add, "Though of course it's clearly none of my business."

He looked at me, smiled, and sipped his scotch.

"I don't operate well with too much freedom—never did. My Da always understood that about me, maybe because he's the same way. After I got back from Nam I knocked around Hawaii and California. Won some money gambling and put it into the stock of a company I'd read about that sounded like a good takeover candidate. I was right and I damned near doubled my money. It seemed easy, and it was fun. I started to study the market and bet on my informed guesses. Most of the time they paid off. That way of life leaves you a lot of free time. I bought a beach house in Santa Monica and most of my days and nights were playtime. Lots of booze, some dope. Women. Anyway, Pat came out to the coast to visit me. He came without Rosie. I guess he wanted to check me out. I was proud as hell of myself and I showed off for him—not the dope, of course, or the girls, but the rest of my fancy life of leisure. The third morning he was there, he marched into my room and hauled me out of bed, dragged me to the window and ripped the curtains open. I thought my head would split from the brightness. I couldn't imagine what was happening. He looked at me and said, 'Ike, you're a bum.' 'What the hell are you talking about, Da?' I said. 'I'm rich. I can have anything. Do anything. I move my money around and I'm damned good at it. How can you call me a bum?' He dragged me over to the bathroom mirror and practically shoved my face through it. 'Look at yourself. In my book anyone who's sleeping it off at one o'clock on a Wednesday afternoon is a bum. And I'm ashamed of you.'

"I showered and kind of pulled myself together. When I came downstairs ready to give some mouth back to him, I found him drinking coffee. His bags were packed and he was obviously ready to leave. He poured me some coffee and, before I could say anything, he said, 'The police exam is next Thursday in New York. You'll be good at the work and you'll like it. This Monopoly-game play money is swell for your spare time, but that's all.' Then he left. I was furious. Felt put down—betrayed. But I thought about what he'd said—couldn't get it out of my head. And I didn't drink or smoke grass that day or the next. I put the house up for sale and caught a Monday morning flight to LaGuardia. Made a bundle on the house, too," he added with a grin.

"That would be a long time ago. Why aren't you a captain by now?"

"A captain's basically a paper pusher and a politician—not my strong suits. I like the action just where I am. And I don't need captain's pay. I've kept my Monopoly money in action in my spare time, just like Pat suggested." He smiled as he mentioned his father. "He is something, my da."

"He sure is," I agreed, "so is Rosie. How are they?"

"The king and queen of Fort Lauderdale? They're great. You know, I wanted to call you or write or something when your father died, but I . . . well . . . He was special to me, too."

I glanced at the piano as he spoke about my father. "I see you still play the piano." My father, who never met a musical instrument he couldn't play, had started twelve-year-old Ike on the piano, bringing to his instruction all the enthusiasm which would have been wasted on two tin-eared daughters.

"Yeah, I do. Funny, I use it just the way your dad did—to unwind, get away from it." For a moment, I thought he was going to reach for me, but he got up to make us another drink instead. We were back in the present. A man had been murdered. Ike wanted more information from me about my London contact and I had news about the erased message to deliver that he wasn't going to like any more than I did. I took a deep breath and readied myself to plunge in.

"Ike, there's something I've been meaning to tell you, but I kept forgetting. I didn't think it was important, but apparently someone else did."

I told him about the message and the "phone repairman." His face tensed.

"Do you remember what King said? I mean his exact words?"

I had no trouble with that one. I'd heard the message twice and replayed it many more times in my head. "He said, 'Liz, this is King. Our meeting tomorrow morning is canceled. There's no point in involving you, unless—' he paused and then he said, 'I'll have to handle it another way.' "

Ike got a pen and pad off the kitchen counter and asked me to write down what I'd just said. When I'd finished and handed it back to him, he sat down beside me on the sofa and asked me who I'd told about the message.

"Four people," I answered, "the three partners—Rog Durand, Les Charlton, Dave Goldstone—and Mandy Greathouse." In deleting Angela, I'd lied to him again, and I felt rotten about it. "But," I added, "I have no idea who else might have heard about it from any of them. Mandy could have told Charlie

Kaye. As you probably know, they date each other. But the message didn't *say* anything."

Just then the phone rang. Ike strode over to the kitchen area to pick it up. All I heard on his end were uh-huh's, yeses, and other noninformative monosyllables. When he hung up, he walked back to the sofa without stopping at the bar to pick up our drinks. His face was drained.

"What is it?"

"We can probably cross Mandy Greathouse off our suspect list. Somebody's murdered her."

16
....

Ike's Volvo made its way from the West Village to the FDR Drive in about a minute and a half. Or maybe I was so spaced out that it just seemed that way. I'd insisted on going with Ike to Mandy's apartment, where she'd been found strangled with a pair of pantyhose. He'd offered to drop me home. My response was a "No," which exploded out so loud that it embarrassed me. I tried to cover by saying I wanted to come because I thought I might be helpful, but I really was terrified at the idea of going back to my apartment where a bogus telephone man with a garotte in his hand could be lurking in any corner. As we swung onto the Drive from Fourteenth Street, I broke the silence. "All of this is bound up with that damn mystery meeting that King and I were supposed to have. Mandy called me last night to ask me what the meeting was going to be about, because someone had asked her and she was ashamed to admit that she didn't know."

"Ashamed?"

"Yeah. Mandy's—was—King's top assistant. It was a matter of pride to her that she always knew what was going on, so she told this person—whoever it was—that the matter was confidential. When I told her that I knew less than nothing, she sounded agitated and then she got off the phone real quick because her call waiting beeped. I said I'd give her a ring today, but the time got away from me and I never did."

"Jesus Christ. That stupid broad!" Ike's foot took his frustration out on the gas pedal and we surged forward past a couple of astonished, law-abiding drivers. "I guess it would be too much to hope that she gave you any idea who was trying to pump her?"

I thought hard. "I'm afraid it *is* too much to hope for. I don't have a clue." I paused and chewed on my thumbnail. "I guess it's the telephone man, huh?"

"Not necessarily. The telephone man could be a hired hand. We don't know what we're dealing with here yet, but we've been talking to a lot of people and we're beginning to make some assumptions—or at least to rule out some possibilities."

"What about Sir Brian? Hasn't he told you what his private detective was up to? That should tell you something."

"I'm sure it would—if we could get our hands on Sir Brian."

"What do you mean?"

"He seems to have, as the Brits say, 'gone missing,' and that's all I'm going to say at the moment."

"Suit yourself," I said huffily.

"Look, Liz, for your own protection it's better that you don't know. It could be dangerous for you."

"Dangerous!" I shrieked. "That's really too funny. Everybody who calls me on the phone seems to end up dead the next day. A murderer, or at least a murderer's helper, gets into my apartment and monkeys with my message machine and you're talking 'could be dangerous'? Damn right it's dangerous, and I'll feel better if I at least know who I can trust."

"You can trust nobody, got it? Nobody. After tonight you just stay out of this, okay? I know you have to write your press releases and whatever else you're doing in damage control for your client or I'd tell you to get on a plane and go to the Bahamas or someplace till this is all over. Instead, I'm telling you to be very careful around everyone involved with Carter Consultants; not just the partners, everyone connected with the whole damned organization. Don't go off alone with any of them and don't be a big shot. As far as anyone is concerned you don't know nuthin' about nuthin'. Got it?"

This sudden tongue-lashing had a tonic effect on me. It made me so mad I forgot to be scared.

"Exactly who the hell do you think you're talking to? I'm not a retarded twelve year old."

"No. You're a smart-ass forty-three year old who I would like to see live to become a smart-ass forty-four year old."

As we turned onto Eighty-ninth Street from Second Avenue, I saw that the street was blocked halfway up by three black-and-whites with red flashers. Ike stopped the car with a lurch.

"I'm perfectly capable of taking care of myself, but thanks for your warm sympathies and sage advice," I said coldly as I undid my seat belt and got out of the car.

The building Mandy lived in was a six-story, not-very-weathered brick. It and its like had sprung up in vacant lots and replaced derelict brownstones in many good residential neighborhoods all over the city during the 1970s. They had afforded no-frills living, mostly to singles and young couples, at relatively cheap rents. The accommodations were still no-frills but the rents had developed delusions of grandeur.

The wall of uniforms blocking the front door to the mingy little vestibule parted for Ike. The inner door was propped open. Immediately beyond it to our left was a small, battered elevator which took a few beats to open, even though it was on the so-called "lobby" floor.

Ike pressed "three" and we rattled up, each facing opposite corners of the little corrugated silver box. The gum-chewing cop standing sentinel opened the chipped blue door to Mandy's apartment.

At first glance, it looked as though a cocktail party too large for the small apartment had gotten out of hand—a drunken guest passed out on the floor and others engaged in assorted strange acts.

I tasted scotch at the back of my throat and had to fight hard not to throw up. Mandy, sprawled on the floor, her bright hair fanned out against the side of a cream tweed sofa, was unspeakable. Her face was blue and her pale eyes bulged. Porky Remley and an older, stooped man—the medical examiner, I guessed—were crouched on either side of her. I turned away as fast as I could unglue my eyes and spotted a dark head, bent and buried in its owner's hands. The chunky body attached to it was a bit too wide for the bentwood soda fountain chair it sat on, elbows propped on a pine drop-leaf table. I was startled to realize it was Charlie Kaye.

"Charlie!"

He looked up. His eyes were red and his face damp with tears.

"Liz. What . . . what are you doing here?" His voice sounded clogged.

"I . . . well, I . . . It doesn't matter. I, uh . . . was . . . uh, with Lieutenant O'Hanlon when he found out about . . . about . . . I came along because I thought maybe . . . maybe . . . I could help." I sped through this incoherent nonsense. My mouth didn't seems able to form the word murder—or even Mandy.

"Thank God you're here. I . . . Oh my God." His head went back down into his hands. I think he was so glad to see a live, familiar face that he didn't much care why it happened to be there.

"Charlie, what . . . Did you find her?"

"Yeah." He didn't raise his head. I took a few steps closer and patted his shoulder awkwardly. The raw grief radiated out of him like heat. My eyes misted as I looked at the tiny room, so lovingly decorated. Pale yellow walls and cream shag rug to make up for the sunlight it rarely saw. Calder and Miro prints.

What kind of monster would kill Mandy? King was powerful; formidable. I could see someone mad enough, or maybe scared enough, to murder King. But Mandy was so . . . so vulnerable. I took a quick glance around and didn't see Ike. I assumed he must be in the bedroom, because that would've been the only place in the small apartment where he'd be out of my sight. From where I stood I could even see the open door to the bathroom.

"When did you get here? Tell me what happened." If Ike wasn't going to give me any information, I'd have to damned well find it out for myself. I operated far better when I knew what was going on, and if Ike O'Hanlon didn't realize that yet, I'd make sure he soon did.

Charlie raised his head. His square face with its blunt nose and well-shaped full lips looked hypnotized as he began to speak. His voice was devoid of its accustomed, cocky briskness. "Dinner. We were going to have dinner. Mandy'd been so tense since King died. We all are, of course, but somehow it was harder on her. She's . . . she's so frail." His voice broke on the word and he took a moment to recover.

"I told her I'd pick her up and we'd go for Chinese. Mei Chung Ho's just around the corner and we both love it . . . Oh God, I can't!" If that man wasn't legitimately grief-stricken then Hollywood was missing its hottest prospect in fifty years.

"When did you make your dinner plans?" I'd been on the answering end of police questioning over the last two days, and found myself switching easily over to the asking side.

"I called her at about six-thirty or so—well, maybe it was closer to seven. Yeah, it was ten to seven. I had the radio on—WINS—and they said the time while we were talking. I told her I'd be at her place in an hour."

"And were you?"

"Uh-huh. Just about. I got here a couple of minutes before eight. I checked my watch, because when I rang the bell downstairs she didn't answer."

"How'd you get in?"

"Oh, I had a key, but I rang to let her know I was here. I thought she might be in the john or something, so I let myself in, and then . . . and then . . ."

"I know, Charlie. I'm sorry to put you through this." If he'd been more collected he might have asked who the hell I thought I was to interrogate him. I pressed on, not knowing how much longer I'd have before Ike, who was quite collected, appeared and asked me the same question.

"Was the apartment door open or locked or what?"

"It was closed, and that automatically locks it, unless you press the button that lets the handle turn. But it wasn't double locked, the way Mandy usually keeps it. I guess the mur . . . he just ran out and closed the door behind him."

"Did she say on the phone—" I never had a chance to finish the question, because Ike strode in from the bedroom, accompanied by Sergeant Libuti, who nodded in my direction.

"I'm Lieutenant O'Hanlon, Mr. Kaye. I know you're feeling pretty rotten, so I won't keep you any longer than necessary. You've already told Sergeant Libuti, but could you run through what happened one more time for me, please?"

Charlie told it exactly as he had to me. Then Ike asked the same question I'd started to.

"Did Ms. Greathouse say anything on the phone to indicate that she was expecting another visitor before her date with you?"

He thought before answering. He said, "No. Nothing at all." He seemed positive of it.

Ike said he'd want Charlie to come in and make an official statement tomorrow morning, and that he was free to go now.

"Come on, Charlie," I said, "let me take you for a drink. You don't want to be alone just now . . . and neither do I." Then something else occurred to me. "Mandy has family, doesn't she? In Wisconsin somewhere. Who's going to tell them?"

"I can't, Liz, I simply can't," Charlie said quietly. "Mandy and I were going to go out to Racine for Thanksgiving. I was going to meet them. We were going to . . . I can't." I didn't blame him a bit. Since I didn't see that the Greathouse family would find the horrible news any easier to take from me, who they'd never laid eyes on, than from the police, I didn't volunteer. One thing was clear: I seemed to have been mistaken in the idea that Charlie was simply using Mandy to get ahead at Carter Consultants.

"I'll contact them," said Ike with a level blue gaze at me. "Civility may not be the specialty of us humble cops, Ms. Wareham, but I'll give it my best shot."

17

CHARLIE AND I HEADED FOR SECOND AVENUE. BEING OUT of Mandy's apartment felt like a reprieve from hell. By mutual unspoken consent, we selected the first quiet, unfashionable bar we saw—not easy to find in the midst of swinging singleland with its fun-promising lineup of "Rascals," "Bloomers," "Red Blazer," etc. We settled into a back booth at McCurdy's. Charlie ordered a beer and I a scotch. Neither of us specified a brand nor, when the drinks arrived, did we take more than a sip or two. This wasn't a social occasion and he didn't feel any more like drinking than I did. The bar was merely a place to go. The price of the drinks was pew rent.

"Look, Charlie," I finally said, "Mandy must have been killed because of something she knew—or something somebody thought she knew—about King's murder. Do you have any idea what it was?"

He shook his head. "If Mandy knew anything about King's murder, she'd have gone to the police. And I think she'd have told me. We were in love with each other, for God's sake. Look, I know what everyone thought: 'Old what-makes-Sammy-run Charlie Kaye, using poor little Mandy to get ahead at Carter.' " I started to protest, but he cut me off.

"Come on, Liz, I'm not a dope. I'm in a people business. Ain't no such animal as a successful headhunter who can't read people. That's what everybody thought, and they were right—for starters. But then it changed. I fell in love with her. She was such a gentle little bird." He wiped his eye. "Maybe that's how girls are in Wisconsin. I dunno. I'm from Brooklyn. In Boro Park I knew bright ballsy Jewish girls—you know, like you." Somehow I didn't think this was a compliment.

"By the way," he continued, "it's a funny thing, talking about Boro Park. I was raised Orthodox. You know, the *cheder*—the whole nine yards."

"Yes, what about it?"

"Well, I've been spending a lot of time with the partners—Dave Goldstone especially, since King was killed, and, Liz, he's no Jewish guy."

Mandy's murder must have knocked his oars out of the water. "What are you talking about, Charlie? Of course he is."

"No. You weren't raised the way I was—and the way Dave claims he was. Boys who went to *cheder*, had an Orthodox Bar Mitzvah, we have certain mutual memories. Never met one who didn't laugh when I talked about tripping Herbie Berkowitz with my tallis. Dave didn't laugh—not until I started to and he got that he was supposed to. I threw out a couple more references. I wasn't trying to test him really, I was trying to bond. He is my new boss, after all, and we're two Yids in Goyland. At least I thought we were. But he's *not*."

"That's crazy, Charlie. I've heard of Jews denying that they were Jews, but never the other way around. You have any surprise curves to throw about Rog or Les?"

"Not really. By the way, I saw Rog over at the Manse today. You know the cops are letting us move back into the first floor, but nobody's allowed upstairs until Friday. Anyway, he was terrified."

"What do you mean?"

"Well, he was looking through some papers and I came up behind him and clapped him on the shoulder and said, 'Hi, Rog.' Well, he jumped three feet. I mean, I thought the guy was going to have a coronary."

The waiter came over and asked if we wanted refills. In other words, order another drink or pay up and move on, which is what we did. I gave Charlie a spontaneous hug and said I'd see him tomorrow at the funeral. He flagged a cab for me. I got in, gave the driver my address, and started to think.

I didn't know the details that the police did about exactly when King had been killed and who had alibis for what times. But I did know about some stuff that Ike didn't: Angela's visit to the Manse the night of the murder and the fact that King had intended to hide a message for her to find. Now I also knew that Rog was terrified, which didn't seem surprising, and that Charlie thought that Dave wasn't Jewish, which didn't seem relevant. But maybe it was. If Charlie was right, and Dave wasn't Jewish, then he wasn't David Goldstone. If he wasn't David Goldstone, then who was he? And how could I find out without sticking my neck into someone's pantyhose?

18

KING, MANDY, AND I WERE PLAYING RING-AROUND-THE-
Rosy. We swung our hands and chanted, "Ashes, ashes, we all
fall down," then the ground gave way and we went tumbling
into space. I woke with the shuddering start that accompanies
a dream of falling. My bedside lamp was on and so was the
tall one on my dresser. It took a beat before I remembered
why. The combination of dark, unknown, and alone has always
terrified me. As a result, I have passed the night in fully lit
rooms in more Hiltons and Sheratons than I care to count.

Usually my own bedroom is safe ground, but last night it
hadn't felt that way. Mandy's death had hit me hard. Not
that we'd been close or anything like it, but the brutal end
to a gentle life seemed excruciatingly unfair. It also raised
disturbing internal questions about my own life and the uses
I was putting it to.

A glance at the clock told me it was seven thirty-five, and
I willed myself vertical, despite the muzziness in my head
and the brown dryness in my mouth. Today was going to be
a tough one. We'd have the media all over us about Mandy's
death. Besides that, King's funeral was this afternoon at two.
I stepped into the shower and lathered up. Last night, I'd tried
to reach Dave and, when he wasn't in, Les, to let them know
about Mandy's murder. Never mind Ike's warning to me, it
would have looked suspicious if I *hadn't* called. After all, I
had been there. Charlie Kaye knew that and had no reason
to keep it secret. I'd left messages with the Regency desk

for each to call me, but neither had. I'd also alerted Seth and told him to draft a statement for the media and a paid obit from Carter Consultants expressing the company's sorrow at Mandy's death. I didn't have to direct him to make both as bland as possible. He was a pro. My last duty call had been to John Gentle, for no reason except that he liked to be in on everything. It had been hard to get him off the phone.

I toweled dry while Elephi and Three licked remaining drops of water off my toes and ankles. As I padded down the hall to the kitchen to feed the cats and start the coffee, I thought about Dave. If Charlie was right, doting, self-sacrificing Sol and Minnie were phantoms and the poor but colorful childhood on the Lower East Side was made up. But why?

After I set the cat dishes on the floor, I went back to the bedroom to dress. If David Goldstone wasn't who he claimed to be, had he killed two people to protect that secret? In a book the motive would be tailor-made. But this wasn't a book, and I couldn't picture Dave murdering anyone. I could see him furious, punching someone out with his meaty fist, but not . . .

Who *could* I picture? I thought as I buttoned my white silk shirt. Les? Rog? Charlie? Gillian?

I zipped my navy suit skirt and it caught the hem of the shirt.

As I tried to work the bit of silk loose, the doorbell rang and I ran down the hall to get it, preoccupied with jiggling the zipper so as not to tear the delicate fabric. My efforts met with success. I turned the Segal lock and the other lock and threw open the door.

In my defense, I can say only that my mind was on the stupid zipper and that I'm used to opening a ringing door—to deliverymen, friends, kids' friends, whatever. This was no friend. I could tell that by the blue-black gun he held pointed at my chest.

My stomach dropped.

"Don't even think of hollering, lady."

I *was* thinking of it, actually, but my throat didn't seem able to produce a sound.

"Inside. We're gonna have a talk."

I backed into the apartment, not wanting to turn my back on him. He was tall and solid with dark hair and eyes. His olive skin bore the traces of acne past, but not by that many years. He didn't look more than twenty-two, tops. He was dressed in black jeans and turtleneck under a zipped black leather jacket with wet shoulders. Apparently it was raining. He looked familiar somehow, yet I was sure I didn't know him. He waved the gun toward the long red sofa.

"Siddown."

I did. He did, too—at the other end. Elephi appeared from the kitchen, sniffed his ankles, and began to rub against his leg. So much for animal instincts. Maybe I should have stuck with ex-husband number two's example and kept Dobermans.

"How did you get up here?" I whispered.

"Easy." He was proud of himself. It made him seem even younger. "It's raining. I just waited till the doorman stepped out to get a cab for some old guy."

"What do you want?"

"Tell me about that meeting—with Carter."

"I never *had* that meeting. You must know that."

"What was he gonna talk to you about?"

"I have no idea. He never said. And he canceled the meeting anyway, only I never got the message. But you know that from the tape."

"What tape?"

"My answering machine tape. The one you erased." But he hadn't erased it, I realized suddenly. He didn't look at all like Freddie's description of the phony phone man. Besides, he didn't seem to know what the hell I was talking about.

"You didn't have to kill Mandy. She didn't know what the meeting was going to be about either."

"Who's Mandy?" He looked confused—trying to make up his mind about whether I was putting him on. His face *was*

CAROL BRENNAN

familiar. So was the voice. He reminded me of someone, but I couldn't quite figure out who.

"Mandy was King Carter's—" The phone rang. I looked at him for permission to answer it. He didn't give it.

"I'm expecting early morning calls," I said quickly. "They'll get suspicious if I'm not home. They'll call the police." Was that a smart thing to say, or a very dumb one? The phone rang again.

"Go pick it up. But watch what you say, lady. I mean it."

I ran for the kitchen phone and caught it at the end of the third ring, just before the answering machine would have picked up.

"Hello." My voice sounded surprisingly normal to my own ears.

"Liz. Dave. I was out at dinner with Les when you called, and then the police got to me. Jesus! Where's this gonna end?"

The man was standing about ten feet away, his nasty little gun pointed straight at me. It didn't seem like a good idea to try anything cute.

"I wish I knew, Dave, I just wish I knew." His olive face went sickly yellow. His gun hand lowered slightly. As I watched him, I suddenly had an idea. But did I dare stake my life on it?

"Dave," I said into the phone, "those brothers we were talking about? Well, the younger one . . ." The look that crossed his face was part puzzlement, part astonished terror. I was terrified myself that he'd tense up and pull the trigger, but now I was sure I was right. I continued, keeping my voice as steady as I could, "the one that was arrested for breaking into that woman's house—" His gun hand fell to his side. He turned abruptly and ran out the front door, letting it slam behind him. My knees started to shake.

"What the hell are you talking about? Have you gone nuts?" I couldn't get my knees to stop, so I sat down on the kitchen floor.

"I'm talking about your brother, Dave. He was just here. With a gun."

"My what?" David's voice exploded in my ear.

"Your brother, Dave. Your younger brother. He ran out when he heard it was you on the phone. Look, I'm going to call the police in the next two minutes, so don't even think of arranging for anything to happen to me."

"Liz, wait. Please, please wait. It . . . it's not what you think. I . . . I didn't kill King . . . or Mandy, and my brother didn't either. I swear. I . . . Look, Liz, you have nothing to fear from me, or from him. Goddam asshole with his dramatics. Watches too much television."

"What you call dramatics scared me half to death and with good reason. Why should I believe you? If I don't call the police, what's to prevent you or some goon of yours from knocking me off?" I asked, sounding as though I, too, watched too much television.

"Liz, listen. My life is at stake. My whole life. I beg you. Meet me. Let me explain. It's not what you think."

That was probably true, since I had no idea what the hell was going on. "Okay," I said, "this is what I'll do. I'm going to write all this up the minute I hang up and fax it to someone I completely trust with instructions not to do anything about it unless something happens to me." I'd been delighted six months before, when the office installed a fax in my apartment, but not as delighted as I was at this moment. "So you'd better make sure that nothing does."

"But that means someone else will know."

"That's right. It gives you a vested interest in my continued well-being."

He didn't say anything for a long ten seconds.

"Can you meet me in an hour? Not at the Regency, though. Make it . . . Lindy's, right across from Madison Square Garden."

That suited me fine—big and public. I figured what suited him was that we'd be unlikely to run across anyone we knew—or at least anyone *I* knew. I was no longer at all sure about what kinds of people Dave might know.

"Okay. Lindy's in an hour."

19

D AVE WAS WAITING AT AN ISOLATED BACK TABLE JUST behind the swing of the kitchen door when I arrived at Lindy's, which is tucked into the Penta Hotel on Seventh Avenue and Thirty-second in the middle of the garment center. It took me a couple of minutes to spot him amid the garmentos animatedly doing business over bagels and coffee.

It'd taken longer than I'd expected to get my report onto the word processor—a testament to my ineptitude at typing. I had included Charlie Kaye's certainty that Dave wasn't Jewish and, after some hesitation, had thrown in Angela's story about her meeting with King at the Manse the night of his murder and the message he'd supposedly hidden for her. After all, if I came to no harm, no one would see any of it, except Sam Boyd, to whom I'd faxed it, and he was totally trustworthy and unflappable. If anything *was* about to happen to me, loyalty to Angela would be far down my list of concerns—if I lived to have any.

After faxing the stuff to Sam's apartment in Washington, I'd hidden the diskette in the jumble of my scarf drawer, where I defied anyone to find anything, and put the hard copy in my bag to secrete somewhere in my office.

I approached Dave's table. The *Wall Street Journal* was open in front of him, but he wasn't reading it. Instead, he was staring into space. My arrival startled him.

"Good morning, Dave."

"Good morning, Liz." He motioned to the waiter to bring me some coffee. Amazing how we observe these rituals that have been imprinted early.

"Good morning, class."

"Good morning, Miss Grundy."

"Good morning, we've come to electrocute you."

"Good morning, just a minute while I finish my last breakfast."

The waiter filled my cup and refilled Dave's. We ordered a basket of hot rolls. Neither of us knew how to begin.

"David, I don't know what to say to you, and I'm not going to make small talk. Why don't you just tell me what the hell is going on and why I should believe that you and your gun-waving brother aren't running around killing people."

"I guess the only way to tell it is to tell it." He let out a deep breath and took a slug of coffee. "I am David Goldstone." I started to interrupt, but he cut me off. "I've been David Goldstone for seventeen years, and I have every damned right to be him—I've earned it. But I wasn't born David Goldstone." He took a deep drag on his Marlboro and exhaled. Sol and Minnie went up in a puff of smoke.

"Who were you born?"

"Mario Mastrantonio." The name meant nothing to me—told me nothing except that he was Italian not Jewish. "My father's connected. Nothing big time. He's a distant relative of *the* Mastrantonio family. He's spent his life running errands for them—some, I'm sure, pretty grisly, but nobody ever talked about it at home. My mother protected us from it. Till I was fourteen I thought my father installed cigarette machines, which in fact he did. It just wasn't *all* he did."

"How'd you find out?" I asked, caught up in the human details of his story despite myself.

"My mother died a week after my fourteenth birthday. Heart attack. Jesus, she was younger than I am now." He dragged on the cigarette as though in defiance of his genes. "After that the wise guys started coming to the house more. I overheard things—and then I knew. I was the oldest. My sister Josie was

109

twelve and Carlo was nine. I kept it from them as long as I could."

"Wait a minute. Your brother—the one I met. He was younger than that."

"Yeah, that's Frankie. He wasn't born until I was sixteen. My father's second wife. He's their only child—and he's a good kid." My eyes rolled upward in disbelief. "No, he *is*, Liz. Christ, he's not even *in* the mob. He's going to be a vet, for God's sake! He must have gotten some cockamamie idea that he was going to protect his big brother. I'll kick his ass from here to Brooklyn when I get my hands on him, and he knows it." That would explain why Frankie had looked so scared at the mention of Dave's name and why he'd beat it out of my apartment so fast when he'd heard me go on with that double talk about brothers.

"Let's get back to how you got to be David Goldstone— and why."

"Why is easy. I always wanted to be Jewish." I looked at him skeptically. "Nobody always wanted to be Jewish," I said. "Lots of Jews always wanted *not* to be Jewish, but—"

"No, really. All that stuff about Sol and Minnie was my childhood fantasy. All the smart kids in my class were Jewish— all the ones with families that pushed them to become professionals. You know—Mom and Pop would stand over the pickle barrel and talk about 'my son the doctor.' Well, my family wasn't like that—at least my father wasn't. He thought being connected was the hottest thing going. He figured maybe his Mario would make it bigger in the mob than he did."

The corner of his mouth turned down in irony. He took a deep drag on his cigarette.

"Some ambition, huh? My mother was different—like a Jewish mother. She wanted me to be a lawyer. A *real* lawyer, she said, not a mob mouthpiece. Her name was Theresa." He smiled slightly as he pronounced it. "The up side of my father is that he'd do anything for me. He did the biggest thing of all. He let me go."

"What about your brother and sister?"

He grimaced ruefully.

"They liked the family business, it seems. Josie married into it and Carlo died in it. Anyway, you have the why part of your answer. The how is a little more complicated." The waiter gave us another dose of hot caffeine from a scratched silver pot.

"David Goldstone was a real person. He was a foster kid in the neighborhood. It *was* the Lower East Side, by the way. I didn't lie about that. David practically lived at our house. The foster family didn't care. They got their checks every month from social services. After high school we both got drafted. David got shipped to Vietnam. I stayed in California—Fort Ord. Just luck. David got killed."

"And you became him?" It seemed incredible. It couldn't be that simple, could it? "Aren't there papers and things . . . Social Security cards, birth certificate?"

"Yes, there are. My father handled that for me." He smiled, embarrassed. "He knows people who do that kind of stuff. When I heard about David buying it in Nam, I was in a funk for weeks. Then I started to think. I could be a successful Jewish boy. I could be David. His name would be my passport to the world I wanted. I'd make it for both of us. David had no family. No one who really cared, except me. Not even a girlfriend. It was a chance for a whole new beginning.

"I was twenty-one, ready for discharge. I called my father and asked him to fly out to California and not to say anything to anyone. When he came I outlined my plan. He'd tell everyone—everyone except my brothers and sister and my stepmother, and they had to swear to secrecy—that I'd been killed in action."

"And your family. Did you . . . did you just stop seeing them?" I'd read stories this incredible, but I'd never heard one over the breakfast table. This was David Goldstone, about to become president of one of the country's top executive search firms (after enough years in PR, you even think like a press release). How could he suddenly turn into Mario Mastrantonio?

"You're staring at me, Liz. I'm a different person now, huh?" he said, reading my mind. "But to answer your question, no. We Italians and we Jews—I'm really both by now—don't break with our families. I stayed away from New York for a year or so. Had a little plastic surgery on the nose and chin. Meantime, the family moved out to Jersey—South Orange, so when I did come to New York it was easy to sneak in a visit."

"How'd you get into the University of Chicago?"

"I didn't. That's what I should have done, of course, but I guess I didn't have enough confidence to feel I could really make it in college. I knew I had to have the degree if I was going to get anywhere, so I—" He shrugged.

" . . . just said you had it." I finished for him. "Wasn't that taking kind of a chance? What if someone checked?"

"They don't. They just want to see a transcript. Transcripts are a piece of cake to forge compared to birth certificates."

"What did you major in?" I asked, winning the morning's prize for dumb questions.

"Psychology." That broke the tension and we both smiled real ones. "I thought it'd be a safe bet. I bought a bunch of books and found I really liked the stuff. I got a job in personnel at Consolidated Industries in L.A. I moved to Quigley four years later and got to be the number two guy in the department after three years. When the V.P./Personnel job at ABN in Chicago opened up, I was a natural for it, except that I needed an MBA to qualify."

"So you decided to become an instant Stanford alumnus?"

"Exactly."

"Jesus." Was it worse to have a client who might be a murderer, or one who'd lied about his credentials?

"A few years later, King offered me the partnership and I jumped at it. Life was perfect. I married Shelly . . . the kids . . . Oh God, Liz, it *can't* be over. I've worked too hard. Never mind the college. I've worked my tail off to get where I am. And I'm goddamned great at what I do."

"All of which would give you a perfect motive for killing King, wouldn't it?"

He sighed and lit another cigarette. "Yeah, I know it would. But I didn't. I don't deny my heart was in my mouth about the Green Star merger—would Salter do a deep background check on all of us and blow me out of the water? But then nothing happened and I thought it was okay. King never said anything. Why would I kill him, for Chrissake? Besides, I spent that night at my dad's in South Orange. We were up drinking coffee and anisette till after two. Then Frankie came down and he and I stayed up the rest of the night talking. I didn't leave there till after seven."

"Did you tell the police that?"

"Are you kidding? Nobody knows about my family, except Shelly. We've never even told our kids. They think that Pop and Serafina are just friends—from the old neighborhood."

"Maybe you could tell the police where you were without telling them the rest of it."

"Nah. I've thought of that. It would all come out. I know it would. How could I explain why I was there? And what makes you think they'd believe an old Mafioso anyway?"

I saw his point. His story rang true to me, but so had Charlie Kaye's—and Angela's. Maybe I was just gullible.

The subway car smelled of wet cloth and leather. The bodies were packed tight enough to eliminate the possibility of falling down and to discourage conversation as the E train lurched its way uptown. Fine with me, since my sense of balance had never been great and Dave and I had said all we'd had to say to each other for the moment. Many of our fellow passengers were engrossed in the tabloid coverage of Mandy's murder. I winced at the loud black *Post* headline, HEADHUNT II: KING'S SEC'Y STRANGLED. Dave was greenish white, his forehead dotted with sweat.

I lowered my head to get a look at my watch without being accused of sexual molestation by the guy on my left. It was nine-twenty. Shit! I'd promised Seth I'd be in early to discuss media strategy for King's funeral and Mandy's death. Ordinarily the subway would be half empty at this hour, but every rain, not to mention snow, took New York by surprise, as though it had never happened before, so how could we possibly be prepared to cope? Trains were delayed. People were late to work. And forget about getting a cab, which is how come pillars of the taxi community like Dave and me happened to be in the E train at all. We got out at Fifth Avenue, rode the long escalator to toll-booth level, and trudged up the steps to 53rd Street.

"Look," I said, breaking the silence, "Seth'll be there to handle the media at the funeral. I'll also have a couple of other people from the agency to help get all of you in and out with as little hassle as possible."

"Umhm." His mind was somewhere else—no surprise.

We covered the two blocks to my office in silence under our umbrellas. Just as I was about to enter the building, he touched my shoulder.

"Liz, please," was all he said.

"Dave, I promise I'll do all I can. If I told you more, I'd be lying."

He turned and started to walk east toward the Regency.

"Dave," I called to him before thinking about it. He turned. "I believe you." As I said it, I realized it was true. I *did* believe Dave. I also believed Angela and Charlie Kaye. Maybe if enough people told me they didn't kill King and Mandy, I'd convince myself that both of them had died of natural causes.

20

....

"DROPPING LIKE FLIES AT CARTER CONSULTANTS," WAS Morley's greeting, instead of his accustomed "Gracious good morning."

"Looks like," I answered as I walked past him into my office.

"Any calls?"

"You gotta be kidding. The message slips start from eight o'clock. I've bucked the media calls to Seth, but here's a list of them. Your mother called and your sister and Barbara. I told them you'd get back to them, but maybe not right away. Angela needs you, and Seth asked me to buzz him when you got in."

"I'll call Angela," I said, my heart pounding suddenly with the realization that her putative hidden message from King might have prevented Mandy's murder if we'd told the police about it. "Go ahead and buzz Seth, but tell him to give me five minutes, okay?"

"Sure. He may still be signing autographs. Wait till you see him."

I punched Angela's extension and she answered with her name.

"It's Liz. I just got here."

"I'm going in tonight. You still want to come?"

"Yup." The prospect was terrifying, but there was no doubt in my mind that I wanted to do it.

"Meet me at P. J. Clarke's at eleven-thirty. It's only two

blocks away. They haven't changed the lock, so we won't have any trouble."

"How do you know?"

"Oh, I tested it last night. My key worked fine."

"You mean you . . ." Had she gone in alone last night and gotten the message? I was instantly furious.

"No, no, I didn't go in. I just tested the key." Was that the truth? How the hell could I know?

"Okay," I said, "eleven-thirty at P.J.'s." I had to play by her rules, if I was going to play at all.

A knock at the door announced Seth. As he entered I saw what Morley had meant. New charcoal suit, blue shirt, yellow power tie. This was the new Seth: Media Personality. What was really startling, though, was his naked upper lip and the absence of the horn-rimmed glasses that always covered and further magnified his prominent brown eyes.

"Seth, you're . . . you're beautiful," I said, aping the hero in a thirties movie. He smiled shyly, showing as much gum as teeth. "But will you be able to see okay without your glasses?"

"Oh, I'm wearing contacts—soft lenses. I put in a rush order yesterday. Think I can charge them to the client?"

"We'll find a way. Couple of media lunches and some cabs should do it."

"I thought clean-shaven was more sincere, and the yellow tie'll let them know they can't push me around."

There's no business like show business.

The phone bleeped and Morley told me that Dennis Quayle was on the line. God! I'd forgotten all about him and the British Board of Trade proposal. That damned budget . . .

"Look, Dan Rather," I said quickly to Seth, "you got everything lined up for the funeral?"

"Yeah, Patti's gonna help me out. Also, the funeral home'll lay on a few extra bodies." He chuckled at his joke and then continued in a serious tone. "I've been stonewalling the media on Mandy. Not hard—I just tell 'em all I know, which is nothing. But Carter's gonna be in big trouble when their office reopens on Monday. Bud Campeau, who's covering the story for the *News*, says he talked to a couple of employees who just ain't gonna show up—too scared."

"Terrific," I said glumly, "but I guess it figures. Look, I've got to take this call." As he turned to leave I added, "You know, Seth, they're all wrong about you. You're not just another pretty face."

He gave me the finger accompanied by a gummy grin as he left, shutting the door behind him.

I picked up the phone wondering how to put the best face on the delayed proposal budget, and how to finesse a reference to the late Antony Swift.

"Hello, Dennis, sorry to keep you waiting," I began, taking the bull by the horns rather than throwing it. "I must apologize for the—"

"Liz, I don't know how you do it," he cut me off, "with all that's going on, I mean. The budget is fine."

"It is?"

"Yes. It arrived yesterday, along with the proposal addendum. Some excellent ideas there."

"I'm glad you think so," I replied carefully as I riffled quickly through the pile of papers on my desk, stopping when I reached a document covered by a note in Angela's dramatic hand: "Fed Ex'ed the budget and a couple of the additional thoughts we discussed to Dennis Quayle with attached note from you. A."

"Yes, they were super. My team is just as enthusiastic about the prospect of working with you as I."

"Wonderful!" For a moment nothing was in my head but the triumph of having made the sale. "You're going to love my team, too. Especially Angela Chappel, who's nothing short of amazing." God knows that was true.

"The only thing is, of course, it's not entirely our decision." Uh-oh. The sweat broke out on my upper lip. It always starts there when I'm nervous.

"We—the staff—think your proposal is by far the best. We like the Buy Britain theme and love 1-800-CHEERIO as the

117

number. Your budget makes sense too." He paused. Someday I'm going to win a game of Pause. But this wasn't going to be the time.

"I'm not sure I understand, Dennis. You're the executive director. You and your staff agree that you prefer our program. What's the problem?" I knew as soon as I'd said it that I was pushing too hard—especially with a Brit. They just froze up into terminal politeness when pressed. I had to retreat to more comfortable terrain for him.

"Dennis, excuse me, I didn't mean to put you on the spot. I guess I'm a bit frazzled with, uh, everything and . . . well, you certainly don't have to answer that."

"No need to apologize. I share your frustration." With the pressure off, he volunteered. "The board of directors have stuck their noses under my tent. Normally, decisions such as this *are* totally my province, but two of your competitors have offices here, and some business—not to mention golfing— bonds have been formed with certain directors. I've had several phone calls and one lunch offering strong suggestions that a large firm with a London office, such as Hill and Knowlton or Burson Marsteller, would be the way to go, even though their budgets would be considerably larger."

"Of course the budgets would be larger." I couldn't restrain myself. "With their overheads they have to charge more, or assign some junior to run the account. Anyway, what does it matter that they have offices in London? This is a program directed at Americans."

"I couldn't agree more, Liz. I'll make those points, but I'll have to do it in my own way. Perhaps I'll prevail." He changed the subject, shutting the door on further discussion. "By the bye, did you ever hear from my friend Swift?" Oh shit!

"Uh no, I didn't." Well, it was true. So Ike had been able to keep news of Swift's death out of the London papers—so far. He also hadn't sniffed out Dennis for questioning, at least not yet. I didn't quite believe he'd backed off trying to find the person who'd referred Swift to me just because I'd refused to name him.

We hung up cordially enough, but the conversation had put me in a worse mood than being threatened with a gun and finding out that my client was a masquerading son of the Mafia. I pressed the intercom button.

"Morley, I need more coffee."

Just then my door opened—no knock. John Gentle's silver head appeared. His face had a slightly chagrined look. What now?

"Liz, I'm really sorry but something's come up—a chance for a great piece of business, and Briggs and I have to catch a flight to Chicago in an hour." Another body blow. He'd just given Briggs Farragut Products, why . . . ? My rational self popped out of the closet to point out that *I* certainly wasn't available to go to Chicago in an hour, so of course he'd take Briggs. But it felt rotten anyway.

"Oh, who the hell cares!" I thought. At least I thought I thought it. When John Gentle strode into my office and shut the door behind him, I knew that the words had blasted out of my mouth. I was going nuts—really losing it. Hollering at my boss that I didn't care about the central thing in his life—and my own.

"John, I . . ." but I never finished the sentence. Maybe because I had no idea what the rest of it would be. It all seemed so stupid, suddenly, scrabbling around like a mouse in a maze to sell more paper napkins and cashmere sweaters, just so I could buy more paper napkins and cashmere sweaters. My whole world of selling and buying, of intense work and casual sex, of clothes and facials seemed contemptibly shallow. I was a great success at a bunch of things that didn't matter, and such a failure at the things that did. And my time was running out. Oh, I knew somewhere in the back of my mind that I wasn't looking at the whole picture. I had children I loved—a mother, a sister, friends, but . . .

John parked himself in one of the chairs opposite my desk, his long legs stretched out in front of him. He rested his elbows on the arms of the chair and made a little tent of his fingers. He didn't speak. Just looked at me. The light caught his glasses in a way that hid his expression.

All at once, with no warning, I started to cry. Deep, racking sobs—for Mandy, for King, for me. I'm not sure how long I cried, but it felt like forever. As my sobs subsided, I saw John's hand held out across the desk offering an immaculate white handkerchief. I took it and used it.

"Feel better, kid?" he asked in a tone I'd never heard before.

"Ye-yes," I said, my voice catching in a leftover sob. "I'm sorry, John. I didn't mean—"

"Yes, you did." He was right. I did. "You won't believe this, but I know how you feel." I doubted that, but didn't say so. He smiled slightly. "You're wondering how you can sit here caring like anything about things as meaningless as new accounts when these people you knew and worked with—maybe even liked—are suddenly dead." My surprise must have shown. "You're thinking what a crock of shit it is—your whole superficial life." I was astonished.

"How . . . how could you know that?" I asked, and gave my nose a final blow.

"You think I've never felt it, huh? After my wife died—that was thirteen years ago, before I knew you—the thought of work made me sick. Literally. I gagged at the idea of coming to the office. All I could think of was the time I didn't spend with Cassie when I had her."

He paused, hands flat on my desk. His jaw muscles worked like an engine revving up to start after a stall. He reached out for a framed eight by ten of my children smiling, squinty-eyed in a Sunfish up on Martha's Vineyard. It's not a recent photo—Scotty's thirteen and Sarah, eleven—but it's always been a favorite of mine. As his thumb ran slowly up and down the edge of the frame, I felt a flash of intimacy between us that didn't need words. He was caressing what was most precious to me.

"She used to say this agency was my number one wife and she was number two and hanging on. Of course we never had any kids—lousy break, more for Cassie than for me. Cancer.

It was quick, took less than a year from the time they found it." He let out a breath and shook his head slowly. "But you know, Liz, you get over it. The toughies like us do." He got up, walked around to my side of the desk and put his hand on my shoulder. "Look, I won't be at the funeral today. I know it looks bad. I had Mary send flowers, but—"

"It's okay. I'll explain that it was a long-standing meeting that couldn't be canceled." He opened the door and started to leave. "Thanks, John," I said to his back. He turned and gave me a full-fledged smile, which I found myself returning. "Break a leg in Chicago."

Morley's elegant arm placed a cup of coffee in front of me. He executed a delicate salaam.

"I hope this is to madame's liking."

"Sorry for making you wait on me, Morley," but I scowled as I said it. My sense of humor had gone on strike.

He looked at me, one eyebrow raised over the top of his glasses. "Who do you think it is?"

I shook my head slowly. "Beats hell out of me. King knew a lot of folks. Some of them had damned good reasons for not liking him a whole lot."

"What about Mandy? If being the secretary of someone who isn't a hundred percent popular is that dangerous, you can have my resignation right now."

"Touché, but if you resigned nobody'd have to knock me off. I'd do it myself."

21

....

I HAD THE CAR SERVICE PICK ME UP AT ONE-FIFTEEN,
even though the funeral was scheduled for two and Frank
E. Campbell was only a mile uptown. I wanted to be there
early on two counts: one, to support Seth and Patti in case
anything went wrong with the media, and two, to see if I
could learn anything about the murders that I didn't already
know. Something that might, for a change, make some sense
to me.

As the driver crawled his way to 81st and Madison, I
reviewed what I knew. King clearly had come by information
that was highly dangerous to somebody. He'd planned to
discuss it with me, which had to mean that the bombshell,
whatever it was, had PR implications. Dave's background and
nonexistent MBA would certainly fill that bill, but it didn't
mean that his was the only nasty secret floating around.

Maybe King had recommended against Gerry Klose for the
top job at Seagrave on grounds more sinister than mediocrity.
Maybe Les was a child molester. Maybe Charlie Kaye was a
Russian spy. Maybe Rog . . . well, maybe Rog wasn't as stupid
as he looked. For that matter, maybe Angela was a lot more
devious than *she* looked. And maybe Gillian Carter murdered
rich husbands every five years. The trouble was I knew so
little. Hell, I didn't even know who had alibis and could be
eliminated from consideration. I realized with a twinge that my
growing determination to figure the thing out myself was not
quite explained by the fact that my client had been murdered,

or that I had found his body. There was another fact: I was feeling as competitive as a World Series pitcher.

The other team's pitcher was Ike O'Hanlon.

I could see from two blocks away that the television vans had arrived, so I had the driver drop me at 80th and Madison. I'd walk the extra block and enter as unobtrusively as possible. The front of Campbell's was mobbed with reporters and passersby who figured that if reporters were there, something interesting must be going on.

Four husky Campbell employees seemed to be doing a good job of letting those attending the funeral in, and Seth was holding his own keeping the proliferating swarm of reporters at bay. The partners had insisted on allowing no press to attend the funeral.

I spotted Patti handing out releases and watched Seth being taped by the Channel Two minicam. He was having the time of his life. I caught his eye when he was finished and gave him a quick wink. It was obvious he didn't need my help. I walked around to the side entrance, gave my name, and was admitted by another brawny Campbeller.

I walked up a single flight of stairs into an anteroom where people were stowing their rain gear. I gave my sopping umbrella a shake and put it in a rack. As I started to take off my raincoat, I saw Les's trench-coated, slouch-hatted back, partly masked by a potted palm. He was talking with a portly gray-haired military-looking man whom I didn't know. I thought I ought to tell him I'd arrived. I walked over and clapped a hand on his shoulder.

"Les, excuse me for interrupting, I just wanted to—"

He started as though from electric shock and spun to face me. Only it wasn't Les, nor was it a he. It was Gillian Carter and her face was chalk white and furious. To say I was embarrassed didn't quite cover it. I felt my face go scarlet with mortification.

"Oh God, Gillian, how stupid can I be? I can't imagine how . . ."

"Who are you?" she shot at me.

"I'm Liz Wareham. I . . . my agency handles Carter Consultants' public relations. We met once. I . . . I'm so sorry." She recovered her composure with some effort.

"Yes, yes, of course. I apologize for jumping at you, Liz." She used my name with visible effort. "You startled me."

I began to apologize for my gaffe again, but she cut me off.

"I'd like you to meet Geoffrey Severing, my attorney. Geoffrey, this is Liz Wareham." Her pale, fine-boned face restored itself to the cool calm that encouraged Dave to refer to her as the Ice Queen. None of the dramatically cropped hair I remembered from our first meeting was visible beneath her hat and her eyes were shaded by dark glasses. She was an arresting woman with a touch of 1930's Berlin about her.

I cleared my throat and managed "How do you do" as we shook hands. He responded with what a pity it was to meet on such a sad occasion. I looked around, not knowing what to say to either of them.

"I guess we should get out of these wet coats," I said inanely. As Gillian doffed her trenchcoat and hat, I saw that the pale blond hair was as I remembered. She was wearing a simple, long-sleeved black sheath with a heavy, but not ornate, gold cross on a chain around her neck. Low-heeled black boots met the hem of the dress.

"Leslie's off having a word with Reverend Flowers, Liz. You were looking for him?" she asked dismissively.

"Yes, I was. But just to see if I could help out in any way."

I was grateful to glimpse Rog shepherding the Family Durand through the door. He made a beeline for us.

"Gillian." Rog put a hand on her shoulder and leaned to kiss her cheek. She turned her head just enough to make his mouth land on her blond crop instead. He winced at the snub.

"Liz, I don't think you've met my wife, Peg." I hadn't. She reached out a blunt, sensible hand.

"Hello, Liz, I've heard so much about you and your good work." I liked her at once. Not just for the graceful compliment, but for the intelligence and humor in the short-lashed brown eyes that lighted her plain, round, slightly weathered face. I imagined her sensibly short-haired salt and pepper head bent, tending a serious garden and acquiring the sun wrinkles which had etched themselves into the back of her neck.

"I'm so pleased to meet you, Peg," I replied, meaning it. I don't know what I expected of Rog's wife—perhaps that she'd be his female clone—but Peg was a pleasant surprise. She reached out and took Gillian's hand. She was not about to risk the rebuff her husband had received by attempting a kiss.

"What can one say, Gillian? I'm so terribly sorry about King . . . and Mandy, though I'd never met her." She introduced her children, a boy of twenty and a girl, eighteen, the same ages as my own kids. Roger, Jr., called Chip, was short and solid like his mother, while Harper resembled her father to a striking degree, except (good luck for her) for the glint in her eyes which was clearly matrilinear. Both were at Yale. They seemed like extremely nice kids.

The anteroom was filling up rapidly and the Campbell crew herded those of us who had already stowed our rain gear into a much larger standing-around room right outside the chapel. As I left the anteroom, I glimpsed Ike lurking in the far corner. He saw me notice him and flashed me a grin, which I did not return.

I cased the standing-around room and noted some familiar faces: Chet Sturtevant, chairman of Baker Bank, deep in conversation with William Safire; the mayor with his arm embracing Les's shoulder; Felix Rohatyn trying to escape Rog Durand.

I waited until the mayor had moved on to greet the chairman of Morgan Stanley and made my way toward Les. I figured that he probably knew about Marcella Grimm leaving Robotrac, but we were living in strange times, to say the least. He might have missed the report.

"Hi, Les. You bearing up all right?" Though his face looked paler than normal, and drawn, he was elegantly composed in a dark blue double-breasted suit whose fit on his slender frame would have gladdened the heart of his Savile Row tailor.

"Sure," he said, "it's rotten for all of us, but we'll get through it."

"Les, I know it's not your top concern right now," I said, dropping my voice a bit, "but you *have* heard about Marcella Grimm, haven't you?" He looked mildly surprised, but just for a second.

"Has it made the papers already?"

"Yeah, yesterday's *Journal*."

He shook his head slightly. "I should have trusted my instincts about her at the time. I felt there was something . . . unstable. But she was so qualified for the spot." He smiled ruefully. "Breaks of the game. Robotrac's not happy with me at the moment. They've given the replacement search to Wilbert Speed. But I'll get them back," he said with a quiet intensity both in his voice and in his glacial gray eyes.

"What exactly happened? How did she screw up?" I asked.

Les never got a chance to answer. Gillian Carter appeared alongside him and spirited him away with a brief, chilly glance in my direction.

Coincidentally, I spotted Grace Wilbert, a tall, rawboned redhead, who with her partner, Nora Speed, were the only major female powers in the headhunting field. While considerably smaller than Carter Consultants, their firm was growing fast. The Robotrac assignment would be the biggest they'd ever had. Marcella Grimm had been hired at a compensation package of salary and perks worth upwards of half a million dollars—per annum. Grace caught my eye and walked over.

"Liz, hi."

"Hi, Grace. Thanks for coming, and congratulations."

"Of course I'd come." She looked slightly abashed. "King and I knew each other a long time, and even with the recent situation . . . well, all that seems so unimportant compared to . . ." She let the sentence trail off. People were self-conscious about saying the word *murder*. It sounded so melodramatic.

I hadn't meant to make her uncomfortable by congratulating her on Robotrac. "I mean it, Grace. I don't know exactly what happened. But if Carter had to lose Robotrac, I'm glad it went to you and Nora."

"Thanks, Liz. I appreciate it." She smiled, flashing a row of strong, yellowish teeth.

"Nora's out in California on it now, which is how come she's not here. It's damned awkward, of course—ethics questions always—" She broke off abruptly and turned her head. "Oh there's Roger. Gorgeous daughter. Looks just like him. Where's Dave? I hear he's going to move to New York and take over."

"News travels fast. His wife Shelly is coming in from Chicago for the funeral. Maybe the rain delayed her flight. I'm sure they'll be here any minute."

A tap on her shoulder from Matt Freiman of Affiliated Brands turned her around. I shook hands, thanked him for coming and discreetly drifted away to think seriously for a second. Grace had mentioned ethics before she'd stopped herself. Did she mean that Robotrac suspected a breach of ethics? And whose—Marcella Grimm's? Les's? King's?

Dave had arrived with Shelly in tow and was shaking hands with various people—just what I should have been doing, earning my keep as PR representative instead of playing detective. I crossed the room, which was getting stuffy as it filled, to where they were standing. Dave was still greenish, and when I said hello to Shelly, the anxiety in her dark brown, carefully made-up eyes told me that she knew I was in possession of the family bombshell. I tried to look reassuring, but doubted whether I was in a position to reassure them of anything.

Suddenly, the world brightened perceptibly. Sam Boyd entered the room. He has that effect on almost everyone. He made straight for me and enfolded me in a bearhug—a term which, in his case, is especially accurate. Sam looks like a benevolent cinnamon bear with horn-rimmed glasses. He's short—five foot seven tops—and bulky without being fat. His strawberry-blond hair is a touch longer than most management consultants wear it and his beard and mustache manage to be appealingly woolly, without looking in the least unkempt.

"How you holding up, lovely?" He stepped back and surveyed me. "A little peaked, but you'll do."

"Thanks, I think."

His eyes canvassed the room, taking in the heavy hitters who were now pouring in—including a deputy mayor, a U.S Senator, and assorted corporate and financial types. I saw Charlie Kaye come in, looking corpse-pale, and realized he must have spent the earlier part of the day with Mandy's family and the police. Dave strode over and put his reassuring arm around Charlie's shoulder.

"Some crowd," Sam was saying.

"Give the people what they want and they'll turn out for it." The comment—originally made at some Hollywood mogul's funeral—came in a deep slurred voice from a tall, thin man who had just entered. He had a high domed forehead and thinning blond-gray hair. I didn't know who he was, but his slightly askew tie and the boozy flush in his face signaled trouble. To make matters worse, I caught a glimpse of Bud Campeau of the *Daily News*, who'd managed to sneak his way in. Terrific.

Sam put his hand on the newcomer's arm and said, "Easy, Gerry."

He introduced us. This was Gerry Klose, the man King had ruined at Seagrave Bank. If he'd murdered King, as Les had suggested, he'd be pretty stupid to show up at the funeral. But who knows what a drinker will do?

"I couldn't resist," Klose said, as though he'd been reading my mind, "I hadda make sure the bastard was really dead." He followed this by a mirthless bark of a laugh that turned those heads that hadn't already responded to the decibel level of his voice, which was a cut louder than anyone else's. Les caught my eye and made a discreet get-him-out-of-here sign, which I, in turn, conveyed with eye signals to Sam. Between us, we edged him toward the door where Sam took his arm and said he was eager to have a private word with him somewhere quieter. I accompanied them down the hall to the anteroom.

As we walked, Klose said, "I was there that night, you know." His tone had the shaky defiance of a swaggering but scared adolescent.

"You mean at the Manse? At King's house?" I deliberately made my tone casual.

"Yeah. I'd never faced him with it—what he did; how unfair it was. I knew that job like I know my name. I'd have been fine, but he . . . Ah, what's the damn difference?"

"When, uh, what time did you get there?" Was he drunk enough to answer me? I noticed that Sam was looking at me in a funny way, but I didn't care. I'd explain later.

"About seven-thirty or so. I thought I might have to fight my way in, but I didn't. He let me in all right. Took me right up to his office. Then he made mincemeat out of me. Playing with that fucking dagger the whole time. Shit heel. When he looked at you and called you incompetent, you couldn't even defend yourself. You knew he was right." He shook his head and shrugged. "Hell, it didn't take him more than fifteen, twenty minutes to destroy me all over again. He didn't even have to throw me out."

"Hello, Mr. Klose."

I jumped at the sound of that unexpected, slightly sandy voice. I'd been so intent on Klose's revelations that I hadn't realized that Ike O'Hanlon was standing near a coat rack a few feet behind us.

"If you tire of the public relations business, Ms. Wareham, I'd be glad to let you know the date of the next police exam. Of course, you'll have to spend some time in uniform before you make detective, but—"

"Knock it off, Ike, okay? I'm not in the mood." I wasn't. What I was was embarrassed and flustered. I fought to not let him know it. "Sam, this is Lieutenant Ike O'Hanlon. Ike, Sam Boyd. I gather you know Mr. Klose."

"Sure he does," said Klose. "What do you think I am, stupid? When I heard that someone put that knife through the bastard's heart—like I would've liked to do—I went right to the police."

I heard the sound of organ music down the hall. "Gentlemen," I said, "if you'll excuse me, I have something pressing to attend to before the service begins." It was true, as well as an excuse for a quick getaway. I found Bud Campeau and ejected him, which left me with one friend less at the *Daily News*.

Les led Gillian Carter up the chapel aisle to a front-row seat. The other partners followed with their wives and, in Rog's case, children. King had no living blood relatives. He'd left the bulk of his estate to the Metropolitan Museum of Art and Harvard, and given his partners first-refusal rights to buy the Manse at fair market price.

As Reverend Flowers began to eulogize, my eyes searched the rows for Gerry Klose's balding head. I didn't see it and guessed Sam had persuaded him to leave. I wondered if the police considered him a suspect; after all, Ike didn't know that Angela had been with King after Klose left. But what if Klose had returned much later and actually done what he loudly claimed he'd wanted to? Why then, going to the police and fessing up about his pathetic visit to the Manse would have been very smart. And doing a drunken scene at the funeral perhaps even smarter.

22

$\cdots\cdots\cdots\cdots\cdots\cdots\cdots$

AFTER THE FUNERAL, I PUT IN A FEW PRODUCTIVE HOURS at the office, catching up on some dangerously neglected chores for other clients. At six o'clock, Seth, Patti, Carmen, Morley, and I gathered around my office TV to catch Seth's debut. A star was born and he glowed. He'd stood up beautifully to Sally Fiorella's pounding, which had included a barrage of questions on Mandy's murder, as well as King's. Seth had managed to come across as credible and helpful, while giving no more information than we'd planned on giving, and slipping in a clear but not pushy plug for Carter Consultants' eminence. A straight-A performance. I'd taped Channel Two and had Morley order tapes of the other channels from Video Monitoring Service. I looked forward to playing the tapes at the Monday morning senior staff meeting and getting off some discreet I-told-you-so's.

Seth informed me, with what passed for a modest blush, that his debut was also being taped by his parents, his Bubba Ida, his Aunt Bessie, his brother Murray's wife (Murray couldn't get home in time), his old camp friend Herbie, and his psychiatrist, Dr. Klingwasser—each one assigned a different channel. As we disbanded, I handed him a stack of assignments. Even stars don't get away scot-free.

The hours between seven-thirty when I'd gotten home and eleven o'clock when I'd left to meet Angela were pure hell. I killed a little time catching up on phone calls to my mother "Maybe you could come down here right now, till Ike catches

131

this maniac"); my sister ("Godinheaven! How do you know who you can trust?"); Barbara Garment, amateur shrink ("I mean it, Liz, O'Hanlon's in the dominant position here. It's like you're still seventeen and you're setting yourself up to get hurt again"). I tried to nap and couldn't; tried to eat and couldn't do that either. I'd have loved a drink, but felt it would be imprudent.

I replayed the funeral in my head. Gillian Carter didn't seem like any bereaved widow I'd ever seen. Maybe Dave and Angela were right that King's death had come at a convenient time for her. But she'd been somewhere else at the time of his murder. At least the papers said so. I wished I could ask Ike whether it was true, but there was zero likelihood he'd answer me. Could she have hired a killer? It was possible. She could have given him keys, if she had them, and told him the alarm combination, if she knew it. God, it all would be so much simpler if the killer were Gillian or Gerry Klose! The firm could walk away clean and . . . I remembered Grace Wilbert's disturbing reference to ethics. I'd have to talk with her again and see if I could pry out anything more.

When I realized I'd bitten off my thumbnail while I'd been ruminating, I knew I was in tough shape. I decided to try some hydrotherapy. Just as I was stepping into the shower, the phone rang. My hello was answered by a slightly familiar voice, but I couldn't immediately come up with a name. She supplied it.

"This is Peg Durand. I'm terribly sorry for calling so late, but I must talk with you."

"Certainly. And it's not too late." My puzzlement must have been apparent in my tone.

"I know this must seem strange, since we don't really know each other, and of course it's Roger who's your client, not me."

"Oh no, Peg, it's perfectly fine for you to call me. What can I do for you?" I had a full hour to kill before I had to leave and this was as good a way as any.

"I can't discuss it on the phone. Might we meet? I could come to your office tomorrow, if that's convenient."

"Sure. Can I take you to lunch?"

"No. Thank you, but no. It's a rather sensitive matter and I'd prefer as much privacy as possible. But if lunchtime is good for you, perhaps we can have a sandwich in your office."

I told her that would be fine and we settled on one o'clock. After we hung up I noted that though she'd sounded tense not one "uh" had interrupted the flow of her words. I took my shower. It didn't help.

23

I SAT IN THE CAB ON MY WAY TO MEET ANGELA AT P. J. Clarke's trying to psych myself into being Emma Peel off on a caper. I was dressed entirely in black—jeans, turtleneck, sneakers, and leather jacket against the unseasonable chill that remained, even though the rain was taking a rest. I was having no luck in summoning up even a scintilla of devil-may-care. Instead, I felt a losing combination of stupid and scared. As I reached into my capacious black bag for a mint to pop into my dry mouth, I felt the head of an oversized flashlight—one of four such relics of the children's camp days and the only one that still worked.

The first person I spotted as I entered P.J.'s was not Angela, but my client, Chris Maclos of Baker Bank. She was perched on a stool near the front, talking animatedly to a weak-chinned, pale man with thinning fair hair, whose open pin-striped jacket revealed red suspenders imprinted with yellow ducks. Her black hair was freed from its office bun, and her purple silk shirt was unbuttoned one crucial extra notch. The cigarette between her long burgundy-nailed fingers punctuated whatever she was saying with little stabs. Since her thirty-ninth birthday two months ago, Chris had become acutely concerned with her "biological clock" and was infusing the issues of finding a husband and producing a baby with the same focused energy that had made her a Baker Bank EVP at thirty-six. I was betting on her to have the whole assignment accomplished in two years, at the outside.

Fortunately, the place was packed with rollickers and I was able to hide behind a laughing foursome until I was well clear of Chris. I finally found Angela way down at the end of the bar, nursing a glass that could have been Perrier or gin. I tapped her black leather shoulder.

"Hi, Angela. I guess we saw the same *Vogue* layout on what chic burglars will be wearing this year."

"It does give us a certain comradely esprit." She looked around. "There doesn't seem to be another stool. Why don't you take this one." She started to stand up. "Want a drink?"

I suddenly felt irritated. "No. I don't want to settle in. Finish yours and let's get out of here and get it over with."

"Look, Liz, you can still change your mind."

"I'm sorry for snapping at you. I'm not going to change my mind. Hey, you'll never guess who I saw up front making Mr. Right."

"Chris Maclos—winding her biological clock. I said hi to them when I came in. His name's Dennie Talbot. He's at Shearson. I know him from Southampton—kind of a nerd."

"How'd you get away from them?"

"I said I was meeting a friend. Believe me, she was no more anxious to prolong the conversation than I was."

East 64th is a quiet street and luckily no one was strolling on it at a quarter to midnight. The very official-looking sticker slapped across the Manse door proclaimed, "Police Crime Scene. Do Not Enter." The sight of it made me queasy. I thought of the time when I, a reckless seven year old, had persuaded my six-year-old cousin to join me in ripping the "Do not remove under penalty of law" tags from all the pillows in my house. We'd waited, breathless, for the sound of police sirens for the next hour.

Angela and I looked at the police sign, and then at each other. She reached into her purse, retrieved a Swiss army knife and slit the sticker decisively, freeing the door to open.

"Do you suppose we should have brought gloves?" I asked weakly.

"What for?" she shrugged. "I'm sure they've already done

whatever they do about fingerprints. Besides, mine are all over the place already, and so are yours. Come on, let's do it."

I stood lookout while Angela opened the door. As soon as she'd turned the key, I bounded up the front stairs and we slipped in. Immediately my eyes turned left to check the alarm. The red light was on. We had sixty seconds before a hellish screech would summon the police. I grabbed the Camp Shanapa special from my bag, focused its beam on the alarm panel and punched in 24680. I held my breath. God was good. The cops hadn't changed the code. I pointed the flashlight beam downward and headed for the stairs. Angela, holding her own much smaller flashlight, was already halfway up.

"Let's hope they haven't changed this lock," she said as she prepared to try her key.

"At least we don't have another alarm to contend with," I whispered, half hoping, as I looked at a second crime scene sticker affixed to this door, that the cops *had* changed the lock and we could get the hell out.

Angela's key worked. So did her little knife. She closed the door behind us. We were fully committed to it now.

"Where are we going? The office?"

"No, King's bedroom. Follow me." I did. This was new territory for me. I'd never been above King's private office floor. The third floor landing was a miniature of the main entrance rotunda—circular and paved in white marble. Our sneakers made little mouse squeaking sounds as we crossed it. At the ten o'clock position was a wide open archway. I gave it a quick beam of light and saw that it was a sitting room furnished in the graceful French Provincial style and luxurious pale fabrics that King had favored. At two o'clock was a closed fruitwood paneled door with a heavy, intricately worked brass handle. Angela grabbed the handle and gave me a brief appraising glance. Was she thinking that I'd chicken out at the last second after all? I gave her a quick affirmative nod. Suddenly, I was eager to get on with it— excited at the prospect of knowing who'd done the murders, and why.

Angela twisted the handle and pushed the heavy door open. I panned my flash around the spacious bedroom. Heavy damask curtains masked the pair of tall windows opposite the door. A large peach and blue Kerman rug covered most of the wideboard floor. The room was dominated by an elegantly canopied tester bed, its covers drawn back and rumpled, confirming what I'd read in the papers about King having gone to bed before his murderer had arrived. If Angela had left at midnight, that would mean . . . God, this was hardly the time to be working out the timetable arithmetic.

"Where're we supposed to be looking, Angela?"

"Here, in the escritoire," she said as she crossed to a delicately curved polished writing table which stood catty corner in front of the windows. I followed her, thinking she must have lost her marbles.

"In a desk drawer? Some hiding place! The police probably found it on their first sweep. If there was anything to find, that is."

"Not unless they know the tricks of certain antique French furniture." She opened the table's long drawer and then bent down and reached way under the table itself. I heard a little ping, and saw the back of the drawer snap open. Then, suddenly, Angela slammed into me full force, knocked me to the floor, and landed on top of me. The clunky flashlight flew out of my hand and clattered onto the wood floor.

I am going to die, I thought. It was Angela all along. She lured me here with this cockamamie story and now—

A voice barked "freeze" and all at once the room was bathed in light. I turned my head. Ike O'Hanlon stood in the doorway. His right hand came swiftly off the light switch to join his left in grasping the very serious-looking gun he had trained on us. His face was heavy-duty grim.

"Well, well. Nancy Drew and friend." His tone was controlled, but the normal sand in his voice had the rasp of gravel. The white line around his mouth I recognized. It said that he was furious.

"Can we . . . can we get up?" I asked, figuring that even

though things had hit rock bottom, I might be better able to cope on my feet.

"Sure. Both of you get up . . . real slow. Take off your jackets and toss them over this way, toward the bureau. What did you two do, have a wardrobe consultation?"

"Ike, would you put that damned gun down. You frightened the life out of me. This is Angela Chappel. We work together. I mean, for God's sake, we're not criminals!"

"I beg to differ, madam. Criminals are *exactly* what you are. You have broken into a sealed crime scene. You have good reason to be frightened, because unless I hear something that changes my mind, I will slap your ass in jail—and that goes for your buddy too. Now toss those jackets." We did as he said. He put the gun in its shoulder holster, crossed his arms and leveled a steely blue gaze at us. "Okay, let's hear it."

Angela and I glanced at each other. Each of us decided simultaneously to do the talking and take the heat. The result was "It was my fault," in two-part harmony.

"Oh Jesus, not Alphonse and Gaston," Ike groaned.

"Let me, Angela," I said quickly. Suddenly an irresistible question popped out of my mouth. "Hey, how did you know we were here?"

"Courtesy of a public-spirited neighbor who saw a light downstairs." He looked down at the camp lantern. "If you plan to continue your B&E career, I advise something smaller." I wanted to smack him. "But please go on. You were about to explain that it was your fault, I believe."

I ignored the sarcastic civility with some effort. "Angela and King were very special friends. He told her that he had a serious problem—one he thought he could handle, but just in case he couldn't . . . just in case anything happened to him, he'd leave information about it hidden here in the house for her. And he'd trust her to know what to do with it. Ike, it has to be the same situation that King was going to meet with me about, only he changed his mind and—"

"I'm fascinated," Ike cut in icily. "Is there some special reason—Ms. Chappel, is it?—that after your great and good friend was murdered you chose not to share this information with the police? We are, in our own bumbling way, in the business of dealing with these kinds of things."

"King was quite explicit, Lieutenant. He gave me instructions the night he died. I was to get the information he'd leave for me by myself and decide what to do with it. Most likely I'd have come to you."

"Most likely," Ike said, raising a skeptical black eyebrow, "but you didn't come here by yourself, did you?"

Angela didn't answer. I knew that she couldn't figure out anything to say that wouldn't mean more trouble for me.

"I made her take me along," I said, taking the plunge. "I found Angela's earring in King's office and I . . ." The look in his eyes gave me pause.

"You *what*?" he said with a dangerous quietness.

It'll only hurt for a second, like tearing off a Band-Aid, I told myself. "I picked it up and put it in my pocket. I knew damned well Angela didn't kill him and . . ." It came back to me in a guilty flash that I hadn't been so sure of her just a few minutes ago when she'd jumped me. God, she'd been trying to protect me!

"You didn't know *anything*!" His voice cracked like a slap. "You took evidence from a murder scene, you idiot!" He advanced on me.

"Don't you call me an idiot!" I flared automatically.

He stood no more than six inches away from me.

"Idiot is not even a start on what you've got coming." I began to reply, but didn't get a sound out before he cut me off. "If I hear one more syllable out of you, I will allow myself the luxury of beating you almost as soundly as you deserve."

I almost believed him, and decided to take no chances.

"Now, Ms. Chappel, go get whatever it is." Angela reached into the true back of the desk drawer and pulled out a sheet of folded white paper. I was afraid for a second that Ike would simply grab it. Instead, he said, "Read it aloud."

She took a breath and I noticed that her hand was trembling slightly: "It . . . it's dated at the top. It says two-twenty

A.M., September twelve. 'My dear Angela: If you ever get to read this, it will mean that I've overestimated my own capabilities. I'm sorry to have been so cloak and dagger with you tonight, but the problem at hand is the most sensitive and grave someone in my business could imagine. Yesterday, I had a call from a detective called Antony Swift, in the employ of Green Star Industries. His investigation on their behalf confirms suspicions I've been having during the past months. Action cannot be postponed. If this is mishandled, it will kill a business I've worked extremely hard to build. The issue, you see, is industrial espionage and' . . ."

"And what?" I burst out, risking being beaten almost as soundly as I deserved.

"That's it," Angela said, "it just stops." Ike took the sheet from her, looked it over, and put it in his pocket.

Industrial espionage! My mind spun. It all fit. Robotrac firing Marcella Grimm and dropping Carter Consultants. Grace Wilbert mentioning ethics. Someone at Carter was involved in a spy ring! I could see why King would first think to discuss it with his PR consultant, and then decide it was too sensitive even for that. Could a whiff of industrial espionage bring down Carter Consultants? You bet it could.

24

I̲t wasn't that I minded going home. I had a great deal of thinking to do, and there was no place I'd rather have done it. What I minded was Ike's high-handed dismissal. He'd marched me downstairs and into a cab with terse instructions to go home, as though I were a naughty child being sent to her room.

I summoned up a pallid smile for Juan who was on the door.

"Evening, Mrs. Wareham. Wait a second. I have something for you."

"For me?"

"Yeah. Fella dropped them off 'bout ten or so. Hope they still okay." He disappeared briefly into the package room and returned with a tall bouquet wrapped in florist's paper. Douglas? He'd never sent me flowers in two years.

"Thanks, Juan. Night."

When I got inside my apartment, I headed straight down the hall for my bedroom. I was curious about the flowers, but that was outweighed by a sudden eagerness to get out of my stupid burglar togs. I tossed the bouquet on the bed, stripped to the skin, letting the clothes lie where they fell, and enveloped myself in the tatty white terry robe that had been my surrogate womb for the past eleven years. That accomplished, I unwrapped a dozen long-stemmed white roses, still in good shape. The little white card said, "I'm sorry. Frankie." Frankie? It didn't instantly ring a bell. Then it did. David's gun-toting baby brother. I smiled to myself. When you get sent flowers as seldom as I do, you enjoy 'em as you find 'em.

"Industrial espionage," I thought, looking at the roses in my hand. If that was the secret behind the murders, then David's dual identity and forged credentials were back-burner items—at least for the moment. My mind blurred. All at once I realized that I was famished.

I ran down the hall to the kitchen, cats appearing at my heels. After planting Frankie's roses in a vase and setting them on the counter, I investigated the fridge. Not very promising. Freddie was right. Even with Sarah gone, I would have to be better about groceries. I did find a block of sharp cheddar on the shelf and a stick of butter and a couple of slices of Pepperidge Farm Cracked Wheat bread in the freezer. Dinner was at hand. When my kids were growing up, I was known to be the best grilled cheese sandwich maker on the entire Upper West Side.

I chunked some of the butter into a heavy black skillet and while it melted, sliced off some cheese, giving Elephi and Three a sliver apiece. I threw in a bread slice, covered it amply with cheese and capped it with the second piece of bread. As the bottom bread browned and soaked up butter, I pressed down hard with a spatula to help the melting cheese bond the sandwich. At the strategic moment, I flipped it. Ninety seconds later, it lay luscious and ready on one of the beloved cobalt plates that I'd pirated from my mother.

The Heart Association would probably not give me a merit award, but I was living dangerously anyway. I retrieved a half-finished bottle of California fumé blanc from the fridge door, pried the cork out, and poured most of it into a jelly glass—the kind that never break. As I left the kitchen, I noticed that the wall clock read ten of three.

I curled up in the Eames chair and devoured the sandwich in about seven and a half seconds, leaving a residue of buttery crumbs on the plate. I rewarded the reasonably patient felines who sat at my footstool with the opportunity to lick them off—an opportunity of which they took full advantage.

As I sipped the smoky wine, I conceded that finding the murderer was Ike's turf, but my client's industrial espionage time bomb was mine, and I had to find some way to disarm it before it blew us all out of the water. Industrial espionage. Any executive with access to privileged information could steal it and sell it. Actually, it was surprising that it didn't happen more often.

But then who really knew how often it *did* happen? Companies usually swept such things under the rug. They tended to ease the culprit out, quickly and quietly. The headhunter who'd innocently placed the spy might not be likely to get more business from that company, but that wouldn't be enough to destroy the search firm. And King had said that Carter Consultants was in danger of being destroyed. That had to mean that someone within Carter was guilty of collusion with the spy.

It was unthinkable! But was it? Who'd be in a better position to recruit and deploy industrial spies than a prestigious headhunter? The exhaustive search process brought him so close to his candidates that he'd be able to spot who was corruptible, who could be tempted, and then subtly slant his report to the client to favor the potential spy. And the money to be made selling classified corporate research would make even fat executive search fees look undernourished.

Did he put his proposition to the spy during the search or after? After, I guessed. Before would be too risky. Suppose . . .

All at once my train of thought derailed and my eyelids wouldn't stay open. A crowd of identical, anonymous people in raincoats and hats were football fields away from me. I could hardly see them through the mist. I wanted to catch them, but my legs . . .

The phone was ringing. I reached over to pick it up, but it wasn't there. I opened my gummy eyes and realized that I wasn't in my bed, and it wasn't a phone ring sound, anyway. It was the buzzer from downstairs, and it was insistent. I got my body, stiff and kinked from sleeping in the chair, vertical and over to the intercom. What time was it? My watch said five-thirty. Morning? Night? Who the hell . . . ?

"Yes?" My voice came out hoarse and sounded as irritated as I felt.

"Sorry, Mrs. Wareham. I didn't want to wake you up," Juan's voice was apologetic, "but the gentleman say I had to. It's Lieutenant O'Hanlon." That son of a bitch. If I didn't let him up, he'd probably go get a warrant or something. Maybe he had one already.

"It's okay, Juan. He can come up."

I answered Ike's ring and let him in, but didn't speak. Neither did he, but a slow, full-scale O'Hanlon grin materialized on his face as he looked at me. I understood what "seeing red" really meant. I lost all reason and went for him. I wanted to punch his teeth in. He caught my arm and held it in a grip that was more than firm.

"Easy, now." His voice was firm, too. "Don't hit. I'm an egalitarian. I hit back." He led me into the kitchen, his hand still grasping my arm.

"I want to talk to you. Can we have a cup of coffee?"

"I do not want to talk to *you*. And no, we can't. This is not a social occasion. I'm not making you coffee. Can I have my arm back?"

"Only if you'll promise to make it behave," he said, letting go. "I'll make the coffee."

I left the kitchen and settled myself on the long red sofa in the living room. He could do as he pleased, but I wasn't going to help him. After about five minutes he came in carrying two steaming mugs of black coffee.

"How the hell did you know where the coffee was?" I always keep it in the freezer.

"I'm a detective, remember? Here. It'll make you feel better."

"I doubt that."

"Look, Liz," he said as he sat down on the sofa next to me, "we are going to talk." He spaced the words evenly. "And we are going to talk truth now. It will make a nice change." I didn't answer. "And stop being the aggrieved party. After the fool stunts you pulled, you should thank your lucky star— or me—that you got off so easy. By the way, I'm satisfied that your friend is clean. Her doorman and elevator man both swear she came home by one A.M. and never left till eight that morning."

"I could've told you that," I mumbled.

"No, you couldn't. That's the point. But I think you can tell me some things that I don't know, and that's why I'm here." His face looked strained and his blue eyes were red-rimmed with fatigue. He could've used a shave, too.

"Okay," I said, "I'll trade you."

"What do you think this is, a collective bargaining session? Listen—"

"No, *you* listen. I think you know things that I need to know, too." He started to interrupt, but I overrode him. "Not to find the killer. I agree that's your job. But it's my job to find out whose little spy ring is threatening to wreck a firm that happens to be my client."

"You *will not* blackmail me."

"Then I guess I don't know anything you can use," I answered calmly. We did a brief Mexican stand-off in the staring department.

"Okay," he said. "Pretty flowers," he added casually. "Must have lifted your spirits to find them waiting when you got home."

"How do you know they didn't come yesterday morning?" I asked, matching his casualness—or trying to.

"The vase is wet; it's standing on the kitchen counter in a puddle of water; the florist's paper's crumpled in the sink. I may not be a very *good* detective, but—" He broke off. "By the way, who's Frankie?"

"A friend of mine," I snapped. "Look, are we going to trade information here or what? Because if you don't have anything better to discuss than floral tributes to my unrivaled loveliness, you can get your ass down to Charles Street and . . . and call your broker!"

"Okay, shhh, sorry."

I took a breath and willed myself to calm down. Frankie was the last person in the world I wanted to talk about with Ike.

"All right, Lieutenant," I said with a smile of noblesse oblige, "you go first. How do you think I can help you?"

"For one thing, I want to know the name of your British friend—the one who suggested that Swift call you."

I hesitated for a minute and decided to give him Dennis. "His name's Dennis Quayle—executive director of the British Board of Trade. But look," I raced ahead before he could say anything, "I didn't tell him that I knew Swift was dead, or that he'd tried to call me. I have a heavy-duty proposal in to this guy, and if you make me look like a liar or a fool to him, I'll—"

"Peace. Swift's identity will be in this morning's papers, and as far as I'm concerned, you never heard from him. Now, can you tell me—"

"Hold on, friend, my turn." He rolled his bloodshot blues toward the ceiling. "Who has what alibis for which murders?"

An explosive chuckle. "You don't want much, do you? I thought you were going to confine yourself to the issue of industrial spying."

"I am. But the murderer and the spy—it's the same person, isn't it?"

"Probably," he admitted.

"Then I've got to know which of the players I can forget about, and which I . . . which I have to watch out for."

He gave a crisp military salute. "Lieutenant Isaac Redmond O'Hanlon reporting, ma'am. If we operate on the assumption that your spy and my murderer are the same person—a person whose discovery could bring down Carter Consultants, then the suspects are the three partners, Kaye, and Mrs. Carter. They're also the only ones with keys to the private floors. To be more precise, she and the partners had keys and Kaye could have gotten one from his girlfriend, Mandy.

"Gerald Klose, of course, wouldn't fit into this scenario at all," he swigged down the last of his coffee, "though I must say I admired your interrogation technique at the funeral." He paused, waiting for me to bristle. I disappointed him. I was far too interested in what he was going to say next.

He continued, "Klose wasn't a serious candidate, anyway. He's got solid alibis for both Swift and Mandy's murders. Which brings me to your question.

"The scoreboard, madam: ladies first. Mrs. Carter was, as you've read in the papers, out of town while her beloved husband was being knifed. What you haven't read, and what we finally dragged out of her just before the funeral, was that she spent that night up in Boston with one Leslie Charlton." I choked on the coffee I was about to swallow and went into a paroxysm of coughing. After he'd provided a few helpful whacks on my back, the fit subsided, leaving me flushed and teary-eyed. "That surprises you, does it?" he asked.

"Yes." I considered for a second. "Yes, it does. I've always thought of Les as asexual, I guess. Not gay, just . . . But, come to think of it, when I was meeting with the partners the evening after King's murder Dave Goldstone made some crack about Gillian—called her the Ice Queen and suggested that maybe she'd killed King because he was about to divorce her— anyway, Les was furious, but it didn't occur to me . . ."

"She's also covered for Swift's murder—getting her car filled up at an Exxon station on Long Island, with receipts and the gas jockey's word to prove it—and for Mandy's: the servants say she was in all evening."

"But you only have Les's word that she was in Boston, and if they were lovers . . ."

"True, he's her alibi, validated, I should add, by a liquor store deliveryman, who swears she paid him for a bottle of gin he delivered to Charlton's house a little before midnight. For that matter, she's Charlton's alibi—along with the shuttle. He was on the seven A.M. flight from Boston. American Express receipts—also two stews remember him. He *is* kind of unusual looking. That also covers him for Swift. He appeared at the Carter house at eight-forty. The shuttle landed at eight-o-six. Definitely no time in between for him to pop over to the Plaza and do Swift. Once he got to the house, he was with Libuti and Remley until well after the outside time the M.E. gave us for Swift's death. Of course he's got no clear alibi for Mandy's death, but who's perfect?"

"Kind of a coincidence them being together while King was being murdered, isn't it?"

"Happens."

"Could they have hired someone to do the murders for them? I mean they could have given him a key."

"For that matter, any of the suspects theoretically could have hired someone. But I don't think it happened that way."

"Why not?"

"First of all, the murders don't look like rent-a-hits. Pro's work quick and simple: guns with silencers, not antique knives and pantyhose garottes. Second, the street's a gossipy place, if you know who to talk to. None of my snitches or any of my squad's snitches had a whiff of it. That'd be more than unusual for a three-point hit. Heavy bucks riding on it. Someone would've heard something."

"So you're saying Gillian and Les are clear. What about the others?"

"Goldstone's vulnerable on all three. He admits he was in New York the night of the first murder and the morning of the second, but won't say where. Could be a tootsie, of course. We're working on him. Swears he was in his room at the Regency alone the evening of Mandy's murder until he met Charlton for dinner at eight-thirty. She was killed sometime between seven and eight."

"What about Rog and Charlie?"

"Roger Durand's wife says he was with her all three times— and I don't believe a word of it. Story's too pat and she's too nervous. Kaye's shit out of luck. Mandy's his alibi for the first two, and, as you know, he has none for her murder."

"I want some more coffee," I said, picking up both cups. "No, sit, I'll get it." I walked into the kitchen, hoping he wouldn't follow me. I needed a minute to think. As I rinsed the cups and poured fresh ones, I debated whether to tell Ike that Dave *did* claim to have an alibi for King's and Swift's murders. But if Ike didn't believe Peg Durand, why would he believe Dave's father and brother? Puzzling out what to do had the effect of strengthening my trust in Dave's innocence. I refused to give houseroom to a tiny voice in my head that suggested that my touching faith might be based on wishful thinking—that having Carter's new president emerge as an industrial spymaster and a three-time murderer would be more of a PR nightmare than the intrepid Elizabeth Wareham was prepared to deal with.

I returned to the living room and handed Ike his coffee.

"My turn to tell you something." I hoped I was doing the right thing. "Dave *does* have an alibi for the first two murders. He was visiting an old family friend in New Jersey, and it's a difficult situation."

"I assume so, if he didn't care to mention it even at risk of being suspected of murder. Would you care to elaborate?"

"He was with a man called Mastrantonio. He lives in New Jersey. He's . . . well he's not all that respectable, but . . ."

"You mean *Vito* Mastrantonio?"

"Yes," I said, in a slightly truculent tone, feeling suddenly proprietary and protective of David's appalling relatives.

"Some alibi! That old Maf would swear to pink elephants flying over his house if some capo told him to. What's he got to do with Goldstone?"

"As I understand it, they were neighbors when Dave was growing up on the Lower East Side. Dave's parents are dead and he . . . well, he's a very loyal person." I stopped, fearing an onset of foot-in-mouth disease.

"Ummhmm," Ike grunted, a skeptical look on his face. I'd have to get to David quickly and let him know what I'd told Ike. He'd go through the roof. It was going to take every tool of persuasion in my kit to convince him I'd acted in his best interest, but I was pretty sure I had. If Dave and his family stuck to the story, the police probably wouldn't stumble onto the truth of his identity. My conscience zinged a little as I lied to Ike once again, but I told it to be quiet and go back to sleep.

CAROL BRENNAN

"Grace Wilbert's firm—that's Wilbert Speed—has picked up a former Carter client under funny circumstances. At King's funeral she started to say something to me about ethics, and then stopped herself real fast. I'll bet she can give us some answers." I gave this in the spirit of a philandering husband presenting flowers to his wife.

"Thanks," he said and looked at me with narrowed blues.

"What's the matter?" I asked, with the uneasy fantasy that he could read my mind.

"Nothing—I hope," he said softly.

"I . . . I'll, uh, get some more coffee," I stammered and started to reach for his cup. I never made it. Instead, Ike's hand grabbed mine and his eyes looked at me in a totally different way.

His other hand cupped my chin and gently raised my face so that our eyes met. He reached into my robe and began to stroke my breast. I heard a moan. It must have been me. I reached inside the open neck of his blue shirt. His chest was warm, so warm. I pulled my tie belt open and shrugged my robe off, eager to be free of it. Ike felt the same way, judging by the speed with which he was shedding his shirt and jeans. I was almost sick with delight at the sight of his naked body. His shoulders were broad for his five foot ten. The triangular curly patch on his not very hairy chest was just as I remembered. So was the flat belly. As he turned to step out of his underpants I saw his back. It was still the best male back I'd ever met— muscles subtly rippling, but not aggressive, tapering down to a slim but solid waist and then to a round, hard, hollow-cheeked ass with appealingly improbable dimples above it. I opened my arms to him and spent the next hour thrilled to be a woman.

25

....

W HEN I WOKE UP, IKE WAS GONE. HE COULD HAVE BEEN in the shower or the kitchen, I suppose, but somehow I knew he wasn't. I pulled aside the patchwork quilt that covered me—he must have brought it from the bedroom—and gave a long, yawning stretch, which Three, nestled in the small of my back, mimicked. A piece of lined yellow paper lying on the coffee table caught my eye. I reached for it, but had to blink my eyes a few times and hold it an extra eight inches or so away before the letters stopped blurring. One of these days I'd have to give in and get reading glasses. The message made me smile:

"7:05. I didn't want to wake you. Take good care of yourself, you belong to me. Ike."

"Take Good Care of Yourself, You Belong to Me." That was the first song my father had taught Ike to play. Dad had picked it for its easy chords and catchy tune. I'd made it my business to learn all the words and thought of it as "our song," though I'd never have risked saying such a soppy thing to Ike and getting zapped with his derisive chuckle.

I put my feet on the floor and grunted myself vertical, which elicited a reproachful look from Three. Elephi, the eternal optimist, wasted no time on reproach, but bounded off the end of the sofa and dashed into the kitchen, expecting breakfast.

I followed him, naked except for my watch, and served the cats with creamed liver and a clean bowl of water. A faint breeze through the kitchen window touched my body and triggered a flashback of recent pleasures. Was it only a few hours ago? I thought lazily, as I stretched my arms up and yawned. I noticed that Ike had washed out the coffee mugs, but left the Toshiba turned on. There was enough left for a wake-up belt. As I poured it, some coffee dripped on the florist's card that had come with Frankie's flowers. Dave! My muzzy mind snapped to attention. I'd told Ike about his alibi. What if the police had gotten to him—blind-sided him before I'd had a chance to warn him? My watch said seven fifty-eight. I grabbed the kitchen phone, dialed the Regency, and gnawed my thumbnail while I waited a full eight rings for Dave's room to answer. They've picked him up. They've arrested him. His life will be ruined—and so will mine, because he'll fire me on the spot. How could I have been so dumb? How could—

"Yello." His voice cut off the ninth ring. It sounded as though he'd been running.

"Dave, it's Liz. I'm sorry to—"

"Nah, that's okay. I was in the shower. In fact, I thought I heard the phone ringing a couple of minutes ago, but I was all soaped up and decided the hell with it. Was that you?"

"Uh no." I was certain it'd been Ike. "Look, Dave, I have something important to tell you. It'll make you blow your stack, but please let me explain," which I proceeded to do.

"You what?"

"Holler at me later. There's no time now. You have to get to your father and your brother and go over the story with them. The only lie they'll tell is the one you've all been telling for years: that you're David Goldstone and they're friends from the old neighborhood. Keep it simple and don't provide any embroidery. Otherwise, just tell the truth. You were with them while King was being murdered—and the detective."

"What detective?" Oh shit! I'd forgotten he didn't know about Swift. Ike had sworn me to secrecy, and on that one at least I'd kept my word—so far. Ike had said Swift's identity would be in the papers this morning, but he hadn't mentioned whether the police had disclosed a connection with King's murder. Should I level with Dave now? I make my living reading people in order to persuade and manipulate them, and I'm pretty good at it. I asked myself, as my brain raced, whether Dave could be a spy and a calculating triple murderer. My answer, once and for all, was no. Even though he'd lived with a false identity and two bogus degrees? Yes, even so. If David Goldstone killed someone it would be in the heat of a moment. As for spying, he'd never risk losing the prestige and respectability he treasured.

"A British detective was killed at the Plaza a few hours after King. It'll be in this morning's papers. His name was Antony Swift. The police say he was investigating Carter for Green Star."

I said it straight and tonelessly. There seemed no point in adding that Swift had tried to reach me. Silence on the other end of the line.

"Dave?"

"Oh my God," he said softly, "I wonder if . . . Liz, do they know what he turned up? Maybe he found out about me. Maybe the police . . ." His voice rose to near hysterical pitch.

"Dave," I cut in firmly before he lost himself, "if Swift uncovered your past, the police don't know about it yet, or they'd have been knocking on your door before now. But it's important for you to have an alibi, that's why I told O'Hanlon what I did. Now the thing is for you and your family not to panic. The call you didn't answer—the one that came right before mine—was probably from the police."

"But—"

"Look, yesterday you begged me to believe you. And I do. I've put myself on the line by concealing your identity from the police. Doesn't that prove anything to you?"

"Yeah." He sighed. "Thanks, kiddo. I mean it."

"Now call your father right away, and let's pray the police haven't gotten to him yet," I said, hoping he'd have too much on his mind to wonder why I hadn't called him earlier. It would have been a bit awkward to explain what I'd been doing instead. "And then call me back. I have something else important to discuss with you."

After we hung up, I took a truncated shower and shampoo. Just as I'd finished, the phone rang. I ran to catch it. I hoped David's news would not be disastrous. Only it wasn't David, it was Les.

"Liz, have you seen this morning's paper?" Any PR person who doesn't know when to answer that question from a client with a lie, when to tell the truth, and when to finesse it had better go into some other business. In this case, the finesse was the ticket.

"You're talking about that detective. I just got off the phone with Dave." That was unexceptionally true. Now to find out what the story said. "Seth and I'll be getting to the reporters to see if they know any more, and I'll call O'Hanlon. Did you see *all* the papers?"

"You'd better believe it! That *Post* front-page headline, HEADHUNT MURDER III, hit me on the way to breakfast and I bought every paper I could find, including the *Globe*, of course, which features a picture of me as its—what are you always calling it? local angle."

"Is the out-of-town coverage any different from the New York papers?"

"Basically they're all the same, some more purple than others." Goddamnit, would he never get to it! I was dying to hear how much the press actually knew. "All they say is that this Swift was working for Green Star, checking us out. Then they quote O'Hanlon that the police are assuming he found something out about someone, went to King with it, and King confronted whomever it was." No mention of industrial espionage. My stomach unclenched in relief. "But don't you see, Liz, it's a no-win situation. Until they find the murderer, we're all under a cloud. The longer it all goes on, the worse."

"You're right. I wish I could tell you something more hopeful, but it simply isn't there. I also would like to say we can get the media to back down, but I'm afraid I'd being lying. If I learn anything more from O'Hanlon, I'll let you know. Meantime, needless to say, don't talk to any reporters—refer them to Seth." That really *was* needless to say. Les was the most reserved of the partners, and didn't love dealing with the press, even under normal circumstances, though he gave a good interview if the writer was smart and prepared. "Probably the most valuable thing the three of you can do is to talk to your own staffs—reinforce their confidence in you, personally. I've drafted a staff memo. It should be in your box in the lobby. You'll probably want to personalize it for your people, but it may help a little."

"That's good advice. I'm flying back up to Boston this morning to do just that. I'll be back here for the weekend, though. David's going to need my help—and I want to drive Gillian to the airport. She's taking the noon flight to Little Dix Bay—clear her head a bit."

"Ummhmm," I replied noncommittally, feeling uncomfortable at his mention of Gillian. Should I tell him I knew about their affair? What could I say, except to recommend discretion. And to someone as naturally discreet as Les, such advice would be superfluous, not to say insulting.

I was saved by the beep of a call waiting, and said a quick good-bye. The new call was from Dave, reporting that he'd reached his father—and not a moment too soon. While they'd been talking the doorbell had rung, and shortly after that his wife had come upstairs to tell him that two detectives were waiting for him in the living room. Frankie, however, had not been home. We'd have to keep our fingers crossed that Dave or his father reached him before the police did.

"I was on the phone with Les when you called," I said. "He's seen the papers. Though some of the headlines are pretty lurid, the press doesn't know what that detective found out and told King." I paused, not for dramatic effect, but because I knew this was going to rock him and I wasn't sure how to break it. I decided plain was best. "But I do," I continued, "and I need to tell you about it."

"What . . . Do I understand what you're saying to me? You know what this guy turned up? *You know who killed King?*"

His voice was hoarse with amazement.

"Yes to the first. No to the second, unfortunately. What Swift found out is that someone in the firm has been running an industrial spying operation." I heard his sharp intake of breath. "Swift reported it to King, who must have faced the guy with it and told him he was out. He apparently killed them both before they had a chance to tell anyone else."

"What about Salter? He was employing this Swift. Doesn't he know?"

"Maybe he does, but Sir Brian seems to have disappeared. The British police can't find him."

"Liz," his voice was wary and I knew what was coming, "how the hell do you know all this?"

"O'Hanlon and I grew up together. He's told me more than he would a stranger." That was as true as it needed to be. "Dave, I have no idea who it is, except that I'm sure it isn't you. But it has to be someone near the top. O'Hanlon's not going to release this—at least not yet. What's on your agenda today?"

"I'm planning to spend the morning with the New York staff and fly to Chicago to meet with my own people this afternoon, but I guess the cops'll blow that plan to hell. I'm sure they'll track me down as soon as they're finished in New Jersey. Thanks for that staff memo, by the way, it was good. I put in some of my own stuff and faxed it to both offices."

"Dave, don't say anything about the espionage thing to anyone. It could be dangerous for both of us."

"This could bring down the firm." His voice was entirely flat.

"Not if it's settled fast. King's reputation was brilliant, and so is the firm's. If the murderer is caught soon, you should be able to recover. David, these people are your colleagues. What do you think? Any ideas on a likely spy?"

"No . . . well . . . no, not really. I just wish it were King's damned wife. That'd solve all our problems." The call waiting beeped again.

"Let me catch this call, Dave." It was Seth. He'd seen the papers and the "Today" show—which I'd totally forgotten to flip on. He was at the office and had already left a message with his shrink's service canceling that afternoon's appointment.

Hearing that, I was ready to believe anything.

26

By THE TIME I RODE THE ELEVATOR DOWN TO THE LOBBY, it was well past nine. I should've jumped in a cab and been at my desk in ten minutes. My work on other accounts was backed up to alarming proportions. Paperback sleuths seemed able to put their day-to-day chores on endless hold while they cleverly whipped around solving murders. I, on the other hand, had Arthur F. Oldburgh and Partners waiting to hear some brilliant new strategies to help them come from number fourteen to within sniffing distance of the magic "big six" circle of accounting firms that included Arthur Andersen.

However, the September sun was shining and the temperature was a delightful sixty degrees. For the first time in a week I needed neither an umbrella nor a jacket over my hunter green crewneck and black leather skirt. The hell with it, I'd give myself the luxury of a walk down Central Park West and catch a cab at the 66th Street transverse through the park.

Gus was on the door and I detected some concern in his "good morning." Juan had probably filled him in on O'Hanlon's early morning raid during their changing of the guard. I smiled a bland good morning and small-talked about how good it was to see the sun to convince him that life was relatively normal and I was fine.

It was three and a half blocks before I got the idea that I was being followed. Central Park West wasn't crowded at that hour. Worker bees were already at their downtown desks, and mommies and nannies were not yet out and about. I'd stopped for a second in front of the museum to shake an irritating piece of something out of my shoe, and noticed out of the corner of my eye a brown glen-plaid sport jacket about half a block behind me make a too-abrupt stop.

I kept walking past the museum, hoping that he was merely an innocent salesman who'd been halted in his tracks by the abrupt realization he'd left his order book home, and that when I sneaked a peek behind me he'd be gone. At 75th Street I did, and he wasn't. I could have hailed a cab; I also could have stopped, turned around, and confronted him. But I was curious now and more afraid of scaring him off and leaving my questions unanswered than I was for my own safety which seemed well-protected by the battalion of doormen that lined Central Park West. At 72nd Street I abruptly turned west and walked quickly to the stone guardhouse which protects the entrance of the Dakota—the vast Victorian castle which in its time has housed John Lennon, Lauren Bacall, Rosemary's Baby, and other notables.

I stepped back into the courtyard, where he wouldn't be able to see me as he turned the corner, ignoring the guard's peremptory "yes?" It took him no more than a running thirty seconds to round the corner and reach the guardhouse. I stepped out and almost collided head on with Frankie Mastrantonio. His plaid sport coat, white shirt, and brown striped tie testified that clothes make the man. He was almost unrecognizable as the leather-jacketed hoodlum who'd menaced me with a gun. It occurred to me fleetingly that his outlaw outfit had been almost identical to my own and Angela's. The psychology of clothes. Maybe we could adapt the theme to our fashion-design client, Evelyne Stacey.

Frankie jumped as though choreographed. The guard, now agitated, spat out a "Look now . . ." and I began to laugh uncontrollably.

"Frankie!" I sputtered between peals, "I had no idea it was you. You look so different."

"Miss Wareham...I...I'm..." His face was as greenish pale as it had been when he'd hightailed it out of my apartment.

"You're just the person I need to see," I said, as my hilarity subsided. "Come on, we'd better get out of this guy's face before he calls the police and has us locked up for loitering." Alarm crossed his face. "Only kidding," I added. I took his arm and steered him toward Columbus Avenue.

"Miss Wareham, I am so sorry about yesterday morning. My brother, he really reamed me for it. I ... did you get the flowers?" He sounded as shy as a school kid apologizing to his teacher for acting up in class.

"I did, Frankie, they're lovely. Thank you." I thought fleetingly of asking him if he regularly sent flowers after pulling a gun on someone, but I was not sadistically inclined. "Look, I have something awfully important to talk to you about. Let's find a coffee shop." Arthur F. Oldburgh and Partners would have to wait a little longer.

When we were safely tucked into a booth with coffee and bagels on the way, I filled him in on what I'd told Ike and that the police had already paid a visit to his father. "So it was really lucky that you were up here tailing me, instead of ... by the way, why *were* you following me?"

"To apologize, only I didn't want to come to your building. I thought you'd be too mad to let me come up, and you might— you know—have me thrown out, so I waited for you outside. Then when I saw you I ... well, I felt kinda scared to talk to you. I figured if I just walked along behind you for a while, I'd ..." he smiled sheepishly, but it was a disarming smile— not unlike Dave's, "I'd get braver. Then you disappeared around that corner and I was sure I lost you."

The bagels arrived hot, mine with butter and a smear of cream cheese as ordered. I bit off a healthy, properly chewy chunk. After I'd swallowed it, I said, "You're not very good at tailing, you know." I was treated to another smile.

"No, I guess not. What the hell does a veterinary student know about that kinda stuff? Or about guns? When I was a kid my mom used to say she'd cut my hands off if I ever even thought of picking up a gun. But I felt so bad for Dave. He was so fucking worried that—" He blushed deeply. "I'm sorry," he mumbled.

"It's okay. I've heard the word before," I said, noting how amused anyone who knew me would be to hear me being apologized to for the F word.

"Anyway, he felt so bad. You know, he busted his chops to get where he is, and, ah sh—I mean, he wouldn't kill anybody! You gotta believe that."

"I *do* believe that, Frankie, that's why I didn't blow the whistle on him. But it'll help him to have an alibi, and you and your father are it. He's an old family friend from the Lower East Side. You were just a baby when your family moved to South Orange. You don't remember those days, okay? About the night and morning of the murders, just tell the truth."

"Uh huh." He frowned and took a bite of his bagel, which he hadn't previously touched. "You're a smart lady, Miss Wareham, who do *you* think could've knocked those people off?" He looked at me expectantly with Dave's black eyes.

Maybe it was that he expected an answer from me—trusted that I'd have one—that made me look at the whole mess from a slightly different angle. I laid aside the issue of alibis and focused on the players. Who really would be capable of these particular crimes? Frankie didn't say a word as I gnawed my thumbnail and thought.

Dave wouldn't be. I'd decided that already, but I reconfirmed it in my mind. Roger Durand, as I knew him, wouldn't have the brains or guts either for the spying or the killing, but I didn't rule him out. Rog was such an empty suit that his whole persona could be a carefully executed, long-term cover.

Les Charlton had brains and guts to spare—also the cool determination to carry it off, though I couldn't see why he'd want a spying sideline. He was making millions as a reasonably honest headhunter.

Charlie Kaye was a perfect candidate, a smart, ruthless, risk-taking climber. I had trouble, however, picturing him choking

Mandy's life away. He'd seemed so entirely devastated by her murder, but maybe I'd mistaken tears of regret for tears of shock. Charlie'd been with the firm only a year and a half, and it'd be a lot less damaging to the Carter reputation if . . . I bludgeoned that thought. Not fair to intrude what I'd prefer from a PR standpoint. Which brought me to Gillian Carter, my favorite potential perpetrator—and Dave's.

I'd met her twice. I didn't like her. There was something about the woman. Perhaps she was just what we used to call when I was growing up "a man's woman," meaning that she had boyfriends but no girlfriends. But I thought somehow it was more than that. And her affair with Les didn't make sense to me. One really had to be swept away to bother risking the consequences of an affair that close to home. I'd done it, and in retrospect it didn't come close to being worth the anxiety. Neither Gillian nor Les seemed to me like people who tended to get swept away. But who really knew about other people's passions?

"Well, whaddaya think?" Frankie's voice startled me. I must have been ruminating for a long time. I took a sip of my coffee. It was cold.

"Frankie, I think two men in your brother's firm could have been capable of the murders. One has an alibi, one doesn't. There's a third one, but I'm not sure about him."

"What about the King's wife?" I noticed that he'd picked up the *Post*'s way of referring to King as "the King." "Dave thinks she's a real creep, ice water in the veins, he says."

"I know he feels that way, and I agree with him. I think she'd be capable of it. My problem is I hardly know the woman. I don't know anything much about her. Besides, I should tell you she has an alibi—one the police are satisfied with."

"Maybe she put out a contract."

"O'Hanlon doesn't think so. He and his cops have poked around pretty thoroughly and come up empty. Also, he says that the style of the murders doesn't look like a hit man."

"Yeah, he's right about that," he said glumly.

"Still, something about Gillian Carter is, I don't know, wrong," I mused, more to myself than to him. A sudden off-the-wall idea struck me. It was probably a lousy one, considering Frankie's track record, but I didn't have many other resources—any, to be precise. "Frankie, how would you like to help in a way that might be more, uh, useful than what you've been doing so far?"

"Anything, Miss Wareham. I'll do anything. Just tell me."

"I guess you can start by calling me Liz, since we're going to work together." He smiled and I hardly noticed the acne scars. "You're going to be a vet. What do you know about horses?"

"Lots. I do some part-time work for a vet in Far Hills. That's hunt country, and horses—that's his whole practice, almost."

"Great. Gillian Carter is leaving tomorrow for Little Dix Bay." A faint ripple of puzzlement crossed his face. "That's a resort in the Caribbean. Anyway, by tomorrow afternoon she'll be gone."

"You want me to follow her?" he asked eagerly.

"God, no!" I answered quickly.

"I'm not very good at following, huh?"

"No, not very. But you're smart. And you're very likable—when you leave your gun home." He looked pained. I reached across the table to pat his arm. "I'm sorry, I shouldn't joke about it. As I understand it, Gillian's one real passion is her horses. Is there some good excuse you can think of to get chatting with the stable staff? Could she have ordered some new experimental horse vitamin or something?"

"Let me think about it. I'll come up with something, I promise. So I start shmoozing them. What am I looking for?"

"I wish I knew." The waiter started to refill our cups. "Just a drop, please," I said, indicating an inch or so with my thumb and forefinger. As I did so, I caught a glimpse of my watch. Almost a quarter past ten. I could visualize a posse of irate clients organizing a lynch party. "Anything you can find out about her. Has she radically changed any of her habits in the past—oh—month or so? Has she been seeing any new people?

Has Leslie Charlton been out there much?"

"Charlton? You mean Dave's partner?"

"Yeah. He and Gillian have apparently been having an affair." His eyes widened in surprise. "I had the same reaction," I said. "And that information is confidential—at least for the moment. By the way, I think we'll skip telling Dave about your undercover assignment. He'd clobber both of us."

I took out my Filofax, tore out a page, and wrote out approximate directions to Carter Farms and both my phone numbers. "Don't make an appearance there until tomorrow afternoon. And keep in touch." I put out my hand. "Partners?" He grabbed it and we shook firmly.

"Partners," he agreed.

27

....

It was almost a quarter of eleven when I arrived at the office. I'd hoped John Gentle was out, or that I could duck him on the way to the safe haven of my corner. No such luck. When I got past his empty office, I thought I was home free, but he nailed me midway down the corridor on his way out of the conference room.

"To what do we owe the honor?" he asked with a deep bow. John has a misplaced pride in his sense of humor.

"The honor is all mine," I responded in kind, bobbing a curtsy. We were back to business as usual.

"Do you have a second to come into my office." It wasn't a question, and he didn't make it sound like one. I braced myself for what I knew must be coming. He shut the door and perched on the edge of the gray slate table that was his desk. I stood. It was my best chance of making a quick getaway. "I just had a call from Clem Farquharson," he said. Shit! Clem was the president of Arthur F. Oldburgh.

"John, I'm terribly sorry. I've been so tied up with the Carter—"

"Clem thought that perhaps you'd been the latest victim. He has left two messages for you during the past two days and hasn't gotten a return call."

"Angela—"

"Angela isn't you, and you know Clem doesn't deal with underlings—even ones like Angela. May I remind you that Arthur F. Oldburgh and Partners," he rolled out the client's entire name for added impact—unnecessary, the point was

165

CAROL BRENNAN

hitting my gut with quite enough impact, "is a far larger account than Carter Consultants, and if you're not equipped to deal with it effectively, I can . . ."

"Put it into Briggs's group," I finished. "I know, John. But Clem would not like such a switch. He's happy where he is—well, most of the time, and that's all you can expect with any client. Don't you always say 'if it ain't broke, don't fix it'? I will call Clem and apologize. He will have next year's program on his desk Monday, in plenty of time for his board meeting. We're raising the budget to three hundred fifty thousand dollars."

The prospect of a thirty percent fee increase put a little color back into those pinched cheeks, and he favored me with a more or less mollified smile as I left. I figured this wasn't the moment to tell him I was going to have to hire an additional body to help do the work.

When I reached Morley's desk, he looked up from his screen with his left eyebrow peeking out above the tortoise-shell frame of his glasses.

"Well, well."

"Don't start with me," I snarled, "I've just had my wrist Gently slapped for neglecting our other clients. That's the bad news. The worse news is that nobody leaves here tonight until we get the Oldburgh program finished." Morley didn't snarl back. That's not his way. He just looked at me stonily—much more effective. I sighed and shook my head. I could feel i beginning to ache. "Morley, I am really sorry to do this t you, especially on a Friday. Would you get Angela for me and the boys—in about five minutes. I have to make nic nice with Clem Farquharson first." I started into my offic and paused in the doorway. "Oh, and order in some lunch fo me and Peg Durand. She's coming at one."

"Peg Durand? Any relation to Roger the Beautiful?"

"Only by marriage," I answered and shut the door.

I was bidding good-bye to a relatively happy Clen Farquharson when Angela arrived with Kirk Aristidos an Cormac McCafferty in tow. We all thought of them as Angela' boys, and she took in good spirit a lot of kidding about how she mother-henned them. What she *did* bristle at were my periodic observations that if only we could combine Kirk's drive with Cormac's brains, we'd have one dynamite PR man. I motioned them to the round table while I reassured Clem one more time that the program would be on his desk Monday morning. After I hung up I retrieved a large yellow lined pad from under the pile of white paper and pink phone messages on my desk, grabbed a pen, and joined them. Since other people were there, Angela and I could do no more than exchange "Are you all right?" glances and assuring nods. We couldn't have done much more even if we'd been alone. This was crash time.

"I'm sorry to do this to you guys, but Son of Farquhar has my word, on the lives of my children, that he'll have his program Monday. And since said program doesn't yet exist, we're going to have to make some fast magic."

We spent the next hour brainstorming what we might do to justify the thirty percent fee increase I'd promised John, and came up with some pretty good stuff. I split up the writing chores so that each of us had a chunk. Just then Morley buzzed. Sam was on the line.

"I have to take this," I said. "Give Morley your drafts ASAP. I'll review them and we'll get back together at . . . four-thirty, okay?" Kirk turned a little pale.

"Five-thirty's more like it, I think," Angela said quickly from the doorway, protecting her chick from the Wicked Witch of the West Side.

Morley buzzed to tell me that Peg Durand had arrived. I said I'd be right with her and took Sam's call.

"I'm so glad you called, Sammy. I'm afraid dinner's going to be all screwed up. We're crashing on a proposal. I don't know what time we'll be done, and I'm stuck here till when-ever. But I really want to see you."

"Easy, lovely, don't get so strung out. Finish your proposal, however long it takes. Then pour yourself into a cab and come to my place, where I will have food and drink waiting—not, by the way, in that order."

Why are friends so much nicer than lovers? Sam and I had contemplated falling in love with each other—not at the same time, thank God—but I guess we both found the friendship more valuable. The proof that we were right was that after seven years, we were still together, while my Bob, Frank, and Douglas were gone, along with Sam's Susan, Marilyn, and Cindy.

"Sam, you're the best. See you later."

Morley ushered Peg Durand in. She was wearing a violet tweed suit, which might have dated from her first job interview after Vassar graduation or been bought last week, and a discreet string of good pearls. Her face was tense, but determined.

"Sorry to keep you waiting, Peg. Can I offer you a drink?" She looked like she could use one, and I was glad that the minifridge in my cabinet was stocked.

"No, thank you," she smiled weakly. "I don't think it'll help, really."

"Let's sit over here, shall we?" I asked, indicating the sofa. She sat and put her small, square alligator purse down next to her. I pulled up one of the paisley chairs and sat facing her across the coffee table. "How can I help you?" I asked.

"My grandmother was a real Yankee. She never could tolerate beating about the bush. I can hear her saying, 'Out with it, girl. Tell the truth and shame the devil.' I think I'd better listen to her." She paused, but not very long. "My husband is a very foolish man, but perhaps you already know that since you work with him. He has stolen money from his partners—'cooked his books,' I think you call it." I just looked at her. I had no idea what to say.

She continued, "He did not, however, kill King Carter or those other people. Roger could never carry off one murder, let alone three. He can't even steal efficiently. Besides, he has alibis for all three murders, though not the ones we gave the police." So Ike had been right about Rog's phony alibis. Now, in addition to an industrial spy and multiple murderer, Carter Consultants' talent bank included a thief. Terrific!

"Did King know about . . . about the money?"

"He did, yes."

"Did that detective, Swift, tell him?"

"No, he did not. Roger told him—two weeks ago. When I found out about the situation, I told Roger I'd give him the money to make good. I have quite a lot of it, you know. But I said I'd do it only if he faced up to what he'd done."

"I don't think I quite understand," I said. "If you have all this money, why would Rog need to . . . to steal?"

"Because," her lips compressed with the effort she was making, "because of Jamie." I was about to ask who Jamie was, but I stopped myself. She was going to tell me. "Jamie is the young man who is my husband's lover. Roger wished to buy him an apartment." She related these facts tonelessly, as though she'd said them to herself over and over to remove all emotion.

Whatever I'd expected, it hadn't been this. I was stunned. All Morley's kidding about Roger the Beautiful. Had he known?

"I'm so sorry," I said. I didn't think my sympathy was what she was after. "So Rog was with Jamie at the times of the murders?"

"Yes."

"And you want my public relations advice?" She nodded. "Go to the police and tell the truth. Speak only to Lieutenant O'Hanlon. If you level with him, he'll protect the confidence. As far as the money is concerned, unless it's already been returned, Rog is going to have to tell David and Les—face up to it the same way he did with King—and take the consequences. I can't say what they'll do, but I know one thing they *won't* do, and that's go public with it. That would damage the firm's reputation, and be as bad for them as it would for Rog."

She processed that and nodded. "Thank you. That's sensible advice." She stood up and put out her hand. "If you don't mind, I think I won't stay for lunch after all. I'm not very hungry, I find."

I took her hand and said, "You're an extraordinary woman, Peg Durand. Good luck."

28

....

After peg durand's abrupt exit, morley walked in and inquired with raised eyebrow, "Didn't she like the menu?"

I replied that she'd come to discuss matters tense enough to deaden the appetite, even for a smoked turkey sandwich with Russian dressing. "However," I added, "I'm starved. Why don't you bring me my sandwich and have the other one yourself?"

"Well," he hesitated, "Sirpan and I did agree that we were going to eat only veggies this week, but . . . you no talk, me no talk." As he was leaving my office to get the food, he casually threw over his shoulder, "What happened? She find out after all this time?"

"Wait a minute!" My voice was sharp. "Find out what?"

"That Rog is gay," he answered simply.

"How the hell did you know?" I was astonished.

"Oh, I figured the first time I met him. Then later we got to know Jamie at The Saddle and heard all about his new apartment and this guy who was buying it for him—it's a small world, you know, 'specially around Christopher Street. Want a Perrier or coffee?"

The rest of the day had been Arthur F. Oldburgh and more Arthur F. Oldburgh. We'd drafted, added, subtracted, redrafted, re-edited. By the time we'd done the last double proofread—Cormac reading aloud to me and Kirk reading aloud to Angela—and Morley'd corrected the last error, a crucial missing zero in the budget, which we'd all previously overlooked, it was almost nine o'clock—too late to Fed Ex. Morley'd take care of that in the morning. I'd broken out the booze, toasted them for valor and smarts above and beyond the call, and instructed them all to give me dinner bills to charge to the client.

Angela and I had a few minutes alone together in the ladies' room. She was ivory pale and looked exhausted. I put my hand on her shoulder.

"Angela, I'm afraid I botched the whole thing. It was that damned camp lantern."

"That's okay," she responded with a weary smile, "I'd have had to go to the police anyway. What else could I have done? No clue about which partner would have been safe to talk to about it." Tears started to follow one another down her perfect face. "Oh Liz, I've let him down. He turned to me for help and I . . ." She couldn't finish. I put both arms around her.

"No, you didn't let him down. You said it yourself, and you were right. What could you have done, except go to the police?" I reached in my bag for a tissue and handed it to her. "It'll all be over soon, and with any luck the industrial espionage part will never come out."

"It's strange," she said as she dabbed the tears away and pulled a compact out of her Hermes bag to touch up her face. "The industrial spy thing was such a surprise. I didn't think it would have to do with business."

"What were you expecting?"

"I don't know, exactly, but something to do with Gillian— perhaps that she and one of her cute little stable boys were stealing money from him or something, and when he faced them with it they . . ." She held her hands out, substituting the gesture for the words she was having trouble saying.

"Killed him," I finished for her.

"I thought something like that at first, but I wanted to see what he'd left for me in the writing table before I said anything. Then, after Mandy, I wasn't so sure. King would never have discussed anything personal with Mandy, although who knows what she might have seen or heard? Besides, the papers said Gillian was away when he was killed. So when we went into the Manse last night, I didn't know what to expect."

"Hmm," I mused. I powdered my own nose and ran my fingers through my curls. "It must be almost nine-thirty," I said blandly, "and the guys are waiting for us to lock up and leave."

"You know more, don't you, Liz?"

"Not really," I said truthfully. "I think some things, but I'm not ready to talk about them." I knew Angela wouldn't press me. It wasn't her style.

The shape I was in when I rang Sam's downstairs bell gave new resonances to the expression "wiped out."

He buzzed me in and I began the three-flight trudge up to the skylit top floor that served as his New York pied-à-terre. He met me at the first landing, holding two globular stemmed glasses half-filled with liquid a little darker than straw. He handed me one.

"Thought you could use some fuel to make it up the rest of the stairs." I grabbed the glass gratefully and took a long sip. California Chardonnay—tasted like ZD or Sonoma Cutrer, strong and oaky, just the taste Sam knew I loved. That was Sam. Given his druthers, he'd have preferred bourbon.

"Yum," I said and kissed him. "I've just approved your canonization. How does Saint Sam sound to you?"

"I think I'll take to it real well," he said as we mounted the second flight. "Has a nice ring."

I walked through the open door of Sam's apartment and felt, as I always did when I came there, away and protected against whatever might be plaguing me at the moment. It was one large, airy room, with a small separate bedroom off to the left. Two tall windows looked south over Gramercy Park, and a peaked skylight framed the first stars we'd seen after a rainy week. I plopped down on one of the two blue homespun sofas that faced each other across a slate-topped coffee table in front of the fireplace, where a Duraflame log was burning.

"Even a fire," I said as I kicked my shoes off and curled my legs up under me.

"I hate designer sawdust logs, but I haven't had a wood delivery yet this fall." He walked over to the open kitchen on the other side of the fireplace. "Hungry? Or should we just drink for a while?"

"Yeah, let's. Come on, sit with me. I want to pick your brain about something you said on the phone the other morning."

"Okay." He walked over with a basket of corn chips and the wine bottle. He put them on the coffee table, and sat on the sofa opposite me. "By the way, Pam said there was a fax from you at the house. What—"

"Oh, my God!" I just about jumped off the sofa. "Sam, don't read it. Throw it away. Did Pam read it? Who the hell is she anyway? I've never even heard her name before." All this tumbled out of me rapid fire. I'd forgotten totally about the fax, incriminating Dave and his brother.

"Hey, easy." He came round to my side of the coffee table and put his bear arm around my shoulder. "Sit down, it's okay." I did. He sat down beside me. "Of course I'll throw it away, whatever it is. I won't even cheat and read it. As for Pam, she checked the fax machine because I asked her to— I was expecting something—and she told me that it hadn't come, but there was something with a cover sheet that said 'Sam Boyd from Liz Wareham.' I told her to just leave it; I'd be seeing you in New York. I'd bet she didn't read it. She's a painter, and shows an almost dismaying lack of interest in what I do in the so-called real world. To answer your last question, Pam is living with me in the Georgetown house. You haven't heard of her yet because she's new."

I took a healthy sip of the wine and felt a little calmer. "I'm sorry, Sammy, I'm so damned strung out. That fax was, uh, a false alarm, and if anyone read it . . ."

"No one will." He held up his right hand, three fingers out. "Scout's honor. Tell you what, I'll call Pam right now and tell her to tear it up and get rid of it."

"Look, I feel like an idiot. It can wait till morning."

"Nope," he said, reaching for the phone on the teak end table. "I know you, lovely, you will obsess and worry the thing to death until it's destroyed, and I want to enjoy the goodies I bought for us at Balducci's in peace." He dialed. Pam, apparently less of a goer than her predecessor, Cindy, was at home. I felt reasonably certain by the time Sam hung up that the fax would soon be history.

"Thanks, Sam. I'm sorry to be such a pain in the ass." I reached for the bottle and poured us both more wine. "Do you remember you said to me that there'd been some pretty interesting reactions around the table at Robotrac when what's his name walked in with the news of King's murder?"

He crunched on a corn chip and took a contemplative sip of wine. "Yeah?" he questioned, and waited for me to continue.

"Well, you don't throw language around, so when you say 'pretty interesting' I assume you mean more than the shock and sadness you'd expect from clients who'd just heard that the president of their search firm had been murdered—I guess I should say a former search firm."

"Yes, I did mean more than that, but I probably should've kept my big mouth shut—even to you. After all, Robotrac is still *my* client, and I'd prefer to keep it that way."

"Maybe you don't have to tell me, Sammy. Let *me* tell *you.* I think that when those guys around the table at Robotrac heard about the murder, they wondered if it had anything to do with their little problem, namely that an executive they hired through Carter turned out to be an industrial spy. How'm I doing?" The question was rhetorical. His face told me I was on target.

"How did you find out? Everybody's trying to slip this one by real quiet."

"Nobody's more eager to keep it quiet than we are, believe me, but I have to know one thing from you. Is it Marcella Grimm? And what did she do?"

"That's two, and my question's first in line: How did you find out about it?"

I mentally shrugged my shoulders. Even Sam wasn't

sweetness and light all the time. "I read about Marcella's sudden resignation in the *Journal* and put it together with some things the police turned up." I'd trust Sam with my life, but I just didn't feel like going into the whole megillah of Angela and our break-in and King's note. "Please, Sammy, it's important for me to know."

"Yeah, I guess it is. Okay, you're right. But I didn't tell you."

"Well, what did she do?" He looked distinctly uncomfortable and didn't answer. "Come on, Sam, it'll be a real help if you tell me."

He hesitated another beat and then said, "It was NightWatch, Robotrac's new burglar alarm robot. She copied the designs and shopped them to Takahayo."

I was speechless. Takahayo was the IBM of Japan. This was big stuff. My God, the money . . .

"Les brought her to Robotrac," I said quietly. My head was on overload. So many facts fit—almost—but didn't quite match. Like taking twelve black socks out of the dryer and no two of them make a pair.

"Right. But if you're looking to lay blame, it's not that simple. Seems Charlie Kaye had placed her in her last job at Aventech four years ago when he was still with Korn Ferry. It was Charlie who threw her chapeau into Les's ring for the Robotrac slot."

I took a deep breath and let it out slowly. Charlie or Les? Les or Charlie? But Les couldn't have killed King. He was in Boston. Charlie Kaye.

29

IT WAS AFTER ONE BY THE TIME WE'D FINISHED MUNCHING Balducci's shrimp with black mushrooms, chicken with sun-dried tomatoes and cilantro, ratatouille, and sourdough bread. Sam urged me to sack out at his place and leave in the morning. It was tempting. I was more than exhausted. But I needed to go home. I had a lot of thinking to do. Maybe waking up in my own bed would help unscramble my brain and the facts would make better sense.

Sam walked me downstairs and over to the north side of the park where he hailed a westbound cab. We hugged each other tight.

"Be careful, lovely. I mean it. If one of your guys is mixed up in Marcella's game, the PR crisis could be the least of your worries. Watch your back. Promise?"

"Promise."

I fed the cats when I came in, and headed for the bedroom. Midway down the hall, I heard the phone. A ringing phone at two in the morning is unsettling in the best of circumstances. In the current ones, it set my heart pounding as I ran the rest of the way to the bedroom to catch it. Ike's voice answered my hello.

"Good morning. Welcome home. Have a good time?"

"A great time," I answered airily. "I gather you've been trying to reach me."

"Since ten o'clock your time."

"You just missed me at the office then. I was there till almost

176

nine-thirty. What do you mean 'your time'? Where are you?"
As I asked, I knew the answer.

"California."

"You're onto Marcella Grimm, aren't you?"

"Bingo." The edge in his voice told me I'd brought him up short. "If you've just found out about her, my compliments," he said carefully. "But if you knew about it yesterday and you held out on me—" His temperature was rising rapidly.

"Hey, get off it, okay?" I snapped. "I didn't know about it yesterday." Silence. There was no point in protesting further. He'd just have to take my word, which, based on recent record, he had every reason to reject. "Did she admit she was hooked up with someone at Carter on the spying?" I chewed my thumbnail waiting for his answer.

"Yes. She fingered Charlie Kaye."

"What . . . what happens now?" My hand felt unsteady holding the phone. Here it came, and it would blow us right out of the water.

"Libuti questioned him tonight and got nowhere. I'm at the airport waiting for the red-eye to board. I'll have a go at him when I get back. It's borderline, but we may have enough to book him."

How do we keep it out of the papers, I asked myself. I didn't have an answer.

"Who else knows about this?" I willed my voice calm. This was new professional ground. I was going to have to make it up as I went along.

"Not the press, if that's what you're worried about. I promised the Robotrac people and the fair Marcella we wouldn't release the espionage angle if they cooperated. Boy, is she a piece of work! I'll level with you though, if we indict Kaye for the murders, it'll all come out."

I had to get hold of Dave Goldstone. There was a glimmering in my mind of what our strategy ought to be, but I needed his support, and wasn't at all sure I was going to have it.

"Tell you what, Liz, I'm going to be seeing Kaye in the morning, and we will or won't book him. I simply don't know yet. But I give you my word that even if we do, we'll leave the espionage issue out of it—at least for the time being."

"That's fair. Thanks."

"You're welcome," he said with ironic formality. "Look, how about you come to my place for dinner tomorrow night. I'll grill the steak we didn't have a chance to eat the other time, and give you a status report." He paused. "Also, I want to see you," he added in a different tone.

"Also, I want to see you," I agreed.

I knew my call—both the content and the hour—might well push Type A Dave into cardiac arrest, but he needed to know immediately. I checked his home number in my Filofax and dialed. He picked up on the first ring.

"Yello," his voice barked with tension.

"It's Liz, Dave. The police are pretty sure that they've found their man. It . . . it's Charlie." I could hardly make my mouth say his name. It just felt wrong. I sternly told myself to grow up and made an internal promise to stop reading so many thrillers.

"Charlie?!" he croaked. I filled him in on Robotrac and Marcella Grimm. He punctuated my narrative with the occasional "Jesus." He was silent for a moment. I could hear him lighting a cigarette. "It's crazy," he said in a voice uncharacteristically soft. "I feel like someone on a battlefield whose buddy was just shot down next to him. It's like they nailed Charlie and I escaped. Jesus, I'm free! I got away with it, but Charlie . . . why do I feel so guilty? Weird. Hang on a minute." I could hear him explaining it all to Shelly. Then he was back. "Sorry about that. Shell was jumping out of her skin here. Charlie. God, I just can't believe it."

"Can't you?" I jumped in before he had a chance to go on. "Why not?" Since I felt the same way, I was eager to know whether David's reasons were any more concrete than my own.

"I guess it's the spying," he said slowly. "Funny, if you told me Charlie killed someone who got in his way, or even that King was chewing him out—you know how he could strip your skin off—and Charlie just grabbed that knife and did him, I could believe that. But I'd never figure him for a spy. I'd sooner have bet on Les, or even Rog."

"Look at it this way," I said, "it'll be easier to contain the damage. I mean, Charlie's not a partner. He hasn't even been with the firm two years." Another thought hit me. "I wonder if he has any other spies in place. Dave, unless the police get him to admit something, they're going to be talking to clients."

"Shit," he muttered. I couldn't have agreed more.

"Let me ask O'Hanlon how they plan to pursue it. You need to find out every client Charlie's worked with since he joined Carter. If the police are going to talk to them, you have to get hold of them first. Meantime, nobody's released the espionage angle, but if Charlie is indicted, it'll come out. We're going to need a statement from you—and a good one. I'll get a start on drafting something. You and Les and Rog will also have to do a lot of one-on-one client handholding."

"That's for sure." I heard him light another cigarette. "I've got to talk to Les and Rog. Suppose we all get together Monday afternoon over at my office." I noticed that "my office" came out without a stumble. He'd already taken over and he'd do fine. "Can we hold off that long?"

I thought briefly. "I don't see why not. He hasn't been arrested yet. And if he is, it won't be till this afternoon or Sunday at the earliest. Unless or until he's indicted, our policy is strictly 'no comment.' And, as far as the three of you are concerned, Charlie is off limits. Don't call him. I know it seems unfair—hell, he hasn't been charged with anything yet, but he probably will be, and it could compromise you. I'll talk to him." Liz Wareham, the *shtarke*, mediating with murderers. I could hear my mother bellow, "Don't mix in," but it was a bit late to begin listening.

"Okay, Chief," Dave replied, with the first glint of humor I'd heard from him since the murder, "and thanks—for everything."

30

....

I WOKE UP TRYING TO HANG ONTO THE TAIL END OF A dream, but it slipped away, leaving only one image: I was sitting in a corner on a stool, face to the wall with a tall dunce cap on my head, sobbing my heart out.

Though I couldn't remember the dream, I couldn't shake the feeling of being dumb and inadequate, nor the fear that I'd be punished for it. I showered and cleaned my face with extra vigor to atone for all the neglect it had suffered this week. Clogged pores. Maybe that was my dreaded punishment. What could be worse, except perhaps the heartbreak of psoriasis? Trying to kid myself out of the feeling didn't work, though. It wouldn't go away. I pulled on jeans and a man's blue oxford shirt, fed the cats, and started the coffee.

I opened the door and brought in the papers. A quick flip through confirmed that they had nothing new. That didn't stop the *Post* and *News*. Both carried prominent stories on Antony Swift, calling him "Phantom P. I." and "Society Dick," but all they really said was that he'd been investigating Carter Consultants for Green Star Industries in relation to a possible acquisition, and that Sir Brian Salter, chairman of Green Star, was "unavailable for comment." Since that was yesterday's news, the *Times* skipped it.

The *Post* also featured an exclusive page three interview headlined DEATH FIRM SEC'Y: "I QUIT!" in which Iris Paluczyk recounted in florid detail why she'd decided to seek employment elsewhere. We were going to have to launch some serious internal PR or the guys would be typing their own letters.

I wandered back into the bedroom and realized that I hadn't checked last night's phone messages. There was only one, which turned out to be from Scott—also three hang-ups. I felt aimless, which was ridiculous. I had a statement and a damage control plan to draft, as well as a bulging bag full of homework for other clients. But I'd be worthless in coping with any of it until I could shake whatever it was that was nibbling at me. So I went where I always go when life gets out of hand: shopping.

Shopping. My therapy of choice for frustration, anger, self-pity, and brain clog. And when I think shopping, I mean clothes. Groceries won't do it for me—even caviar and chanterelles. Antiques? Well, if you're visiting friends in Dutchess County it's fun to browse the quilts and rockers and come up with a trophy, but clothes, that's my real game. As a sport it has everything. Great exercise: striding through Bergdorf's or Saks, stretching and bending in the try-on room. The thrill of the chase: hunting down the ultimate black jacket, the perfect leather skirt. The titillating touch of danger: knowing you might spring for something fabulous you absolutely can't afford. A crack at beating the system: bagging a Gaultier at seventy-five percent off.

I remember with misty eyes dashing into Bloomingdale's after I'd been fired from my first PR job—the tiny agency which had hired me had lost two accounts during the first month of my tenure—and slapping down a triumphant charge card to claim a Montana leather suit for $159. "Hell with 'em," I'd thought as I signed the charge slip, "they can't tell *me* I'm poor." I loved that suit—wore it for eleven years.

The strange thing is, I get some pretty good ideas while fingering crunchy tweed, sumptuous cashmere, and slithery charmeuse. The "Baker Bank Targets" seminar series was born in the Calvin Klein boutique at Saks, and I decided to divorce Alan Bernchiller while trying on a Perry Ellis sweater at Lord & Taylor.

CAROL BRENNAN

When cosseting is what I crave, boutique shopping on Madison Avenue is the answer, but that day I preferred the luxurious anonymity of Bergdorf's. The two-mile walk took forty-five minutes and I swung through the revolving door at about eleven.

By the time I'd left the Donna Karan department and arrived at Isaac Mizrahi, I'd come to four conclusions: that Charlie Kaye just didn't fit as the spy-murderer; that whatever Les and Gillian were having, it wasn't an affair; that Peg Durand was a determined, resourceful woman who'd do and say whatever she thought necessary to protect her husband; and that the plaid silk blazer would work year round and I didn't *really* have anything like it in my closet.

I put a black suede turtleneck and pants on hold and went down the escalator to Armani. King had said in his aborted letter to Angela that discovery of the industrial spy within Carter could bring down the firm. Charlie hadn't been with the firm long enough to bring it down. Hell, he'd been at Korn Ferry for eight years, and with Carter for less than two. If he'd been dabbling in espionage, it'd be a much bigger potential black eye for Korn Ferry than for us, and King would have realized that. God, Armani's fabrics were brilliant this year, especially the minutely pleated featherweight check. But the prices made the suede pants and top look like a bargain. So Marcella Grimm fingered Charlie. So what? Why should anyone assume that *she'd* tell the truth? Les was the one who'd placed Marcella at Robotrac. But Les had an alibi for the first two murders. Well . . . I didn't have an answer for that one.

"That olive and black check is sensational on you." I smiled and thanked the saleswoman for the compliment. I agreed with her, actually, but . . . could I? No, just too expensive. Get back to the third floor, where it's a little safer. It could have been Roger who'd contacted Marcella and enlisted her. Why not? His alibi was Jamie, by Peg's leave. That hardly meant it was true.

At a quarter to four, I departed Bergdorf's with blazer, pants, top, and a new Coco cologne spritz, feeling flushed cleansed, refreshed. As I marched west on Central Park South, lavender shopping bags on each arm, I savored each moment of crisp, clear autumn air. Just as I crossed the street and turned north up Central Park West, the aggregate cost of my expedition intruded itself for a second on my consciousness. But, in true Scarlett fashion, I decided to think about it tomorrow.

I figured I'd find a phone message from Charlie when I got home. Instead, I found Charlie—pacing my lobby and looking ready to cry. When he saw me he ran to my side and grabbed my arm with the eagerness of a four year old who spots Mommy after having wandered around Woolworth's lost for ten minutes.

"Liz, thank God! I have to talk to you." He pulled me toward the elevator.

I hesitated. "Charlie, uh, maybe we, uh, could go around the corner for a cup of coffee . . . or something," I finished weakly. He looked devastated. He let go of my arm and stepped back from me.

"You're afraid." It was an incredulous whisper. "You're afraid to have me in your apartment. God, Liz," his voice grew louder and took on a hysterical edge, "you think I'm a murderer—just like the cops do. Oh my God . . ." He held out his hands in a tense pantomime of supplication.

The lobby was empty, except for Gus, who stood no more than twelve feet away, poised to protect me, but with his face turned purposefully away from us: the most diplomatic doorman on the Upper West Side.

"Let's go upstairs, Charlie, I'm not afraid of you," I said quietly, realizing it was true. I punched the elevator button.

"Mrs. Wareham," Gus began, his voice apprehensive.

"It's okay, Gus," I said. He looked at me, sure that it wasn't. "It is. Really. Mr. Kaye is a friend of mine." The elevator door opened and Charlie followed me in. As the doors closed, I could see that Gus wasn't a hundred percent convinced.

"Want a drink, Charlie?" I asked when we hit the apartment. "You look like you could use one."

"No. I don't want a drink, or coffee, or . . . anything. I just want this nightmare to be over!"

"Let's sit down and talk." I motioned him to the sofa and perched myself on the ottoman of the Eames chair across from it. I let him begin.

"The cops think I did it. They think I killed King and . . . and Mandy." He looked like he was about to cry, but he didn't. "I think they're going to arrest me," he said tonelessly.

"Why do they think it was you, do you suppose?" I asked, in the offhand tone of my former shrink pursuing Something Significant.

"I . . . I'm not sure," he fumphed. I let the silence hang there for a full ten seconds.

"That's not true, Charlie. Isn't it because Marcella Grimm told the police that you enlisted her in a scheme to steal and sell Robotrac technology, and that King found out about it and was going to get rid of you?"

His eyes opened wide. So did his mouth, but no sound came out.

"If you're asking for my help—and I assume that's why you're here—you are going to have to be straight with me, okay?"

"Okay." He sighed deeply. "I know she said that. I placed Marcella at Aventech while I was still at Korn Ferry. Around the time I joined Carter, she and I were . . . Well, I'd just split with my wife and . . ." He coughed nervously. "Marcella and I were having an affair. When I heard that Les was doing the Robotrac search, I . . . she was perfect for the spot—I would never have suggested her otherwise." He paused. "And that's all." He held his hands out, palms up, and shrugged his shoulders.

"What happened with you and Marcella after she got the job?"

"We stopped seeing each other," he said and cleared his throat.

"Come on, Charlie, don't make me pull it out of you."

"I broke it off. I . . . she was in California and I . . . I'd met Mandy . . . Oh God." He lowered his head into his hands.

"That's good news." He raised his head and looked at me startled. "It gives her a reason to choose you as a scapegoat."

"You believe I'm . . . innocent?" His face cleared and for an instant he looked like the cocky Charlie of, was it less than a week ago?

"Yes, I do. Unfortunately, my opinion isn't the one that counts. We just have to convince the police."

"It must have been Les," he said, his mouth tense.

"Les has a rock-solid alibi, as you do not. It could have been Rog."

"Why not Dave?"

"Because it wasn't—for a whole bunch of reasons you'll just have to take my word for. By the way, Dave believes in you, too."

"Yeah? Well, how come he didn't take my calls today. I tried him four times."

"He ducked your calls because I told him to," I said with a bit of sharpness. "Look," I continued in a kinder tone, "if they book you—and they may—Dave has to stand apart from it for the good of the firm. It may not be fair, but that's the PR advice I'm paid to give."

"Goddamn Marcella. I could wring her neck. I could—"

He stopped, appalled at his choice of words.

"Relax, Charlie, it's an expression. But you keep away from Marcella Grimm, understand? The cops have probably told you not to leave town, but don't even think of calling her. It'll make things worse. Did you tell O'Hanlon about your affair with Marcella?"

"No," he answered, shamefaced.

"You should have." I thought for a minute. "Look, I'll make a deal with you. You go home, call O'Hanlon and level with him, and I'll see if I can keep you out of jail."

31

I THOUGHT I'D WEAR MY NEW BLACK SUEDE PANTS AND top to Ike's, but my session with Charlie put me out of the dress-up mood, and when I walked out my door at seven-thirty, I was still in jeans, blue shirt, and a well-worn Aran sweater. The only addition was my diaphragm.

As I listened to his footsteps coming to the door to let me in, I had no idea what to expect—either from Ike or from myself. We both had enough mixed agendas to supply a mayoral campaign. When he opened the door, our eyes locked for just a second before he enveloped me in a major hug, which lasted a long time. As far as I was concerned, it could have gone on forever.

"I know we have a lot to talk about," I murmured up into his ear, "but could we go to bed first, please?"

"Since you said please," he answered softly and led me up two flights to the bedroom. We undressed each other. Nobody ripped anyone's clothes off. It was slow, sensual—interrupted by kisses long and short—and achingly sweet. Ike drew back the plump down coverlet and we fell upon fresh white sheets and pillows where we got deliciously lost.

I didn't exactly fall asleep afterwards, but it felt so good, lying there curled up against him with my head on his chest, that I couldn't bear to break the mood by talking. Maybe Ike felt the same way, because he didn't say anything either for quite a while, though I could tell he was awake. Then he said, "This would be the time for a cigarette, if anybody still smoked."

"Umm," I responded, wanting it not to be over yet.

"We *do* have a lot to talk about, and some of it could be bumpy, because there are things you're going to want to know that I'm not going to tell you, and other things we might not see eye to eye on. But first I'd like to clear up a little history—while I still have the courage."

"Courage?" I propped my head up with my hand and looked at him.

"Yeah," he said with a rueful smile, putting both hands behind his head, elbows way out. "If I'd had the balls, I'd've written to you years ago. I thought about it enough." He paused. "The thing was—ahh, it sounds stupid and trite—I felt so trapped. We'd had sex together, but I . . . I wanted to be free, whatever that meant to me at the time. Hell, I was only twenty, halfway through Columbia. There was the war, and there seemed something so wrong about us suburban kids commuting to our safe little campus revolution while the black kids were getting their asses shot off in Nam."

I'd gone off to a summer stock apprenticeship a few days after the prom night debacle. When I came home at the end of the summer, my mother told me that Ike had shocked everyone by quitting Columbia and enlisting. I'd been shocked too, but knowing Ike's put-your-money-where-your-mouth-is principles, not surprised. I remember feeling terrified that he'd get killed—knowing he would—and somehow mixing it all up with my own fury at him. It had all come up often during four therapeutic years with Dr. Slater. "I may be the only person you knew who wasn't surprised that you enlisted," I said. "I guess I'm thick, though, I don't see what it has to do with throwing me out of your car after the prom."

"We were both such willful kids, and it was your will against mine. Funny, Rosie always told me I should hang on to you, because what other girl could defend herself? Anyway, I was enjoying us in the moment, *for* the moment. And there you were making plans, locking us up in a future together. Christ, a future was the last thing on my mind. And then when you started giving me a hard time about dancing a few times with

Jeanette, I just wanted to slap you—so I dumped you instead. It was dumb and childish."

I groaned inside. Conventional suburban Jewish girl. With all my avant-garde pretensions, I'd been so busy hiring the caterer that I hadn't even really seen him, only *me*. "Why didn't you tell me?" I asked. "We used to be able to talk to each other." I sat up and crossed my legs Indian-style.

"I don't know. I should have tried." He sat up too, his back resting against the cherry headboard. "My dad found out about it a few days later—your sister must have told my brother. Anyway, he was furious with me, really reamed me. How could I do such a thing to 'the doctor's darlin' little girl'?" Ike had his father's brogue down cold. "He hadn't hit me in years, but I swear I thought he was going to. He said I'd acted like such a shameful baby that it was a pity I was too old to spank, because that's what I deserved. Actually, I'd have preferred it to what he did instead. He pulled my car privilege for that whole summer. Said if I didn't know how to behave like a grownup with a car, I shouldn't be allowed to use one. If you remember, I'd lined up a summer job at the Atlantic Beach Club. Would have taken me maybe half an hour by car. Try two hours each way by bus and train five days a week for two months." He grinned and then looked at me eye to eye. "Pat was right to land on me. I behaved like a shit. Is it too late to say I'm sorry?"

It was over. I'd lived with this grudge for twenty-six years, the anger always there to poke around and worry any time I wanted to. Was I going to miss it like a pulled tooth? "No, not too late," I said. "I'll think up a suitable penance." Then nobody made any intelligible sounds for a while.

After we'd played in the shower and dressed, we went downstairs to the living room—and the real world. Ike went behind the kitchen island and came up with a bottle of Cabernet from a small electric wine cellar. As he opened it and poured us each a glass, I perched on a tall dark wood barstool on the other side of the kitchen work counter.

"I advised a couple of people to give you a call," I said. "I've been doing a bang-up PR campaign on your discretion."

"Thanks," he said with a wry smile. He took a sizable wooden salad bowl down from the top of the fridge and broke a couple of cloves of garlic off a cluster. "I talked with Peg Durand on the phone. I was in California and she wouldn't talk to Joe Libuti. A session with the Rog and Peg and Jamie show is on my agenda for tomorrow. As for Kaye, he got hold of me just before you got here. So far it's his word alone about the affair with Marcella, but it should be easy enough to check. Doesn't mean he's in the clear though." He rubbed the bowl vigorously with one of the cut garlic cloves and chopped both of them fine on the butcher block counter with the purposeful expertise of a Japanese grill cook.

"I know that, Ike, but he is. He's not the one."

"You've got a better crystal ball than I have." He tore up leaf lettuce and chopped scallions and tossed both in the bowl.

"No, really. I knew King Carter, and you didn't. He'd have handled things entirely differently if it had been Charlie." Ike raised his eyebrows and refilled our wine glasses. I continued, "He'd have kept his appointment with me, we'd have had a release out that day about Charlie, 'who came to Carter Consultants after eight years with Korn Ferry' leaving the firm to pursue other opportunities, et cetera—much like Robotrac did with Marcella. Don't you see, Charlie was new to Carter, he wasn't a partner. No way he could bring down the firm, and King wouldn't have gone through all the rigmarole with letters in secret drawers."

Ike didn't say anything. He turned on the Salamander grill above his Garland restaurant stove and took two large shell steaks on an oval steel pan from the fridge.

"Hey," I said, "don't you think *I'd* much rather it were Charlie than a partner?" He nodded thoughtfully, as he chopped anchovies. "But it isn't. It's got to be Rog or Les."

"Charlton's got an alibi—a real one—which is more than can be said for Durand, with his wife and his boyfriend, or David Goldstone, who only has the word of an old hood."

"I know," I admitted. "I don't know the answer, but . . . don't arrest Charlie." It came out before I could stop it, and Ike's expression told me I was on sensitive ground. "At least not yet," I finished lamely.

The threatened storm on Ike's face blew out to sea. "We're not going to book him just yet," he said, "but that has nothing to do with you playing Portia for him." He sliced some mushrooms, heated olive oil in a skillet, and plopped them in. "You do have a point about King Carter's note," he conceded.

Great! I cheered silently. "Tell me about Robotrac and how it actually worked. I mean Marcella photocopied the designs for the NightWatch robot and then who did she give them to? Did she give them directly to someone from Takahayo, or does she say she gave them to Charlie, or what?"

He made a referee's T for time with his two hands and said, "Steak, mushrooms, and Caesar salad. We were going to have baked potatoes, but," he smiled, "something came up." He continued in the same tone, "Nice try, but you know you're not going to get answers to any of those questions. That's FBI territory."

"You mean you don't know the answers?"

"I didn't say that." He handed me forks and steak knives. "Place mats and napkins are in the top drawer." He motioned toward the long walnut sideboard on the opposite wall. "Set the table like a good girl." I stuck out my tongue and did it. "I'll tell you this for free, though, my men are working with the Feebs to run down any other possible links between known industrial espionage during the last five, six years and any Carter people. As soon as we find one, we'll have our perp." He slid the steaks into the Salamander, topped our wine glasses and broke an egg into a small mixing bowl for the Caesar dressing. "Dinner's in four minutes, if you like it rare."

"I wouldn't have it any other way."

32

. . . .

By the time Ike and I kissed goodnight in front of my building night was a misnomer. It was four-thirty-five A.M. He'd invited me to spend the night at his place, but, for about five reasons which came readily to mind, I thought it wouldn't be a good idea. As I said, "No," I felt sensible, adult, and deprived.

We didn't talk during the drive uptown, which took no more than five minutes—early morning empty streets combined with Ike's cowboy tendencies behind the wheel. Just as we turned onto CPW at 84th Street, Ike said, "This thing's going to be breaking in the next couple of days—as soon as we can cross-check some information from the Feebs—and I don't want it to break on your head. I'll give you as much advance notice as I possibly can, but Liz"—he brought the car to a lurching stop at my canopy—"stay out of the way. I mean that."

I managed to say, "But—" before he cut me off.

"No buts. I don't want to hear any feminist bullshit from you. These folks are major league dangerous." He touched my cheek and a faint smile tilted his lips. "Take good care of yourself, you belong to me," he said softly. He jumped out of the car, jogged around to my side, and helped me out. A kiss, brief but comprehensive. Then he was gone. Who was that masked man? I wondered as I pushed the elevator button.

I debated whether to wait till a more orthodox hour to let Charlie know that he wasn't going to be clapped in irons imminently, but decided that in his position I wouldn't mind being awakened with that news. I gave the cats an early breakfast and went back to my bedroom to make the call. His anxious "Hello" hit my ear before the first ring was over. Any fears about waking him had been groundless.

"Terrific! What a relief that's over" was his response to my message.

"Not quite over, Charlie," I cautioned. "They still haven't eliminated you or settled on anyone else. I think it would be a good idea for you to stay low profile and not discuss this with anyone until it really *is* over." We hung up. I could tell that Charlie was on his way back to his old self. "Thank you" had vanished from his lexicon.

I noticed that the answering machine showed zero messages. I stripped off my clothes and crawled under the quilt. The next thing I noticed was the clock informing my one open eye that it was eleven-ten A.M.

Sunday passed under a depressing, yet morally satisfying, welter of work. I spent the day in my bathrobe, with unbrushed hair and teeth, in front of the word processor—a bottle of Perrier and a bag of taco chips at my side. I could see through the shades that the day was sunny, but I didn't even pull them open to take a good look. What for? I wasn't going anywhere. The phone rang only twice—my sister Roo, and Barbara. I kept the conversations short. I wasn't ready to cope with either the enthusiastic approval from Roo or imprecations from Barbara, which I knew would follow a mention of Ike, so I refrained from mentioning him.

By nine o'clock I'd produced three statements for Dave to cover various scenarios, with related releases and letters to Carter clients, caught myself up on Baker Bank, and thought up two new ideas to add to the Arthur F. Oldburgh proposal when I called Clem on Monday. I even managed five miles on the long-disused exercise bike. By the time I fell into bed at ten-thirty, hair freshly shampooed, face tingling from the effects of a green clay mask, I felt virtuous and newly minted. But the bed was big and lonely, and I'd have given a lot for Ike's body in it beside me.

33

THE RAIN WAS BACK. I COULD HEAR IT BEFORE I WAS fully awake. The on-top-of-things feeling I'd gone to sleep with seemed to have decamped and left in its place the vague uneasiness of having forgotten something important. I chose a Christmas-red cashmere dress as an all-purpose antidote. As I slipped it on, I realized I hadn't heard from Frankie Mastrantonio. He probably hadn't gotten to first base in his detective pursuits. Thinking of it, it had been kind of dopey for me to dream that an untrained kid could . . . could what? I wasn't even sure what I'd expected him to do. I gave the newspapers a quick scan, including Sunday's, which I hadn't bothered to look at. Other than an efficient recap in *The Times*'s "Week in Review" there was nothing. Even the *Daily News* had run out of rehash material and was giving Headhunt a rest.

At seven-fifty I stepped into the cab that Gus had triumphantly snagged for me. Actually, I could have hailed my own. It's not hard to get one at that hour of the morning, even when it's what my mother calls "teeming" outside. But Gus had quite enough reason to disapprove of me lately, what with early morning visits by policemen and hysterics pacing the lobby claiming they weren't murderers, and I didn't want to add fuel to the fire with an incursion on his turf.

We made good time crosstown. I was going to give John Gentle the unaccustomed thrill of seeing my shining face on time at that diabolical ritual he'd devised to make sure we knew the weekend was over: the Eight o'clock Monday Morning Meeting.

The reception area was empty and stale-smelling. Sharon didn't arrive till eight-thirty—and not always then. Somebody'd forgotten to throw out last week's reception desk flowers. They sprawled out of the vase, lifeless heads hanging face down off limp stems. I shuddered and told myself it was the damp shoes and cool canned air.

I unlocked the door that led to our offices and the conference room, and stopped by my office to hang up my things, grab what I needed for the meeting, and leave Sunday's output on Morley's desk for him to put in prettier shape. I passed Seth's office on the way to the conference room and caught a glimpse of him combing his hair in front of a round mirror newly affixed to his wall. I decided not to interrupt him.

I hit the kitchen, filled my mug, and went into the conference room. Briggs Drew and his two top people, Tony Scarlino and Martin Godfrey, were already lined up on their side of the long gray table. Only so-called senior staff was privileged to attend these Monday morning sessions. That was Briggs and his two lieutenants, me and mine, and John Gentle and his executive assistant, Mary Spenshaw. Briggs and others referred to Mary behind her back as John's office wife. That was nonsense, except in the sense that she kept the Gentle Group running at a more or less even keel, and often prevented operations from grinding to a glitch-induced halt. Actually, Mary was no one's wife. She was the husband of Gladys Traynor, a real estate agent. They'd been together, quite happily I gathered, for more than seven years.

The guys were replaying the weekend's baseball. The Mets were in play-offs against the Padres. As a kid I'd enjoyed following baseball with my father, but it had been years since I'd watched a game or more than glanced at a sports section. Even so, their enthusiastic reenactments of "that catch" and heated debate on who the Mets would pitch tonight were a vivid reminder—and a welcome one—that there were other, happier things going on besides the cataclysmic events that had absorbed me. "Hi, Liz, I see the papers are giving you a rest for a change," Tony said, by way of good morning. He's a decent guy when he's not trying to imitate an Ivy League WASP. He's also the only one of the Briggs triumvirate I can stand.

"Only till someone else gets knocked off," I replied. Tony grinned, Briggs pursed his thin lips, and Martin, unsure of whether he was supposed to laugh or look disapproving, did something in between.

Seth arrived, sat down beside me, and gave a general good morning that was a lot sunnier than either the weather or his normal disposition.

"Hi," I said, swiveling my chair toward him, "let's get together after this and I'll bring you up to date."

"Sure. And I'll bring *you* up to date. They didn't let me breathe this weekend, the media. That new guy from the *Post*, Kessie? After I talked to him four times on the phone, I come out of my building—this is Saturday—to go to a movie. He's waiting in front for me." I smiled inwardly. He was eating it up.

John strode in with Mary at his side. They took their seats at the head of the table, and we were ready to begin. Angela's chair was still empty, but then it usually was until about eight-fifteen, and everybody had grown accustomed to that.

The drill for these meetings was first to review the status of every account in the house as to profitability, performance, and growth potential, and then progress to prospective new business that we were, or could be, pitching. Everybody at that meeting except Mary was expected to work a new business list and occasionally to hit the jackpot. I was overdue for a jackpot.

"Believe that game, John?" asked Briggs, leaning in with a manly chuckle. We had a reprise of the who-are-they-going-to-pitch-tonight discussions. John joined in vigorously for about five minutes in the interest of internal PR before cutting it off to turn to the only sport that really interested him: business.

"How's our headline client coming along, Liz?"

"Things have quieted down for the moment. Dave's taking over the New York reins pretty firmly, which is good. And he has a solid back-up guy to run things in Chicago." I nodded in Seth's direction. "Seth's media work on this has been out of sight—Dave's delighted," I added. It wasn't a lie. He would be if he had a second to think about it. "I have a video tape of Channel Two's funeral coverage. I'll play it if we have a couple of minutes."

Briggs looked at his watch. "I've got a report to—"

He was outvoted. "Great," John cut in, "love to see it."

When the tape was over, John stood and reached out to an overwhelmed Seth to shake his hand. "Way to go, Seth." Then he turned to me. "You going to be able to bill for all this extra time?" The challenge in his voice made it clear that he thought my answer would be no. I remembered why I usually forgot he had a better side.

"Yeah, I think so," I said nonchalantly. "After it's over, I'll discuss it with Dave. There shouldn't be a problem." I think John was more pleased about getting the extra fees than he would have been at springing the "gotcha" trap on me, but I wouldn't swear to it.

"By the way, Liz," Briggs said in the tone somebody must have told him was disarmingly sincere, "I know how tied up you've been, and I sympathize, but did you ever get a chance to start on that outreach to businesswomen section we talked about for my BMW proposal?" Shit! When the hell had I promised it to him?

"We'll have it to you this afternoon," said a musical voice from the doorway. "Three-thirty okay?" Thus did amazing Angela make her entrance in a cloud of Bal à Versailles. She slipped into her seat on the other side of me with a sorry-I'm-late-but-you-know-how-it-is smile that truly *was* disarming.

"That'll be fine," Briggs said tersely. Foiled again.

Mary looked up from her note pad. "Let's try to stay with the agenda, Briggs, okay? We're not up to new business yet." She liked him about as much as I did.

We went through the rest of the existing clients—Briggs's and mine—and had just begun new business, when Sharon buzzed and said there was a call for me. I checked my watch. It was eight-forty-five.

"I'll take it in my office," I said. "Be right back." No call that I was getting these days would be one I'd want to take in a semifull conference room. I ran around the corner to my office and picked up the phone.

Ten minutes later I almost knocked an arriving Morley down as I raced back to the conference room. As I reached the door, I gave a cheerleader jump and a full-throated war whoop.

"The British Board of Trade. We got it!"

John ran around the table, lifted me off my feet, and whirled me around. I kissed Angela and decreed us the best team since Ben met Jerry. Everyone made congratulatory noises. For the moment, nothing else existed but the intoxication of victory.

34
....

F RANKIE'S CALL CAME JUST AS I WAS PUTTING ON MY coat to leave for my four o'clock meeting with the partners. I got rid of Seth, who'd been telling me that *Forbes* wanted to do a feature on the new Carter Consultants, and closed my door.

"Frankie, I wondered what happened to you. I was starting to figure that you'd just struck out." Or chickened out, I added to myself.

"I pretty near did," he answered glumly. "I found out a couple of things, but I don't see how they can help."

"Why don't you tell me anyway, maybe they'll mean something to me."

"Okay, sure," he said, his voice perking up a notch. "I got talking to this kid, her name's Lisa. She lives around here, goes to college—Hofstra—and works at the stable part-time. Well, she told me that Mrs. Carter is sick."

"Sick?" I didn't know what I'd expected to hear, but this was a surprise. "Sick how?"

"Cancer, she thinks. You see, there's this other kid, Chad, he's a friend of Lisa's from college. He works at the stable, too—he's the one who got her the job. Well, Lisa says Chad and Mrs. Carter are ... were ... uh ..." I could hear him blush while groping for polite words to tell an old bag like me that Gillian was screwing the stable boy. I helped him out.

"You mean they were having an affair, Frankie?"

"Yeah. Except Lisa said that a coupla weeks ago Mrs. Carter just stopped it cold."

"And that makes Lisa think she's sick? Maybe she found someone else."

"No, lemme tell you the rest. Chad and Mrs. Carter were, uh, in bed, and while they were, uh—"

"I know what people do in bed, Frankie," I said impatiently.

"Well, he was stroking her hair, and it slipped off."

"What slipped off?"

"Her hair. It was a wig, see? She was bald underneath. Chad only saw for a second. She jumped out of bed and got dressed real quick. She got rid of Chad real fast. She told him she was having these treatments that made her hair fall out, but that it would all be okay soon. She told him not to say anything to anyone, and he wouldn't've, except he and Lisa are real good friends, and he remembered that Lisa's mom had breast cancer last year, and that the chemotherapy made her hair fall out the same way." He paused. "Well, that's it."

"Good work, Frankie." Cancer. Chemotherapy. I felt a quick pang of guilt for my unkind thoughts about Gillian. "I don't see that it helps us, either, but . . . has Lisa noticed any changes in Mrs. Carter—her habits, her behavior?"

"I asked her that. She says Mrs. Carter's been away more than usual the last coupla weeks, and she hasn't been riding as much. But that would go along with her being sick and all, wouldn't it? Anyway, I'm taking Lisa to a movie tonight. Maybe she'll remember something else. You know, Lisa doesn't even have to work," he said, proud of this girl he hardly knew. "She just does it 'cause she likes it. She's a real nice kid."

"Talk to you later, Frankie. And thanks—you're a real nice kid, too."

As I was waiting for the elevator, Mary came out to leave something on Sharon's desk. When she saw me she said, "Oh Liz, you're leaving? John wanted to talk with you. I'll tell him he'll have to catch you tomorrow. Hey, congratulations again, babe. You were overdue."

"No kidding!" I responded with a grin. "John can get me at home later if he wants."

The rain had tied traffic up so badly that I'd get to the Manse quicker on foot than in a cab. It wasn't cold and I was wearing old shoes, so I wrapped my trench coat a bit tighter, snapped my umbrella open, and started walking east toward Madison. Apparently, lots of other New Yorkers had made the same decision. As I turned uptown on Madison, I joined an army of androgynous tan trench coats and black umbrellas as anonymous as my own. I was so deep into my thoughts that I'd walked half a block past the Manse to the corner of Second Avenue before I stopped myself. I tried to go over the whole thing as though it were a math problem: if this, then that. Only math had never been my subject. I turned it upside down and sideways. It still didn't come out right. And yet I felt that I almost had it. Except for one tremendous trifle: it was impossible.

I pushed the bell and was admitted by a trim blonde I'd never seen before. I guessed that she'd replaced the frightened Iris Paluczyk of *New York Post* DEATH FIRM SEC'Y: "I QUIT!" fame.

"Hi," I said, "I'm Liz Wareham. I handle Carter's public relations."

"How do you do. I'm Trudy Ganz. I started this morning. Mr. Goldstone got me from Norrell Temps, but he says if things work out it could be permanent." She smiled with a crisp eagerness. "I hope so. I like challenges."

"I think you're going to do just fine," I said, and meant it. I looked around. Through the open doorway off the entrance rotunda, I could see people at their desks. The place seemed strangely normal. Trudy took my coat and umbrella and hung them up.

"They're upstairs in Mr. Goldstone's office." Funny to hear that said so smoothly. Of course Trudy hadn't known it as anyone else's office. "Shall I take you up?"

"No, that's okay," I said quickly. "I know the way." I walked upstairs, opened the unlocked door at the top of the stairs and remembered with embarrassment my nocturnal visit of last Thursday.

The door to King's office was closed. I'd get used to it being Dave's now, but I wasn't there yet. Through the closed door, I heard Rog say " . . . and Les . . ." He was cut off by Dave's louder voice answering my knock with a "C'mon in."

As I opened the door I had a brainstorm. Literally. A wild wave of truth rose up, gathered momentum, and crashed against my mind with a force that made me reel. King's phone message replayed in my head with new significance. I took in the three of them, while I fought hard to keep a semblance of equilibrium— Dave Goldstone's intense black head, Rog Durand's patrician white one, Les Charlton's smooth bald oval. Suddenly, I knew it all. I knew who and I knew how. An involuntary gasp escaped before I could check it as I looked into the murderer's eyes.

35

....

I GOT THROUGH THE MEETING SOMEHOW. I WILLED MYSELF to sound normal as I went over the statements, letters, and releases I'd drafted. I avoided eye contact while we discussed how soon Charlie might be arrested. Avoiding eye contact. That was the key. Inadvertently, I met his eyes once more, and just for a split second I thought I saw them narrow in speculation. I had the eerie feeling that he could read my mind—that he knew I knew. I told myself sternly to stop being fanciful. When my part of the meeting was over, I was so grateful for the chance to leave, I had to force myself not to run. All I wanted was to get home and call Ike.

It was almost six when I opened my door. It had been impossible to find a cab, so I'd taken the 67th Street crosstown bus and switched to the Number 10 up Central Park West. I dashed to the kitchen phone and ignored feline food overtures while I dialed Ike's office. He wasn't there; neither was Libuti. The policewoman on the other end told me he'd been out all day and was expected in tomorrow. I left a message and reinforced that it was urgent. I said I'd be home waiting for his call. I tried his house and left the same message on his machine. Then I checked my own machine. Maybe he'd called me. Nothing.

I fed the cats. I paced. I went over the solution. Once I'd found the single, crucial element, everything else fell into place with the quick ease of a double crostic after you've identified the breakthrough word. I was jumping out of my skin with excitement. Why the hell wasn't Ike there when I needed him to be! Should I call Seth? I'd need him standing by. The PR explosion would be nuclear. I decided to wait until after I'd reached Ike. The intercom buzzed and I jumped.

"Mr. Gentle. He can come up?" asked Juan.

Shit! When I'd told Mary that John could get me at home later, I'd hardly meant in person. What the hell could be so important? "Sure," I said tersely. I didn't want to get into any of this with John until I'd spoken to Ike. I'd just have to find some way to get rid of him fast. The bell rang and I opened the door. There was a split second when, if I'd acted quickly enough, I could've shut the door on him—kept him out. But the shock of seeing him froze me, and he walked in. The sound of the door closing behind him was as final as death. I heard the cats skitter down the hall toward the bedrooms.

"Surprised to see me, Liz?" he said softly. "You shouldn't be." The brown wig, mustache, and short full beard changed his appearance enough to heighten the nightmare quality. But the gray eyes he fixed on me were unmistakably his—and glacial.

Think, goddamnit, I told myself, this man means to kill you. "No, Les, I guess I shouldn't be," I said, concentrating on keeping my voice steady. It wouldn't help to let him see how terrified I was. The intercom. If I could get to it and scream for help, maybe he'd be frightened off. No, it wouldn't work. I wasn't dealing with a scared kid. This was no Frankie Mastrantonio. He'd just kill me faster.

Les's eyes gave the place a quick once-over. As he walked purposefully past me, I knew at once where he was headed. In one economical motion, he grasped the intercom phone and gave it a decisive yank out of the wall. At my sharp intake of breath he turned to face me again.

"I want to make sure we won't be disturbed," he said. "Let's sit down. I think we have a lot to talk about." He placed his damp trench coat neatly on the floor beside the kitchen door and propped his elegant long umbrella against the wall.

We moved into the living room in a bizarre parody of hostess and guest. He sat down on one end of the long red sofa and motioned me to sit on the other. I complied as though hypnotized. He hadn't threatened me, hadn't taken out a weapon. He didn't need to. We both knew I was helpless. Slender as Les was, he was a great deal stronger than I. And he'd already killed three people, at least three that I knew about.

"How did you find out?" he asked mildly.

There would have been no point in playing coy games like "Find out what?" Besides, it might have made him angry.

"You were the logical person," I said carefully, "the one with the brains, nerve, and imagination to pull it off." Would he respond to flattery? "The only thing in the way was your alibi. So I figured it must be the alibi that was wrong."

"Ummhmm," he said noncommittally. "Go on."

"It was subtle the way you and Gillian let the police drag it out of you that you were having an affair—much more effective than coming right out with it. But that wasn't the brilliant part. The shuttle switch was." I paused to see his reaction.

"Tell me about it," he commanded quietly. Nothing showed on his face.

"Okay," I said, feeling my voice strengthen a bit, "you and Gillian *did* spend that evening together up in Boston, but only the early part of it—and not in bed, by the way. Her tastes run more to stable boys, don't they?" The look that flashed for just a second in his eyes brought me up short. Was I crazy, being smartass with a murderer? I swallowed and continued, as his gaze demanded. "You gave her your American Express card, and I guess she practiced your signature. It's not a very hard one to fake. And then you drove her car down. I figure you got to New York some time after midnight, and you parked it at LaGuardia. You left the keys and parking lot ticket for her somewhere . . . oh, somewhere hidden in the car."

"Taped inside the right front fender, actually. Continue," he urged, "please, I'm fascinated."

"All right." As long as I was talking, I was okay. He wouldn't kill me yet, and meantime maybe Ike . . . I made myself concentrate only on the moment. "Gillian dressed up like you. The same trench coat, black hat, suit, tie, tinted glasses maybe, to hide the difference in the color of her eyes. And she shaved her head, didn't she?" The flicker of surprise in his eyes confirmed that I'd guessed right. Chemotherapeutic baldness was just too much of a coincidence, once I'd thought about it. "It wasn't hard for her to pass as you. Hell, I mistook her for you myself from the back at King's funeral—I can see now why that shook her up so much. All a busy stewardess would remember is a bald man with a trench coat and tinted glasses." I coughed. My throat felt dry and tight. Was I previewing how it would feel when he. . . . No, if I thought like that, I was playing on his side. And my side needed all the help it could get.

"I'm going to get a glass of water," I said, preserving a scrap of illusion that I was free to do as I liked in my own home. "Can I get you one?" I rose carefully off the sofa.

"No, thanks. I'll join you in the kitchen, though." I hadn't really thought he'd let me out of his sight to fetch a carving knife. But he was playing the civilized game, which meant he wanted to hear more. Well, I had lots more to tell him. Concentrate on the moment and you won't panic.

We walked into the kitchen together. I fantasized making a bold move and savaging him with a carving knife or jamming his head in the food processor, but bold was the last thing I was feeling, so I simply opened the fridge, took out the Evian and poured myself a large glass. I drank most of it in gulps, then refilled it and returned to the living room, Les right behind me. We resumed our places. I put my glass of water on the coffee table.

"Please go on," he said politely. "What did I do then?"

"You went to the Manse. If it'd been me, I'd've taken the Carey bus into the city to avoid a long ride with a chatty cab-driver."

"We think alike," he said, a smile touching the corners of his thin lips.

I'm sure we do, I thought. I think you're going to kill me, and I'll bet you do, too. "How'd you get to the Manse then, after the bus dropped you?"

"What would you have done?" For a second it felt as though we were brainstorming a story angle for *Forbes*.

"I'd have walked—if it hadn't started to pour yet."

"It hadn't. And I did. The rain was unexpected."

I had a sudden flash of understanding that made my skin crawl. "You took my umbrella, didn't you? You were still in the house when I . . . I . . ."

His smile broadened. "You were a surprise. But actually a fortunate one. I didn't have an umbrella with me, and couldn't risk taking King's—someone might have recognized it. When you ran out to call the police, I simply borrowed yours and slipped out after you." My mind registered a quick snapshot of Les standing in the rotunda of the Manse surrounded by police, my borrowed street-corner special clutched in his hand. "I'm sorry," he said in a tone of polite finality that I didn't like at all, "that I won't be returning it to you."

"That's okay," I managed to say flippantly, "I borrowed it myself." I had to keep the conversation going. I was Scheherazade. Until the story finished, I was alive. "When did you get there—about three in the morning?" I saw no point in telling Les that his arrival had interrupted King's naming him in the letter to Angela, and that since King had tagged the letter 2:20 A.M., I knew almost exactly when he'd arrived.

"A bit earlier, but close enough. You're doing fine."

Just then the phone rang. I jumped at the sound and started to get up to answer it. Les's long fingers closed on my arm in a grip that removed any possible doubt about my chances in hand-to-hand combat with him.

"I'm afraid not," he said quietly. A second ring. My mind raced. Should I tell him I was expecting a call from someone who'd call the police if I didn't answer? What would that get me? Killed sooner, I decided. A third ring. He let go. An aborted fourth ring, followed by my own voice asking the caller to wait for the beep and leave a message. I held my breath in fear. What if it were Ike and he referred to my "urgent message" or said he was coming over? If I were Les, I'd kill me quick and get the hell out. A loud click as the caller hung up. I took a deep breath and felt dampness on my forehead and back. Get him engaged again. Quick!

"Did you kill him right away, Les?" I asked, trying to sound like a good reporter—the kind he always cottoned to. "Or did the two of you talk first?"

"There was nothing to talk about. We'd done that the day before on the phone, after that British detective, Swift, called King and blew the whistle on my, shall we say, supplementary business ventures. In any case, I believe that King had begun to suspect something when that ham-handed Marcella got herself caught.

"He was going to expose me. Not just cut me loose from Carter, but expose me. I couldn't have that, of course." His smile added, "You can understand that." I nodded. "He'd have told the others at the partners' meeting. That's why he called you, I imagine, to discuss how to handle things."

"Well, I guess he decided he didn't need my help, since he canceled the meeting, only I never got the message and showed up. King said your name on that message, only I didn't hear it right. I thought he'd said 'unless.' Unless. And Les. Not much difference. I didn't get it until I walked into the meeting this afternoon."

"I thought you might—sooner or later. That's why I decided to erase the message, and keep an eye on you. I saw it on your face when you realized. You'd have made a poor poker player, Liz."

I shuddered at his past tense reference to me and dug my nails into my palms to steady myself.

"You didn't need to kill Mandy, you know. She had no idea about any of it. She was just ashamed to admit that King had excluded her from something."

"Breaks of the game," he said nonchalantly. "She shouldn't have played." A wave of fury washed over me, almost

CAROL BRENNAN

obliterating the terror. I forced myself to be quiet for a moment. He rubbed his hands together. I didn't like the gesture.

"So you killed him right away."

"Yes. It was the best way to go." He was sharing a business strategy with me—enjoying himself. "I clattered around his office loudly enough to bring him downstairs. I was waiting for him with the knife—poetically the right weapon for King, don't you agree? Of course, I was careful about fingerprints—rubber gloves. It was very quick. A medical text will tell you just how to hit the heart. I sat him in his chair. I'm not certain why, exactly, but it seemed suitable. After all, King was my partner and I esteemed him. I really did."

"I'm sure," I said, wondering if he'd say the same about me. "Once you'd killed King, I guess it was important to get to Swift pretty fast. How'd you know where to find him?"

"It wasn't hard to find his number in King's calendar. I called it, learned it was the Plaza, and found out his room number. Then I just waited. The Manse was by far the safest place for me to be. Shortly before you arrived, I put these on"—he pointed to his wig and face hair—"in preparation for my visit to the Plaza. I've found them useful through the years. As you so rightly remarked earlier, a bald man is remembered as a bald man. The same is true of a man with a mustache and beard."

"I gather that the Marcella affair wasn't the launch of your, uh, supplementary business."

"Oh good lord, no. I began that years ago before I got into the search business when I worked at Global Computer. We were doing new things with microchips. Some Japanese acquaintances of mine found them especially interesting and were willing to back up their interest with very substantial cash. It all went quite smoothly. When King approached me about joining Carter, I realized that the search business would suit me perfectly. I didn't need to be just a one-man operation in a single company any longer. I could expand." I'd never seen Les this animated. It occurred to me that it wasn't only

208

the money that turned him on. He loved the hell out of the whole filthy game. "You're a smart woman. Surely you can see the possibilities."

"Oh yes." My mouth felt dry and tasted of metal. "You mean all your hires were . . . were spies?"

"You disappoint me, Liz." I shuddered at the sound of my name on his tongue. "Of course not. Not every company is worth the trouble and risk of placing an agent—I prefer that word to spy, if you don't mind—and not every executive is agent material. Marcella clearly wasn't," he said regretfully.

"How do you know you can trust Marcella now—or Gillian, for that matter?"

"Carrot and stick. Marcella's been paid very handsomely, and Robotrac doesn't plan to prosecute. Also, she'd like to live to be a great deal older, which she may—or may not. Gillian has the world at her feet. She's rid of King and she'll have plenty of money for her horses and," he cleared his throat, "other hobbies. I know how Gillian's mind works. I've known her a long time—introduced her to King in London."

"Why did King marry her?"

"Gillian has certain extraordinary gifts. Namely, she makes the Kama Sutra look like Dick and Jane. King became obsessed with her. He wanted to own her. He was a collector, after all. By the time he woke up to what she was, they were married. But I do worry about her, to answer your question. Gillian is stupid, and I may have to—"

He stopped and looked at me speculatively. I knew my time was up. My heart clutched. I thought I would pass out. I did the only thing I could think of. I grabbed the glass of water from the coffee table, threw it full in his face, and started to run. I knew I couldn't make it past him to the front door, so I dashed for the long hall to the bathroom. Past Scott's room. I was almost there. Good. I'd lock myself in. I could break a bottle by the time he got the door open and—

The pantyhose slipped around my neck and stopped me cold. I could see the beige panty and elastic hanging down on my chest. I reached up, tried to pull it off. It tightened.

This couldn't happen. Not to *me*. Oh God. Tighter. Nauseous. Black circles. I *couldn't* die! I pulled at it again, trying to tear it off my throat. Pain. I couldn't breathe. All black and red.

A typhoon exploded through Scott's door and swept me off my feet and suddenly I could breathe—great, painful gasps of delicious air. I was face down with Les on top of me, and something on top of him.

"How things down at the phone company, Pa Bell?" said the something on top of Les. It was Freddie, awakened from her pre-rehearsal nap. The thundering hooves past Scott's room must have roused her. "Can you crawl out from under there okay, Liz?" Monday! God, I'd totally forgotten she was coming.

"Yes," I tried to say, but it came out a croak. I wriggled out and stood up on legs that had somehow lost their bones. Freddie was sitting astride Les's back, as though he were a legless horse. She held his right arm, seemingly without effort, in a hammerlock.

"Get hold of those pantyhose over there," she made a forward gesture with her head, "so's we can tie this motherfucker up." The pantyhose were lying no more than a foot in front of Les's nose. I walked around the far side of them and picked them up gingerly, as though they could still hurt me. As Freddie held his wrists, I tied them together tightly, with enough ins, outs, and crossovers to confound a Houdini.

"Good thing you had time for a nap, Freddie," I rasped. "I won't apologize for waking you," I added with a laugh that died aborning. It hurt my throat too much. She grinned her gleaming, perfect whites at me.

"You want to call the cops so's I can get off this creep?"

Just then, a key turned in the front door and there was Ike, his gun drawn and ready.

"No sooner said than done, Freddie," I said, feeling my lips curve into a smile.

"Looks like you have the situation well in hand, Nancy Drew," he said. Though his tone was casual, his face was tense, the blue eyes deep and squinched. "Who's Wonder Woman?"

"Freddie Mae Riggins. Freddie, this is Ike O'Hanlon, Lieutenant by title."

"Oh, I know him. He's a TV star. I'm glad to meet you, Lieutenant. You want to take over from here?"

"Sure thing. You can dismount now, Wonder Woman." After she did, Ike said, "Get up, Mr. Charlton, nice and slow." Les rose silently. His wig was perched at a loonily rakish angle over one pale eyebrow. His face looked as though the soul had fled his body. Ike quickly ran through the Miranda warning. Les took full advantage of his right to remain silent. He didn't say a word.

"Want to cuff him to that chair?" Ike asked Freddie, tossing her a pair of handcuffs.

"Do you carry handcuffs around all the time?" I asked in my new hoarse voice.

"You never know who they'll turn on," he said. As Freddie snapped the cuffs shut, Ike put his gun back in its shoulder holster, put his arm around my shoulder and squeezed tightly. "You okay?" he asked softly. He glanced at my neck. "Your throat must feel rotten."

"Not great," I admitted. "How'd you happen to show up just in time?"

"I didn't. *She's* the one who showed up just in time. I got your message saying it was urgent and that you'd be waiting for my call. When I phoned and you didn't answer, I thought there was an outside chance that Mr. Charlton here might have paid you a visit, so I came right over. Your doorman said a man had gone up about an hour ago and was still there, so I took your key from him and joined the party."

"You knew it would be Les?" I asked.

"As of today, yes. Sir Brian finally surfaced. The British police tracked him down at some hideaway in Scotland. His late P.I., Swift, had given him a full report on Charlton. He was terrified when he heard about King's murder and decided to disappear for a while."

The phone rang, and I ran to the kitchen to catch it, like the Dalmatian I am. It was John Gentle.

"Liz, I'm glad I caught you. What's wrong with your voice? You don't want to go getting a cold now—too much to do. You know, I've been thinking that maybe your client relations in this Carter thing could use some creative thinking. I believe we have some untapped opportunities here and—"

"You know, John, it's interesting you should bring that up," I said as I peered out the kitchen door at Les, handcuffed to my chair. "Since I saw you this morning, I've applied some really unusual strategies that've worked out just great. Tell you about it tomorrow. I guarantee they'll knock your socks off."

Epilogue

....

The red-headed cleaning woman pushes her cart down the empty university corridor. She unlocks a door marked "Registrar," enters and quickly locks it after her. She turns on no lights, using instead a slim flashlight, which she pulls from her sweater pocket. She switches on a computer terminal and leans over it, chewing her thumbnail as she waits for it to warm up. She punches in an access code, calls up the data she wants, and makes an entry. She punches in an exit code and switches the terminal off. All of this takes approximately four minutes. She leaves, locking the door behind her.

I walked into my room at the Hillside Motel and plopped down, spread-eagled, on the too-soft bed, my heart still pounding. I stuffed the red wig and cleaning woman's dress into the bottom of my suitcase. I'd dispose of them back in New York.

I was exhilarated. I'd actually done it!

I'd come out here to spend Thanksgiving with Sarah. It had been a grand reunion and a much-needed getaway from the cataclysm that had followed Les's arrest. We'd all been working twelve- and fourteen-hour days for the past two and a half months, putting the Carter Humpty Dumpty back together. Hanging onto clients, Bucking up staff morale. Finding ways to get some positive media exposure and to dissociate the firm's reputation, as much as possible, from Les's unspeakable acts.

CAROL BRENNAN

At this point, I was willing to bet anything that we'd succeeded where all the King's horses and men had failed. Carter Consultants, led by David Goldstone, was going to be okay. Andy Schlagle, the new San Jose-based high tech partner, was a smart, classy guy. Rog was giving a creditable imitation of a mensch—though who knew how long that would last? And Charlie Kaye, who had rebounded into his accustomed high-powered swagger, was a strong right hand to Dave, whom he adored. Even John Gentle was smiling: I'd gotten us a hefty raise.

Sarah had been surprised, not to say a bit puzzled, at my avid interest in the nuts and bolts of her job in the Registrar's office—especially the university-wide computer system, its data bases and access codes.

"You're getting to be a techie in your old age, Mom. What's it all about? You going to plant a computer virus or something?"

"I confess," I'd said, "but you've got to promise not to turn me in." We'd laughed.

Sarah had accompanied me to the airport and we'd hugged and kissed enough to last us both until Christmas break. I'd hung around the passenger lounge long enough to give her time to leave before I'd gone to the Avis desk, rented a compact, and checked into the Hillside, which was sufficiently out of the Stanford mainstream that I'd be unlikely to bump into Sarah or her friends.

My stomach had done a tarantella as I'd waited for the university's night cleaning crew to file out at 4:00 A.M. Which one should I approach? Which one would be most receptive? The first woman I'd picked out wouldn't even answer my "Excuse me, can I talk to you?" Instead, her eyes had grown large with fear, and she'd bolted and run.

But Milagros Sosa had liked the idea of five hundred dollars cash just for being sick and letting me replace her at work the following night. She'd liked it a whole lot.

I reached for the phone and dialed. A voice thick with sleep answered, "Yello."

214

"Hi, Dave. I just called to congratulate you on your graduation from the Stanford Business School. Be careful not to get too carried away with those alumni appeals."

My next call was answered, "O'Hanlon."

"Want to come to my prom tomorrow night?" I asked. "I promise I won't get mad if you dance with somebody else."

"I don't want to dance with anybody else," he said.

IN THE DARK

A NOVEL OF SUSPENSE

CAROL BRENNAN

When actress Emily Silver heard the hoarse, familiar voice in the darkened theater, it all came back: the yelling, the gunshots, the footsteps on the stairs. She remembered hiding in the darkness....

On that awful night twenty years before, Emily's parents had been killed. It was called a domestic quarrel, a murder-suicide. No one believed the little girl who swore she heard that voice in the house. But she knew now: Whoever had killed her parents was here in Los Angeles.

With each step, Emily was closer to reliving that distant nightmare—but this time, she might not escape.

Now available in hardcover at bookstores everywhere.

G. P. PUTNAM'S SONS
A member of
The Putnam Berkley Group, Inc.